Fairytale Killer

JANE BLYTHE

Acknowledgments

I'd like to thank everyone who played a part in bringing this story to life. Particularly my mom who is always there to share her thoughts and opinions with me. My wonderful cover designer Amy who did an amazing job with this stunning cover. My fabulous editor Lisa for all the hard work she puts into polishing my work. My awesome team, Sophie, Robyn, and Clayr, without your help I'd never be able to run my street team. And my fantastic street team members who help share my books with every share, comment, and like!

And of course a big thank you to all of you, my readers! Without you I wouldn't be living my dreams of sharing the stories in my head with the world!

CHAPTER

One

July 23rd
7:54 P.M.

"Once upon a time there was a girl who was an ugly duckling. She *never* grew into a beautiful swan, but still dreamed of finding her Prince Charming."

Georgia Lars stared critically at herself in the mirror.

Her face was too round, her eyes a boring shade of brown, and her shoulder-length dark brown hair insisted on being a frizzy mess no matter what she did to it. She tried to keep out of the sun to keep her freckles to a minimum, and no matter how diligently she dieted and exercised, she couldn't seem to lose those last few bothersome pounds.

She sighed.

Sometimes life just wasn't fair.

Her older sister was gorgeous. Why couldn't she have inherited at least a little of those good looks?

It had been around her twelfth birthday that she started becoming self-conscious about her looks. While her friends were being asked out by boys in their class, Georgia was never approached by anyone. In high school, while her friends spent their Friday and Saturday nights on dates, she spent hers at home watching old movies and studying.

In a way, all the studying paid off and she was awarded a full college scholarship where she obtained a degree in finance and her MBA. Now she had a good job, she had a home she loved, traveled, and she had everything she wanted.

Except someone to share it with.

She was so lonely.

Her best friend had just gone through a divorce and was living with her so technically she was rarely alone. At work she was with her colleagues, and at home she was hanging out with her friend, but it wasn't that kind of lonely. It was the kind of lonely where your heart hurt with longing, and jealousy stabbed at her every time she saw a happy couple. Where her longing to have a man who loved her and children of her own was an all-consuming burden.

Georgia wanted her fairytale happily ever after so badly she was prepared to do pretty much anything.

Even this.

She gave her hair another plump and prayed the curls she had meticulously put in stayed for the duration of the evening.

Maybe a little more mascara.

And another coat or two of lipstick. Perhaps if she could keep his attention focused on her lips then he might actually kiss her. If he kissed her then he might want to make love to her. And if he made love to her then he might *fall* in love with her.

She knew she was being ridiculous.

She shouldn't be so obsessed with falling in love. She was smart, successful, and she lived a full life, but still she wanted to find someone who looked at her like they were dying of thirst, and she was the only one who could quench it. Someone who made her excited to get up every morning, who made her want to grow old just so that she could enjoy every day with them. Someone who made the sun shine brighter, and the stars twinkle more dazzlingly than diamonds. She wanted a partner, someone to share the good times and the bad with. She wanted a partner, a lover, a friend. She wanted her soul mate.

So, she had resorted to this.

Online dating.

Never in a million years would Georgia have thought she would have stooped to this, but she felt like she was running out of options. None of the men she knew had ever even hinted about asking her out. She sometimes went to bars with her friends, but she was thirty-four now, too old to meet someone in a bar. And besides, she wasn't looking for a quick hook-up, she was looking for *the one*.

This had seemed like her only option.

About four months ago, she had started looking into the online dating options. There were a lot to choose from. So many websites, all offering the same thing and yet different. Some places matched you with potential partners based on personality questionnaires, some on hobbies and interests, and some left the matching up to you and left you to search through other users' profiles.

Then one day, quite by accident, she had stumbled onto the 'Happily Ever After Club'. A place for like-minded people to come together and find the person of their dreams.

The idea had appealed to her immediately.

The fairytale magicalness of it all was exhilarating. Who didn't want to feel like a princess about to meet her prince?

Almost as soon as she signed up, she had begun messaging with the most delightful man she had ever met. Well, she hadn't actually *met* him yet, but she felt as though she had. She already knew everything about him; his parents, his siblings, and where he grew up. Where he went to school, his favorite teacher and subject, that he'd played football but always longed to play saxophone in the school band. Where he'd gone to college, where he worked, what his hobbies were, what his hopes and dreams for the future were, and what he was looking for in a woman.

She knew him perfectly.

Tonight, she would meet him for the very first time.

She knew what he looked like, and they had spent so many hours messaging that she felt like she had already met him. But tonight, it would be official. She would see him face to face, hear his voice, touch him, and maybe if she was lucky get to kiss him.

Georgia was so excited.

Like a little kid waiting for Santa Claus.

He was late.

It was quarter past eight, and he was supposed to be here at eight to pick her up.

She fussed with her dress while she waited. It was gorgeous. Breathtakingly gorgeous. He had sent it to her, specially delivered a week ago when they had finalized their plans to meet in person. It was gold, blue, and red and reminded her of a real-life, grown-up version of the dress Snow White wore in the classic Disney movie.

She had been thrilled to pieces when it arrived. Not just because it was beautiful, and not just because he had somehow known her exact dress size, but because she had mentioned in passing that Snow White had been her favorite princess when she was a little girl, and he had obviously remembered that and had this dress made especially for her.

It must have cost him a fortune.

He hadn't mentioned being wealthy, but he obviously was, not that she cared. She wasn't after someone for their money, she had plenty of her own thanks to a successful career. She just wanted to meet a nice, sweet, thoughtful, loving guy, and a cute one was preferable but not a deal breaker.

From his pictures, her date for the evening wasn't just cute he was heart-stoppingly hot.

For a moment doubt paralyzed her.

Was he late on purpose? Had he backed out?

He might be hot, but she was just plain and boring.

Maybe he had decided he didn't want to go through with this. Maybe he thought she just wasn't pretty enough. Or smart enough. Or sexy enough.

"Stop," Georgia admonished herself. "Stop it. You're being ridiculous. He's probably just late. Traffic. That's all. Any minute now he'll be here."

She forced herself to drag in a long, slow breath. Then hold it, count to ten, and let it back out again. She repeated this several times until she felt her doubts and insecurities begin to fade.

One last check in the mirror and then she would go and wait downstairs.

Hair, makeup, dress, shoes, purse—everything looked in order.

Fighting her instincts to keep fiddling with things, aiming for a perfection she could never achieve, Georgia headed downstairs. She was at the top of the steps when her doorbell rang.

He was here.

Forcing back a very unladylike squeal, she clattered down the stairs as quickly as she could. After setting the alarm, Georgia flung open the door then frowned.

No one was there.

Had it just been neighborhood kids up to mischief?

Should she go back inside? She didn't want it to seem like she was out here waiting for him. That would seem like she was desperate.

Georgia was about to head back inside when she noticed something at her feet. In the dark she couldn't make out what it was. She bent and picked it up, it was a rose petal. Surprised, she glanced sideways toward the street.

A trail of petals led from her front door, down the garden path, to the gate.

In the street in front of her house sat a limousine.

It *had* been her date who rang the doorbell.

Straightening, Georgia hurried down the path as quickly as she could while still attempting to remain as elegant as possible.

No one was in sight, which seemed odd. Maybe her date was waiting inside the limousine ready to surprise her with something, but shouldn't there be a driver or someone waiting to open the door for her? Wasn't that how fancy cars worked?

Intrigued by what he had planned for her, she opened the door and climbed inside.

It was empty. There was no one waiting in here for her.

What was going on?

She was edging further away from intrigued and closer toward uneasy. Her instincts were telling her something was wrong. She just didn't know what.

"Hello?" she called out.

There should be her date and a driver, but no one answered.

Unsure what was going on, Georgia decided she should get out of here.

Her heart plummeted when she went to open the door.

There was no doorhandle.

She was trapped.

"No!" Georgia thumped on the door, trying to push it open.

All of a sudden, the engine revved and the car began to move.

Was she being kidnapped?

She began to hammer her fists on the window in earnest. "Help me," she screamed. How could this be happening? How could her fairy-tale first date with her Prince Charming end up like this?

∽

8:33 P.M.

His princess slept peacefully in the back of the limousine.

He hoped this time things worked out better.

Honestly, he hadn't expected it to be this difficult to find a suitable woman. One who was beautiful, smart, sweet, funny, sexy, and obedient. Really it wasn't such an unusual combination. Wasn't it what every other man wanted?

Some might deny it, say that they wanted a strong independent woman, but no one really wanted that. Why would you want someone who argued with you? Who thought they knew better? Who wanted to do their own thing rather than take care of you?

A woman's job was to care for the home and children. She should always look her best, and she should always have dinner ready on the table when he came home each day. She should always put his needs and wants before her own.

The perfect woman.

She was out there somewhere.

But it wasn't the woman in his arms, she had been a failure.

He had tried. He was never one who gave up easily. In fact, he *hated* giving up. So, he had given things with Tillie a real go. She had stayed with him for over a month, and he had spent time with her every single day. He had explained to her over and over again what his expectations were.

He had been patient.

Very patient.

It hadn't done any good.

She wouldn't learn. She kept resisting him at every turn. Fighting him, talking back, burning meals, failing to keep her hair and makeup up to scratch, not getting in her required amount of exercise each day, and in bed she didn't take care of his needs.

He had treated her like a princess.

Literally.

He had given her a beautiful room to live in, gorgeous handmade clothes, the best books to read so she would be able to make polite conversation, and plenty of hobbies to occupy her time. He had wanted her to become well-rounded, good at art and music and sewing, all the things a sophisticated woman should be.

Tillie had thrown it all back in his face.

So really, she had left him no choice. What had happened to her was her own fault. If she had behaved like the princess he treated her as then they could have been happy together for the rest of their lives.

It really hadn't had to end this way.

Carefully, he knelt and laid Tillie out. She should be found soon. Since she was of no use to him then he was happy for the police to find her and notify her family. He wasn't a monster after all, just a man looking for love.

Stumbling on the 'Happily Ever After Club' had been a huge stroke of luck. All of those women were just as desperate as he was to find their other half. And what better place to find the kind of elegant, classy, mature woman he was looking for than a forum where women who dreamed of being princesses were searching for the perfect princely gentleman?

Those women *wanted* a man who would take care of them and treat them like the beautiful fragile flowers they were. He had thought that would make things so much easier, but so far, he was two for two.

He didn't understand it. When they were talking online everything went so smoothly. They got along, their world views seemed to align, they seemed to be looking for the same things in a relationship. The women weren't immature. They didn't spend their time hanging out in bars and nightclubs. They were respectable and he thought that he had developed a real connection with them.

Then once they met in person it was like they changed into completely different people. He certainly didn't change.

One day he would get it right. Maybe even today. He glanced over his shoulder at the limousine. He really should get back to her.

He said his final goodbyes to Tillie, arranging her just perfectly, smoothing her hair, and rearranging her dress. She may have failed as his princess, but she still deserved to look her best.

Then he gave her one last kiss. He was going to miss her, he'd had high hopes that she was the one.

Time to go.

He was halfway back to the car when he saw one of the back windows was open.

His anger spiked immediately. He thought he had given her enough sedatives to knock her out for several hours. Once he had picked her up in the limousine and made sure she was safely locked away behind the bulletproof glass, he had driven to a quiet location then gotten in the back with her and requested that she swallow a couple of sleeping pills.

In case she had been uncooperative he had taken a gun with him for added incentive. Georgia had taken the pills without offering much protest. At least he thought she had.

The sneaky thing must have only pretended to swallow them and then spat them out once he got back in the driver's seat. Then she had just pretended to fall asleep while waiting for her chance to run.

Annoyed, he looked about, judging which direction she would have been most likely to run. He didn't like this. Playing games, tricking him, that was *not* respectful. He had expected better from Georgia. He really had. She had seemed so serious about wanting a successful relationship and a man who cared about her, who made her feel special, who treated her like a queen.

And already he had done that.

He had remembered her mentioning how much she loved Snow

White when she was a child and had that beautiful dress made especially for her. How was this a display of gratefulness?

She would learn to be grateful.

She would learn to respect him.

She would learn to be the obedient wife he expected her to be.

If she didn't, she would wind up like Tillie.

Deciding on the way he believed Georgia had most likely fled, he headed off in that direction. He knew her. He should be able to figure out what she would do without much hassle.

Abruptly he froze.

Georgia wouldn't run, she would hide. Find some place to tuck herself away and then when he walked off, she would run in the opposite direction.

He was not falling for another game.

An alley was right beside where he had parked the limousine. That would have provided her with plenty of places to squirrel herself away.

It didn't take him long to spot a shoe sticking out from underneath a pile of flattened out cardboard boxes.

He didn't pause for even a millisecond, just continued toward the boxes, tossed them aside, glared down at Georgia's wide terrified brown eyes peering up at him, and swung his fist at her face.

"Running is unacceptable," he said tightly.

Georgia cried and cupped her bleeding lip.

"You *will* learn."

He grabbed her roughly around the wrist and hauled her to her feet. She didn't fight back, but whether because she was in shock, in pain, or because she was heeding his warning, he wasn't sure. Nor did he care. Fear was an acceptable motivator. At least at first. Over time, she would learn that she had nothing to fear with him. He wasn't interested in a relationship based on fear of physical punishment. He wanted a relationship based on mutual understanding. He was reprimanding her *only* so that she would learn her place.

At the limousine, he tossed her inside then got out more sleeping pills and handed them to her along with a bottle of water.

"This time you swallow them," he warned.

Georgia took the pills, popped them in her mouth, and drank half the bottle of water.

"Open," he ordered.

She just looked at him.

He wasn't in the habit of repeating himself, so he took hold of her chin and dug his thumb into her cheek. She squawked and her mouth opened reflexively. Wedging his thumb tighter against her cheek he pressed it inside her mouth. "Don't bite, understand?"

Huge eyes welled with tears, but she nodded.

Releasing his grip on her, she obediently kept her mouth open, and he stuck a finger inside and swept it around, checking under her tongue and around her teeth to make sure no pills were hiding in there.

Convinced she had taken the pills as instructed, he released her and nodded, pleased. It looked like he had been correct about Georgia's potential to be trained.

"When you wake up, you'll be in your new home," he informed her. Then softened, a rush of tenderness washing over him as he looked at his new princess. "Sleep well," he told her, grasping her face in his hands, and drawing it closer so he could kiss her forehead.

He closed and locked the doors, just to be safe, then got back behind the wheel. He couldn't wait to deliver his princess to her new castle and begin teaching her.

He had a good feeling about Georgia.

She really could be the one.

CHAPTER
Two

July 24th
9:08 A.M.

"I was hoping we still had time to find her alive." Detective Rylla Franklin gazed sadly at the body that lay at her feet.

"He kept the first one for almost two months, but he only kept Tillie for a little over a month. Escalating perhaps?" her partner Detective Matthew Greer suggested.

"Perhaps," she agreed. "Or Tillie didn't perform as well as Jeannie did."

"What do you think he wants from them?"

"A princess if the dresses are anything to go by," she replied.

"So far we don't know for sure that the two cases are related," Matthew said.

Rylla just arched an eyebrow at him. Of course they knew. Okay, forensics hadn't proved it, mostly because they didn't have any, but there were *way* too many similarities for the two cases not to be related. Her partner just didn't want to believe it.

Her gaze returned to Tillie Schueman. What had she had to endure? Alone, scared, trapped, Tillie hadn't had anyone there with her as she suffered in her final days on Earth.

"Do you think she was alive when he ...?" she trailed off and gestured at Tillie's head.

"Yes."

She and Matthew both turned to medical examiner Tracey Curtis. Her dark hair was pulled back into a tight ponytail, her dark eyes were serious—like they always were at a crime scene—and she was on her knees beside the body.

"Yes?" Rylla echoed with dismay.

"Too much blood for her to have been dead. Her heart was still beating when he pierced her eye."

The shoe sticking out of Tillie's head was grotesque and yet it was hard to tear her eyes away from it. It looked so surreal like something on a movie set. The shoe itself looked perfectly normal, but the six-inch heel had been embedded in the woman's right eye.

"How did he get her to lie still while he rammed the heel of a shoe through her eye?" Matthew asked.

Tracey gave a small wry smile. "That's your area of expertise not mine."

"Any signs she was restrained?" Rylla asked.

The medical examiner picked up one of Tillie's wrists. "I see red marks, so yes, he could have restrained her to kill her."

"Did he kill her here?" Matthew asked.

"No, there's no puddle of blood under her head, and I saw blood drops leading in a path from down there," she pointed behind them, "to here."

"Parked the car there, then carried her over to pose her," Rylla said.

"He was very specific in his posing of her this time around," Matthew said.

She nodded. The killer had laid out a large piece of blue silk that looked like it matched the material Tillie's dress was made from. Then he had laid Tillie out on it, resting her hands on her stomach, and stretching her legs out straight. On her left foot she wore the shoe that matched the one which was now stuck in her head.

"He dressed her after he killed her too, right?" she asked Tracey.

"Yes," Tracey agreed, "there is blood on her skin under the dress."

"He did her hair too," Matthew noted.

"It's important to him that she look the part of a princess," she said.

"And yet he didn't bother washing away the blood. That seems at odds with the meticulous dressing and hair doing."

"He's good at doing hair," Tracey added. "He's done a French twist, that's not the kind of thing I would expect the average man to be able to do."

Rylla wasn't even sure she could put her hair in a French twist. It was long, but she never usually did anything special with it, there wasn't really any need to, she never really did much other than work and hang out with her friends. A ponytail usually sufficed otherwise she just let it hang around her shoulders in a mass of red curls. "Hairdresser maybe, or single dad with daughters, could be why he's picking women from a dating website."

"Yeah, maybe," Matthew nodded.

"I wonder if he made the dress himself," she said. "It's not the kind of thing you'd find in many dress stores, and if it was bought, it would be very expensive."

"Given the princess theme, he could be wealthy, consider himself a prince of sorts and is searching for his princess."

"Where did he kill her?" she asked. "He didn't kill her here, but there are drops of blood, so he had to have moved her very shortly after death. He either killed her in his vehicle then posed her, or he killed her close by and brought her here."

Here was an old abandoned industrial complex. There were several abandoned warehouses and more junk and garbage lying around than Rylla had seen in her life. It was quiet here, the odd homeless person slept in the empty buildings, and kids looking for a secluded place to party, drink, do drugs, or make out, but that was it. No one else came out here, which made it the perfect place to dump a body.

"Rylla, Matthew."

Kane, Tracey's husband and father of their fur babies, was a crime scene tech and was waving at them from the end of an alley about twenty yards away. Leaving Tracey to finish up with the body, she and her partner headed down to Kane to find out what he had for them.

"What's up, Kane?" Matthew asked when they reached him.

"I found blood," he said, his brown eyes excited.

"How do you know it's related to the murder?" she asked.

"It's fresh blood," Kane replied. "*And*," he drew the word out for emphasis, "I found this."

He held out his hand. In it was an evidence bag, and inside the bag was an earring. A diamond earring, and it looked familiar. "Is that like the ones Jeannie was wearing?" she asked.

"Yep, it sure is, different color but same style. I found it over here." He led them down the alley and stopped in front of a dumpster. Around it was a number of flattened cardboard boxes that looked like they had been tossed aside. "I found a little blood here." He pointed a gloved hand at a spot on the side of the dumpster. "When you know who the next victim is I can run a DNA test and match it to this, then you'll know for sure that her case is linked to Tillie and Jeannie's."

Rylla didn't like that Kane assumed there would already be a next victim. Not because she didn't agree with him, she did, but because the prospect of dealing with a serial killer was a depressing one.

"So, he already had his next victim when he came to drop off Tillie's body," Matthew thought aloud. "Having his new victim watch him kill his old victim is certainly a good way of ensuring compliance to his wishes, it makes it very clear what will happen to her if she doesn't obey."

"We might be able to get an idea of what kind of vehicle he drives if we can find a blood trail from here, and match it with the one Tracey found from Tillie's body, we can find where they intersect and see if there are any tire marks," Kane said.

"She got away for a little while," Rylla said. "She probably had an opportunity to run while the killer was posing the body. He obviously didn't have her restrained. She had to decide either try and run for help or hide and hope he didn't find her."

Unfortunately, the woman had made the wrong choice. She had chosen to hide, and he had found her. As much as she hoped it wasn't going to turn out to be the case, most likely this woman, whoever she was, would make another wrong choice that would probably get her killed.

～

10:21 A.M.

Nate Oakland sat and stared out the window.

He was supposed to be working but he couldn't concentrate.

All he could think about was weddings.

Not his own, the chances of that coming around again were slim to none. And not the wedding he would be attending next month. He was thinking of a wedding from over a year ago. When his best friend had found happiness and married the woman of his dreams.

He had messed up that day.

Badly.

He didn't know how to make it right. He'd let fear dictate his answer that day and now he was afraid that he had lost his chance at finding happiness with the woman of his dreams.

If he could go back in time, he would do so many things differently. First and foremost, saying yes to Rylla. Nate really hoped that hadn't been the biggest mistake of his life.

Or at least one of them.

At thirty-three, he had made a *lot* of mistakes. More than he cared to think of. And none of them he knew how to rectify.

Something bounced off his head and he started and turned to see a scrunched-up piece of paper fall to the floor.

"I've been talking to you for the last ten minutes and you haven't heard a word I've said." His boss and oldest friend was staring at him.

Nate had known Sam Zeeke since they were kids. They'd grown apart once they graduated high school, but after he had messed up his life in a major way and needed a fresh start, he'd reconnected with his friend and now he worked at Sam's private investigation firm. Sam knew every one of the stupid mistakes he'd made.

Well, almost all of them.

"The wedding has you thinking about Rylla and you ridiculously turning her down when she asked you out," Sam said.

Okay, so apparently Sam *did* know every single one of the stupid mistakes he'd made, including his most recent disaster. "How do you even know about that?" Nate asked. He hadn't told Sam, he'd been too embarrassed.

"Rylla told Naomi and Naomi told me. We're married, she has to tell me everything," Sam added when he scowled. "I don't get it. Why did you say no?"

No one had ever accused Sam of being tactful, he was always blunt. "The timing wasn't right," he answered lamely. He knew that was a pathetic excuse. He had liked Rylla ever since he'd met her six years ago. Detective Rylla Franklin was Sam's wife Naomi's best friend. The attraction had been instantaneous, the second he had seen her he'd wanted her.

Over time, that attraction had grown into something else. He'd gotten to know her reasonably well since they spent a fair bit of time together with their mutual friends. Rylla was smart, funny, tough, and gorgeous. He loved her crazy red hairy, it perfectly fit her personality, she was like a whirlwind of energy and effervescence. He also loved her beautiful green eyes, they hinted at a more serious side that she kept buried away beneath her enthusiastic and carefree attitude.

He could have found out why her eyes were so serious. He could have gotten to know her so much better. He could be dating her right now, perhaps even planning their own wedding instead of preparing to go to a friend's.

But he wasn't doing any of those things.

Because he was an idiot.

Fifteen months ago, at Sam and Naomi's wedding—he had been the best man, Rylla had been the maid of honor—Rylla had asked him out and he'd said no.

No.

Some days he still couldn't believe he had been so stupid.

"What timing?" Sam asked. "What do you have going on that would prevent it from being a good time to date Rylla?"

"Why are you such a busybody since you and Naomi got together?" he asked. Sam had changed so much since he fell in love, it was hard to believe he was the same person Nate had known practically all his life.

Sam just shrugged. "Stop trying to distract me and divert the conversation away from yourself. Why did you say no?"

"Because I was scared." He didn't want to find himself back in the same hole he was still trying to climb out of.

"But you *want* to go out with her, right?"

"Yes."

"Then tell her you changed your mind."

He'd tried.

So many times.

But Rylla wouldn't talk to him anymore. Whenever they were together with their friends, she ignored him or if she was forced to make conversation with him, she kept it extremely superficial.

Nate didn't know how to fix that.

At first, he'd hoped things would blow over and neither of them would mention it, they'd just go back to the way things had been before, and he would continue to long for her from afar.

However, the more she ignored him, the more he realized how much he wanted her. Some nights he lay in bed staring at his ceiling, unable to sleep for wanting her so badly. He filled those long, dark hours by imagining what it would be like to have her lying beside him. That usually led to a cold shower.

He'd had a lot of cold shower the last fifteen months.

Once he had accepted that he had made a mistake turning her down, he had tried to rectify it. He had apologized, but Rylla had just shot him an icy smile, waved him off, then breezed over to the other side of the room and ignored him for the rest of the night. She did the same thing every time he tried to apologize.

What else could he do?

She wouldn't listen to his apologies. She wouldn't even give him the time of day. How was he supposed to fix this? He wanted to date Rylla, he wanted to see if something could develop between them. He knew she liked him too, if she didn't, she would never have asked him out. What he didn't know was why she was being so stubborn about forgiving him. He couldn't have bruised her ego *that* much with one rejection.

"I've told her I changed my mind," he told Sam. "She doesn't want to hear it."

"Then tell her again."

Sam was always Mr. Practical. "She doesn't want to hear it," he repeated.

"Maybe Luke and Summer's wedding will change her mind."

"Maybe," he agreed half-heartedly. He had hoped that being at another wedding would soften Rylla's feelings toward him, but they'd attended the wedding of Sam's sister-in-law a couple of months after Sam and Naomi's wedding, and Rylla had ignored him just like she did the rest of the time.

He was honestly at a loss about how to bridge the gap that had grown between them.

"You giving up?" Sam asked.

Was he?

It would be so easy to walk away. They'd never even officially dated, just liked each other, so it shouldn't be hard to do. Yet so far he hadn't. Fifteen months and he still got butterflies in his stomach when he knew they'd be spending time together. He still thought about her several times a day. He dreamed about her on the nights when she wasn't consuming his thoughts to the point where he couldn't fall asleep. He still found her beautiful and intriguing. She had turned down his apologies several times and yet the idea of asking out another woman had yet to cross his mind.

There was only one answer to his partner's question. "No, I'm not giving up."

"Then let's figure out a way for you to win her over at the wedding." Sam grinned.

Before he and Naomi got together Sam rarely smiled. He was always serious, always all business, and usually a little scary. Now he smiled all the time, he was relaxed, and he looked at Naomi like she was the most precious thing on the planet. Nate liked seeing his lifelong friend so happy. But was it too much to ask to get a little happiness of his own?

He had lost the most important thing in his life and all he wanted was a chance to have something else important. He could have walked away when it became clear Rylla wasn't going to make it easy for him to win her over. But he hadn't. There was something about her that drew him to her like a moth to the flame. He enjoyed her company and he wanted to get to know her better. He wanted to see where things might go between them. That he still wanted that even though the fear that had him turning down her invitation to dinner hadn't receded told him that she was something special. Really special.

Feeling like he was back in junior high plotting how to get the hot girls to notice him, Nate nodded, he was desperate enough to resort to planning something with Sam. "What did you have in mind?"

~

1:09 P.M.

Georgia felt foggy.

Like she was hungover, only she never drank and had only had a hangover once when someone spiked drinks at a party when she was a teenager. That one experience had been enough to turn her off the whole drinking thing.

But now she felt like she had downed a couple of bottles of wine.

It was the sleeping pills.

She might feel like she had been thrown in a blender, but her memory was intact. She remembered her date that turned out to be a planned abduction, being forced to take the sleeping pills, the sounds of the man who took her killing someone, and running for her life. Hiding instead of making a run for it had been the wrong choice.

Georgia couldn't believe this was happening.

Had she really been kidnapped?

Didn't that happen to other people?

Not to her.

Why would it happen to her?

She didn't know any crazy violent people. She was just a normal person. Her parents had divorced when she was eleven. She had a little brother who thought he was her big brother, and an older sister. She had gone to school, then college, then gotten a job. She worked in an office. She hung out with her friends. She went to the gym when she could garner enough enthusiasm. She dated. She lived a completely normal and non-eventful life. So how could she have been kidnapped?

She didn't want to open her eyes. Didn't want to see where she was.

In her mind she was conjuring up so many scenarios. He could have her in a dingy basement, or a creepy attic, a slaughterhouse, or a cabin in the woods, or maybe a warehouse.

How would anyone ever find her?

Someone was *going* to find her, right?

Georgia couldn't let herself believe anything else. Someone had to find her. They *had* to. She couldn't die here. She wouldn't. She would do whatever it took to keep herself alive and in one piece until someone came to rescue her.

Okay.

Focus.

Stay alive.

That was her first priority.

That was her *only* priority.

The first step was assessing her location. As much as she didn't want to open her eyes and let reality sink in, she had to. She had to know where she was and what she could use to defend herself. Or find a way to escape.

Like it or not, she had no choice but to open her eyes.

Taking a deep breath, she did it.

As she took in her surroundings her mouth fell open in shock.

Of all the locations she had envisioned him bringing her, this was not one of them.

She was in a large room that looked like a medieval castle. The walls were stone and there were several large tapestries hanging on them. There was an enormous oak canopy bed with curtains made from the same tapestry as the ones on the walls. There were two nightstands, an armoire, a dresser, and a wardrobe, all intricately carved. An enormous stone fireplace big enough for ten people to stand in had a fire burning in it despite the fact that it was the middle of summer. She was lying on a couch that was covered with the same tapestry as the rest of the room was decorated with. If this wasn't her prison and she was here on vacation, then this place would be magical.

Georgia glanced down at her body. She was no longer wearing the dress that he had sent her for their date. While she'd been passed out, he had removed her clothing and put her in a beautiful pale pink cotton dress.

What else had he done to her while she was asleep?

Had he touched her? Raped her?

She didn't feel sore, and she didn't feel like anything was different. She slipped a hand between her legs and touched the inside of her thighs, they didn't feel sticky, and when she lifted her dress she was still wearing the same underwear she'd put on for her date. Georgia didn't think he had raped her but that didn't mean he wouldn't.

Overwhelmingly relieved, she set about checking herself for any other injuries. Other than the split lip she had gotten when he'd hit her in the alley at the industrial estate, she couldn't find anything else.

She wasn't restrained. Why she had no idea, but it seemed weird. Why wouldn't he want to keep her in one place. She would have thought he'd have her tied to the bed, or chained to the wall, or something, but she wasn't.

Her feet were bare and when she looked down her body, she saw something on her left ankle. It was a tracking bracelet. That's why he didn't feel the need to restrain her, because he thought he could track her no matter where she went. For her that was great news. She would find a way to get that tracker off, or she would find a way to run and get to help before he could get to her.

But first she had to get out of this room.

Although she still felt groggy, she couldn't afford to wait until the effects of the drugs wore off. She didn't know when he would come back so she had to take advantage of every opportunity that presented itself, and any time she was alone was an opportunity.

Scrambling a little unsteadily to her feet, Georgia beelined straight for the door.

Although she knew it would be locked, when she jiggled the door handle and found it locked she was still disappointed.

She didn't have time to dwell though, he could return at any second.

There was one other door, so she ran to that. It wasn't locked and when she threw it open, she found a gorgeous bathroom. Marble counters and tiles on the floor and walls, there was a large Jacuzzi tub and an enormous walk-in shower. What caught her attention was the makeup set out on the counters. It was all her favorite brands. The shades of lipstick, eye shadow, and foundation were also her favorites.

He knew so much about her.

It creeped her out.

It also made her angry.

Mostly at herself.

She had been the one who had told him those things. She had been the one to so carelessly let a stranger into her life telling him everything about herself because she felt safe. She knew the dangers of online dating. She knew that the person on the other end of the computer could be anyone, that there was no way to know if he was lying or if he was who he said he was. And obviously he wasn't who he said he was.

He wasn't a sweet, charming gentleman, he was a vicious murderous psychopath.

And she was trapped here with him.

~

3:57 P.M.

"Are we positive the two murders are related?" Captain Heidi Kramer asked.

"Yes," Rylla answered immediately, there was no doubt in her mind.

"But he used a different name each time. How do we know it's the same person?" Heidi persisted, her narrow, bony face was serious and focused, just like it always was when they were in the middle of a major investigation.

"Different names but we're positive it's the same person. The chances of two killers stalking victims in the same online dating community are basically non-existent," Matthew said.

"But different names, different stories, it could be two different men," Heidi persisted. "Could be too different motivations for the murders. One personal, one random. Or both personal."

"Too many similarities between both the names and the stories that he gave to the women," Rylla countered. "With the first victim, Jeannie Jones, he approached her in the 'Happily Ever After Club' as Brenden Ranalt, if you look up the meaning of the names Brenden means prince and Ranalt means charming or wealthy. Prince Charming. He did his research Brenden is an Irish name, as is Ranalt, and he told Jeannie that he was originally from Ireland but moved here shortly after his parents' deaths in a car accident when he was in his early twenties. Brenden claimed he was now approaching forty and recently lost his wife to cancer, and her dying wish was that he finds someone special to spend the rest of his life with so he wasn't alone and sad."

"With the second victim he went with a similar story, just changed a few details," Matthew said. "The name he used with Tillie Schueman was Galahault Bonnie, again Galahault means name of a prince, and Bonnie means beautiful or charming. Prince Charming. He took the theme of the website and really played it up. The women there wanted a Prince Charming and he gave them one. Galahault called himself Gal and made a few jokes about being lumbered with such an unusual name. He said his parents were Scottish, as both names have Scottish origins, and that they moved here while his mother was pregnant with him. He said his wife had recently broken his heart and left him after almost ten years of marriage, and that he was looking for someone special, someone the opposite of his wife, who would never hurt him like she had."

"How do we know that their murders had anything to do with them looking for love in an online chat room?" Heidi asked, twirling a pen around her fingers so fast it was a blur. Their boss was a ball of energy who hated to be still.

"Both women disappeared when meeting with their date from the website for the first time," Rylla replied. "Both were excited about finally meeting in person, both believed they had in fact met their Prince Charming, both were sent beautiful princess type dresses by their date, and both were picked up for dinner but never seen again. Jeannie was missing for almost two months before her body was discovered, Tillie a little over a month."

"Ireland and Scotland, could it be true that he is from the United Kingdom since he mentioned it in both his fake personas?" Heidi asked.

"Possible." Rylla nodded. "My guess is he just wanted to choose a name that meant Prince Charming and happened upon those names then made up the connection to the countries to fit in with the name."

"He also mentioned losing a wife in both stories," Heidi continued. "Do we think that's true?"

"Could be a trigger," Matthew suggested. "His wife cheats, or leaves him, and they divorce so he's looking for the perfect wife. Or he lost a wife he loved and wants to replace her with someone he sees as perfect."

"Do we have pictures of him?" Heidi asked.

"Yes. Well not of him," Rylla clarified. "He sent pictures to his victims, but we traced them, and they're pictures of models from a website. He picked a model then downloaded a whole lot of photos of him and used them so that he didn't look suspicious only having one photo of himself. And yes, we tried tracing the account he bought the pictures from but it didn't lead us anywhere."

"We think he has another victim, is that correct?" Heidi asked.

"Kane found evidence of another person there last night. There was fresh blood and an earring similar to the ones Jeannie was wearing when we found her," Rylla explained.

"Do you know who she is?"

"Not yet," she answered her boss. "She might not even have been reported missing yet. If she lives with someone then they likely know she had a date and might assume she just spent the night with him. Her work might notify a relative when she doesn't turn up and doesn't notify anyone. We'll go through all missing persons reports of women in their twenties or thirties. It shouldn't be hard to find one who disappeared after a date with someone she met online. Once we find her, we can confirm she's the next victim by matching her DNA to the blood found at the scene of Tillie's murder."

"The completely different modes of murder is concerning me," Heidi said thoughtfully. "One is extremely up close and personal. The other is much more distant and less hands on. They don't seem like they were committed by the same person."

That was true. The murders were completely different, but she was sure that the same man had committed them. "First one he might not have been confident enough to kill her himself, especially if Jeannie was the first person he had ever killed. Plus, it seemed to fit with his theme. The princess thing is important to him and he's clearly associating each woman with a different fairytale. Jeannie Jones was Beauty and the Beast. She writes and she grows award winning roses. Maybe it wasn't even about being hands on or not it was just about killing her in such a way that fit with the Beauty and the Beast theme."

The killer had broken into the local zoo one night and thrown Jeannie into the Grizzly Bear enclosure.

Alive and drugged.

Unconscious and unable to defend herself or get herself to safety, Jeannie had been mauled to death and found when the zookeepers arrived in the morning.

Killed by a beast.

In keeping with the killer's fairytale princess theme, she had been dressed in a beautiful silk dress, with diamond jewelry, her makeup applied, and hair done.

"And Tillie Schueman was obviously Cinderella," Matthew continued. "She was forced out of a sizeable inheritance when her stepmother tricked her dying husband into rewriting his will and leaving everything to her. And he killed her by stabbing her with a shoe. A glass slipper. A genuine glass slipper."

Rylla hadn't even realized that real glass slippers existed outside of the classic fairytale. But apparently there was a way to manufacture shoes made of glass that a person could walk around in without them breaking. "That murder he committed himself because he wanted to do it with the shoe. He has to kill them in such a way that fits with whatever fairytale princess he identifies them as."

"Can we use that to find who he might choose next?" Heidi asked.

"We've tried going through the women on the website but there are too many of them, and we don't know what exactly it is about them that's going to spark something in him. Once he's killed them and we know which fairytale he matched them to then it's more obvious what attracted him to them, but before that it's too hard to know, it could be anything," she replied.

"Do we have anything on either Brendan Ranalt or Galahault Bonnie?"

"Neither exist," Matthew told their boss. "The killer created them expressly for the purpose of luring potential victims. So far, we haven't been able to trace the person who created the accounts but we're going to continue to peruse that avenue and hope he slips up eventually."

"So far, we don't have any forensics, and we have no witnesses. We know he has someone else, but we don't know who. We don't know how he's choosing his victims even though we know the where and that it has something to do with fairytale princesses. We don't know where he's keeping them. We don't know how long we have before he kills his next victim, but we know the time between abduction and murder is shortening. And we don't know why he's killing them."

That was an awful lot of don't haves and not a single have.

Rylla had no idea how they were going to find this man.

And that meant more women were going to die.

CHAPTER
Three

July 25th
10:33 A.M.

"The media are calling him the Fairytale Killer," Matthew said as they turned the corner into the street they were looking for.

"Yeah, I heard, and I'm not surprised, especially given all the hype of the Nursery Rhyme Killer a few months ago," Rylla replied. The psychotic killer had terrorized the city for weeks and left a trail of bodies in his wake.

"I hate when the media give names to killers, but this one certainly fits. I've never worked a case where the killer was obsessed with fairytales, it kind of puts a dampener on the whole fairytale thing. I had kind of looked forward to reading them to my kids when I had them but now, I'll never be able to look at them the same way."

Rylla flinched involuntarily at the mention of kids and hoped her usually perceptive partner wouldn't notice. She didn't like thinking of children and parenthood. She pasted on a smile and nodded agreeably. "Yep, he's certainly managed to ruin fairytales."

Matthew shot her a look that said he knew something was up, but since they had pulled to a stop outside a freshly painted Colonial, he didn't comment. Instead, they both climbed out of the car and walked to the front gate of Georgia Lars' house.

Georgia had been reported missing late last night when she never returned home after work. Her best friend and roommate had contacted her work and when she discovered that Georgia never showed up, she immediately called the police.

The last time anyone had seen Georgia was when she was preparing for a date with a man she had met on the internet on an online dating website.

The Happily Ever After Club.

She had gone on the date, and no one had seen or heard from her since.

Rylla surveyed the house. It was nice, quite large, painted white, double-story, dormer windows, and a neat and tidy front yard with several fancy topiary trees made into the shapes of animals in a line just behind the fence. "She either loves gardening or she hires a fantastic gardener," she commented.

Her partner nodded. "Rose petals." He pointed to the path that led from the front gate to the front door. "But I don't see any rose trees."

"Maybe the killer left them, it was supposed to be a date after all. He makes a trail of petals, rings the doorbell, then goes to wait for her either at or in his vehicle."

"He could have still waited at the door for her."

"Then why leave the trail of petals?"

"Okay, agreed. And I guess opening the door and finding dozens of rose petals leading you to the man you think is your prince charming is pretty romantic."

"Maybe something to store in mind for when you meet a woman," Rylla teased as they opened the front gate and headed for the house.

Matthew grinned. "I'm *always* romantic. But one thing I've learned is it isn't big gestures, it's little things that usually end up meaning the most."

She couldn't help but smile, Matthew had definitely hit the nail on the head.

They knocked on the bright red front door, and a moment later, it was opened by a beautiful woman with smooth pale skin and long dark hair. Although Georgia had been shorter and a little rounder, there was no mistaking the family resemblance, this was Marissa Tress, Georgia's older sister.

"Good morning, Mrs. Tress, I'm Detective Franklin, and this is my partner Detective Greer. May we come in?"

Marissa's brown eyes were scared and sad, but her face was composed, and she nodded and held the door wider open. She didn't say a word as she led them through the house and into a small and cozy den. The house's décor was simple and elegant, white walls dotted with artistic paintings, minimalistic furniture, lots of vases full of flowers, and nothing lying about out of place.

"May I get you a drink? Coffee? Tea? Water? Soda?" Marissa asked, just one small tremble in her otherwise even voice.

"Coffee is fine," Rylla answered.

"For me too," Matthew said.

"Whitney?" Marissa addressed the room's other occupant. A woman sitting slumped over, with her elbows on her knees, and her head in her hands in an armchair by an oversized fireplace.

Whitney Leroy was Georgia's best friend and roommate and seemed to be taking her disappearance harder than Georgia's sister was. Or at least she was finding it harder to contain her emotions. The constant shaking in Marissa's hands said she was struggling just as much as Whitney, but at the moment was still able to keep tight control on her emotions.

"Nothing," came the mumbled reply from behind a wall of blonde hair.

Marissa nodded once and departed. Matthew gave her a small nod and Rylla took the seat beside Whitney and placed a hand on the woman's shoulder. "Whitney, I'm Detective Franklin, I'm going to do everything I can to find your friend, but to do that, I'm going to need your help."

Slowly, Whitney lifted her splotchy red face. "I already told the police his name. It's Leopoldo Kevay. Leo."

They had already researched the name on the way here. Once again, the killer had chosen a name which meant Prince Charming. Leopoldo was German and meant prince of the people, and Kevay was Irish and meant lovely and charming. She was also expecting to hear that Georgia had been told a similar story about his background as what Tillie and Jeannie had been told.

"I know you told us that, but it's not his real name," Rylla said gently. She suspected that shock was still clouding Whitney's mind and she wasn't yet in a place where she could comprehend what had happened.

"Not his real name?" Whitney echoed. "Why would he use a fake name?"

"Because he was playing her. He always intended to kidnap her," Marissa said from the door. "Right?" she challenged as she passed out cups of coffee.

"Right," Rylla agreed. "That's why it's very important that you tell us everything you know about him so we can try to find out who he really is."

"I don't know much about him," Marissa said. "I'm pretty busy with work, and a husband, and four kids including a teenager and a toddler. Georgia and I don't talk as often as we should. Particularly about things like her love life. She's always been a little jealous of me, and when we were kids I was a little ... not very nice to her." Marissa's cheeks pinked in embarrassment at her past sins. "I knew she was dating someone online, and I warned her to be careful, you never really know who you're talking to. But she was so confident that *her* guy was the real thing. That he was genuine. That he was exactly who he said he was and more. She was really enamored."

"Did she have pictures of him?"

"Yes. Well, she had pictures of what she *thought* was him," Marissa amended. "She thought he was gorgeous. I have to admit, I did too."

"Did you know she was going to be meeting him?" Matthew asked.

"Yes, she mentioned it. She was so excited, especially when he sent her the dress."

"The dress?" Rylla asked.

"He sent her this gorgeous dress about a week ago. It was red, gold, and blue, and a little like the dress that Snow White wears in the Disney movie. Georgia *loved* Snow White when she was a little girl, we used to play it all the time, dressing our cats up as the seven dwarfs." Marissa smiled sadly at the memory. "She must have told him about loving Snow White because he sent her the dress and she was just over the moon about it. Couldn't wipe the smile off her face that day. What she loved the most was that the dress was her exact size."

"How did he know her dress size? Did she send him pictures of herself?" Rylla asked. That seemed odd, she couldn't imagine a guy being able to accurately guess a woman's clothing size. She had dated plenty of men, been in serious relationships, and never once had any article of clothing they had bought her been the correct size.

"If she did, they would only have been headshots," Marissa replied. "Georgia didn't like having photos taken of herself, she was very self-conscious about her looks. Even as a child. I think she would have wanted to hold off on him seeing her properly until they met in person, otherwise she would have been scared that if he saw her too early, he'd lose interest in her."

Rylla had seen pictures of Georgia Lars and the woman was every bit as pretty as her sister, just not quite as tall and thin. But once you got an idea in your head about yourself it could be hard to shake it loose. Sometimes how people saw themselves wasn't the same as the way everyone else saw them. She knew all about that.

"I thought we had a break in," a quiet voice whispered brokenly.

They all turned to Whitney who was still hidden behind her hair. "A break in?" Rylla repeated, that sounded hopeful. Tillie Schueman had lived alone and had never reported any break ins, but Jeannie Jones lived with her elderly grandmother who had reported hearing someone walking around one afternoon while she was home alone approximately two weeks before Jeannie was abducted. She had called 911, but when cops showed up there was no signs that anyone had been in the house. Nothing was disturbed and nothing was taken, it was assumed that the old woman had imagined the whole thing, so no action had been taken.

But maybe they'd been wrong.

Maybe the killer really *had* been in the house.

"When was the break in, Whitney?" she asked.

"About two weeks ago."

"Was anything taken?" she prompted.

A slight shake of the head was the only answer Whitney gave.

"Then why did you think there had been a break in? Was a door left open? A window broken? Dirty footprints on the floor?" she asked.

"No. There were just a few things moved. Some of the flower vases were in different places. And Georgia asked me if I'd been looking at her clothes. Sometimes we borrowed each other's things, she said some of the things in her closet had been rearranged, but I told her I hadn't touched a thing."

That was probably the answer to how the killer knew Georgia's dress size.

Whitney sobbed. "I was the one who suggested online dating. It was my idea and now because she listened to me she's gone. It's the Fairytale Killer, isn't it? I saw it on the news. He killed another woman and now he has Georgia. He's going to kill her and it's all my fault."

Rylla wrapped an arm around the woman and patted her back as she wept. There was nothing she could say to comfort Whitney right now. In all likelihood, the Fairytale Killer *was* going to kill Georgia unless they found her first.

Right now, the best that they could hope for was that Georgia kept herself alive and that the killer stuck to his usual pattern of keeping his victims for several weeks before killing them.

They would do what they could. They would continue to try to track him through the website, and in the meantime, they would take Georgia's computer and search through her conversations with the killer, looking for similarities between what he told her and what he told his other victims, hoping that those consistencies might point to things that were real rather than made up to impress and connect with his victims. But when he killed them seemed to depend on when the women did something that disappointed or upset him.

Georgia seemed to be smart, hopefully she could take her cues from the man and do her best to play along and do whatever she could to keep on his good side until they found her.

They *would* find her, that wasn't in question. The only question was whether they would find her dead or alive.

~

11:47 A.M.

Georgia was bored.

Should she be bored when she had been abducted and was being held prisoner?

It didn't seem appropriate, but it was what it was.

She hadn't seen her kidnapper once since she'd been here. She had paced backward and forward across the room for hours, searching for a way to escape, and trying to work off her nervous energy.

As well as pacing, she had tried screaming for help. She had yelled at the top of her lungs, begging for help, until her throat was raw and aching. No one came. She hadn't expected anyone to come and yet at the same time it had been a blow.

What if no one was even looking for her?

What if he'd managed to trick her family and friends into thinking she had voluntarily gone away with him?

After all, he had tricked her into thinking he was the man she wanted to marry.

So, she paced some more. Rechecked every inch of every wall in case she had missed something useful. Called for help again and again until she had virtually no voice left. And done some more pacing.

Then her bladder had started calling out to her.

For some reason she hadn't wanted to use the bathroom. It was like admitting that this little home he had created here for her was real. That she was really living here. That she really might never walk out that door again.

Despite her resistance to using the opulent bathroom, in the end, her body had other ideas and when her bladder was so full she thought it would burst, she had relented and gone running to use the bathroom. Since she had already caved and made use of the facilities Georgia decided she may as well have a shower.

When she was done, she'd had two choices. Number one, she could put back on the dress he'd put her in while she'd been passed out on sleeping pills, or number, two she could choose something from the closet. Neither choice had been particularly appealing. What she wanted was her own clothes, not these fancy ones he's had made for her.

In the end, she had gone with something she could at least choose for herself, so she had put on a long white cotton nightgown. That was the plainest item of clothing here, so it seemed like the best choice.

After that she had paced some more.

There were no windows here in her prison, so she couldn't tell what time it was, but she was sure she must have been here for hours by the time she was so exhausted she couldn't hold her eyes open a second long. She collapsed on the bed, not bothering to climb under the covers, and promptly fell asleep.

When she awoke a tray containing a glass of apple juice, a salad sandwich, and a small bowl of fruit salad was waiting for her. All her favorites. He knew they were her favorites because she had told him.

It hit her all of a sudden. He had known she was asleep and that it was safe to sneak in the food without having to speak with her.

Georgia knew what that meant.

It meant that he was watching her.

There had to be cameras hidden in here someplace so that he could watch her every move. A horrified shudder rippled through her. It was creepy enough knowing that she'd told him everything about herself, but to know he was sitting somewhere watching her every move completely creeped her out.

Who was this man?

She knew for sure who he wasn't.

He wasn't Leopoldo Kevay. He wasn't her Prince Charming. He wasn't the man she had spent countless hours talking with. He definitely wasn't the man she had believed she would marry, have children with, and grow old together side by side.

Was anything he told her true?

Were his parents German and Irish? Had he grown up in Ireland for the first four years of his life before moving here? Had he gone to Germany for a couple of years after college? Did he really have two brothers and a sister? Had he really played football in school? Did he really want to learn the saxophone? Did he really spend his spare time training for and running marathons?

Now she doubted everything.

How could she not have seen that he was a fraud? Her sister warned her to be careful. Told her several times that sometimes people on the internet weren't who they said they were. And she knew that there had been a woman whose body was found in the bear enclosure at the zoo who had been abducted by a man she met on the internet. But she had been so sure that nothing like that would happen to her. That *her* man was the real thing.

A key sliding into a lock caught her intention.

He was coming.

Leo was about to walk into this room, and she had absolutely nothing with which to defend herself.

Georgia fought the urge to run and hide, instead, she climbed off the bed and stood there, waiting. Leo scared her, she knew he was dangerous, she'd heard what he had done to that woman. But she couldn't show weakness in front of him. She had to show him that she wasn't intimidated, that she was strong and tough, and that no matter what he did to her he would never, ever, break her.

"Good afternoon, Georgia."

Oddly enough his voice sounded almost exactly as she had heard it in her head before they met. "Good afternoon," she returned, forcing her arms to remain stiff by her sides instead of wrapping them around her middle.

He had a tray in his arms and set it on a small table by the door while he locked it, then put the key on a chain around his neck. He carried the tray over to the seating area and set about laying out the food, but all Georgia could focus on was the key. All she had to do was get to it then get out the door and lock him in, then she would be free. But how was she going to do that?

"Come. Eat," Leo ordered.

She didn't move. She wasn't going to let him boss her around. Who did he think he was? He wasn't her father, and she wasn't a little girl. She was an adult. A well-educated adult with a good job where she had a lot of people working underneath her. She was *not* used to taking orders from anyone, and certainly not by a man who had abducted her.

"I said come, eat," Leo repeated firmly, a scowl had creased his face. It *was* a handsome face even if it wasn't the face of the man she had been corresponding with. She wasn't surprised that he hadn't sent her his real photo. Why would he if he was luring her into a false sense of security so that he could kidnap her?

Still, she held her ground. "Is your name really Leo?" she asked.

With surprising speed, he moved toward her. Before she could even process what was happening and do something to stop it, he had wrapped an arm around her waist and dragged her to the bed. He sat on the edge and bent her across his lap, locking one leg around hers and holding both her wrists in one hand. His other hand delivered several swift, painful blows to her backside.

Spanking her.

He was actually spanking her like she was some disobedient child.

Tears of humiliation burned her eyes and blurred her vision as she struggled to get out of his iron grip.

"Refusal to follow instructions will result in punishment," he informed her, delivering another slap to her bottom. "Being insolent will result in a punishment. Speaking when not spoken to will result in punishment. Breaking rules will result in punishment. Not following set routines will result in punishment." With each instruction he hit her again and again until her backside stung.

Why was he doing this to her? The man she had gotten to know in the Happily Ever After Club was a gentleman looking for a beautiful princess to spend his life with. What did that have to do with following rules and not being allowed to speak without permission?

"Do you understand?" he demanded.

She couldn't agree to let him treat her like this. Her pride wouldn't let her.

When she didn't answer he grabbed hold of the hem of her nightgown and pulled it up around her shoulders. Then took hold of the waistband of her panties and yanked them down, exposing her bottom. He slapped it three times in quick succession. "I said do you understand?"

Georgia battled her pride. Her backside hurt so badly. She had never been spanked in her life. Her parents had never disciplined her that way. Her brain was yelling at her to just tell Leo what he wanted to hear but her mouth wouldn't cooperate.

His hands released her wrists and she heard something, a swishing sound. Then a moment later something cracked through the air and pain exploded in her backside.

He had hit her with his belt.

She was crying now. She didn't want to, but she couldn't help it. She was hurting, she was mortified, she was angry. It was all too much for her brain to comprehend.

"Do. You. Understand?" he over enunciated each word.

"Yes," she hiccupped through her tears. Common sense had won out over her pride. How badly would he hurt her if she didn't say what he wanted her to? Her goal had to be to stay alive, and if that meant giving in and playing along maybe she would have to learn how to do that.

"Good girl," his tone gentled, and his hand softly rubbed over her smarting bottom.

"I don't like to punish you, Georgia. It brings me no pleasure, but you must learn. A woman's place is to take care of her man, she must be obedient, she must put his pleasures and wants and needs above her own, she doesn't speak without permission. She should be quiet, respectful, thoughtful, kind, and good. When you have learned how to be these things then you will be able to leave this room and fulfill your duties as my princess. You will cook for me and clean, you will do my laundry, you will provide educated conversation about suitable topics, and you will attend to my sexual needs."

He said it so simply like it was a forgone conclusion. Like what he was expecting of her was common and every woman behaved that way.

"Do you understand?"

It was a test. She knew that. To see if she was ready to fulfill her obligations and do as she was told. If she didn't reply, he would hit her again. Or worse. "Yes," she answered meekly.

"Good," he said approvingly, then released his hold on her and stood her up. "There is ointment in the bathroom, you may put that on yourself, then dress, do your hair and makeup, and join me for lunch. I will choose your outfits until you are better aware of what is suitable for which occasions."

In shock, Georgia just stood there with her underwear down around her knees and her nightgown bunched at her hips as Leo stood and crossed to her closet. He pulled out a mauve satin blouse and a white cotton skirt, a pair of heels, and a pair of pantyhose and brought them all to her.

Unable to see another option, she took the clothes and timidly walked toward the bathroom. What else could she do? She was afraid of what he would do to her if she didn't comply.

Before she closed the bathroom door, she saw the smug smile on his face as he watched her follow his orders.

He thought he had won.

But she would *never* let him win.

She would kill him rather than submit and become his version of the ideal woman.

~

5:39 P.M.

For some reason she didn't feel like being alone tonight.

Rylla parked in her best friend's driveway and climbed out of her car. For a moment she just stood and stared up at the sky.

As a child the sky had perplexed her. You could stare at it forever, but never see the end of it. Did it have an end? Could you get to the end? If you got in a spaceship and just kept flying, could you go on forever? And if you did get to the end, what would it look like?

She would spend hours watching the sky change color, she would sneak out of bed early in the morning to watch the sun rise, and the sky go from dark to light, then yellow and red and pink and gold. Then you would blink, and the sky would be blue again. During the day she would lie on her back in the backyard and watch the clouds change shape as they floated across the sky. She would search for animals or things in the shapes and make up stories to go with what she saw.

She had no idea where this sky obsession had come from, but sometimes when she was stressed, or tired, or sad she would revert back to seeking solace from watching the great, endless expanse. It made her feel both big and small, and sometimes she needed the reminder that there was more to life than her and her pain.

She drew in one more deep breath then headed inside. She had a key to Naomi and Sam's house and never bothered to knock. Besides, she had already called Naomi and said she'd be coming over for dinner. Sometimes after a hard day at work, she just couldn't stomach going home alone to her big empty house. On those days she used to call up Naomi and the two of them would go for a run, or to the gym, or hang out and talk work, but now that her friend was married, they didn't hang out as often as they used to. Rylla didn't like to intrude. While she couldn't be happier that Naomi had found happiness after everything she had been through, it did increase her own loneliness.

Naomi was sitting on the sofa with her feet propped up and a book resting on her huge pregnant belly. "Glad to see you're taking it easy."

Her friend looked up and made a face. "Sam won't let me help cook dinner," she said as she put her book down and struggled to her feet.

"How is it possible that you look bigger every time I see you?" Rylla asked as she went and helped Naomi stand. If it wasn't for her oversized stomach, you couldn't even tell Naomi was almost nine months pregnant. She still worked out every day. After almost losing her life three times in a year, Naomi had worked hard to regain her strength.

Naomi smiled then said, "Sam's making pizza for dinner, and some sort of chocolate stuffed crust pizza concoction for dessert. He's on a chocolate kick at the moment, I think it's because he's nervous about becoming ..."

Rylla frowned as her friend trailed off and didn't finish her sentence. Naomi rarely talked about her pregnancy when they were together. "It's okay to talk about it, I'm excited for you," she said quietly. She appreciated her friend's concerns, but she was genuinely thrilled for Naomi and Sam.

"I know you are, but I also know this might be hard for you."

Naomi's brown eyes were watching her cautiously as though she suspected Rylla might burst into a fit of tears any moment now.

Annoyingly, tears were brimming in her eyes. She didn't want to give her friend the wrong impression, she couldn't wait to meet Naomi's baby, but it *did* bring back memories. Memories that she was so conflicted about. On the one hand, they were so painful that it hurt, physically hurt, to think about. And yet on the other hand, if someone offered to remove those memories she would refuse.

She didn't want to forget.

"You've never shown me pictures of her, and you never talk about them," Naomi said.

Thinking about them was hard enough but talking about them was almost more than she could bear. She and Naomi had met not long after she'd lost her family, when they had both joined the police academy, and had immediately gravitated toward each other because they could both be quite obsessive about always being busy and on the move. Even after they graduated and Naomi decided not to become a cop, the two had remained good friends, and now eleven years later they were closer than ever.

With her loss still so fresh, Rylla had told Naomi about her family not long after they met but they had never talked about it since. Just because she didn't talk about it didn't mean that she didn't think about it. And she did. Every single day. Several times a day. Remembering her family was what kept them alive.

"I'm sorry, I shouldn't have said anything."

"No, Naomi, it's fine. Really," she assured her. If anyone understood loss it was Naomi. Rylla reached into her bag and pulled out her wallet, she retrieved her favorite photo and handed it over. "This is Josh and Elianna about a week before the accident."

"Oh, Rylla, she's so pretty," Naomi gushed as she looked at the photo. "And she's so tiny. She was four months old, right?"

"Yes." She had only had her beautiful sweet little daughter for four months before she was cruelly snatched away.

"You were so young when you had her."

"I was nineteen."

"I could not imagine having a baby at only nineteen. I'm terrified enough to be becoming a mother at thirty-one," Naomi said.

"Josh made things a whole lot less scary. He was always so calm about everything, nothing fazed him, he was so great when I was stressed out about Elianna crying, or midnight feeds, or when she got sick, he always knew how to handle it. He was such an amazing dad. He was so good with her, every time he picked her up, she just lit up, she was such a daddy's girl."

"She might have been a daddy's girl, but she looks just like you. The frizzy red hair, the big green eyes, the attitude, it's all you."

"Elianna was my mini me," she agreed. "Josh and I used to joke about it all the time. He was already dreading her teenage years." She couldn't stop the tears from trickling out. Some days it was still hard to believe that her husband and daughter were gone.

"I'm so sorry." Naomi wrapped her arms around her.

Rylla hugged her back. "Some days I wish I had been in the car with them," she admitted.

"I'm glad you weren't." Naomi squeezed tighter. "And so are a lot of other people."

She tried to move on, to keep living her life, to find happiness again because she knew that was what Josh would have wanted, but it was so hard. In the eleven years since her husband's death, there had been only a couple of guys who had caught her attention, and none enough to encourage her to make another lifelong commitment. She'd thought she had her whole life ahead of her. An adoring husband, a gorgeous child, there was so much to look forward to, so much she thought she would enjoy.

In the end, all she'd had was two coffins and a home she couldn't walk into because it was too full of memories.

Choosing a coffin for her tiny baby girl had been one of the hardest things she had ever done. It was so small. Seeing the tiny white box beside her husband's coffin had broken her. All her hopes and dreams gone in an instant. Part of her died right along with Josh and Elianna, but the other part of her knew she had to honor them by living. So, she had joined the police force, made friends, dated occasionally, and did what she could to live her life.

Rylla rested a hand on Naomi's stomach.

She had loved being pregnant. She had loved knowing that her baby was living inside of her. And she had loved every second of labor, no matter how much it had hurt because she knew that she was bringing her child into the world.

She felt a small kick and couldn't help but smile.

"I can't wait to meet your baby, Naomi. I want to hold her, and kiss her, and cuddle her, and sing to her, and love her to pieces. I'm going to spoil her so much. I don't want you to ever feel like you can't be thrilled about your daughter around me. I loved Elianna. I *still* love her, but I love you too, and I will love your little girl."

"She's going to love you so much, Rylla. She's really lucky to have you in her life."

"She's really lucky to have you as a mom," Rylla told her friend. She knew Naomi had a lot of self-doubts, but if she had been in the car that day and not Elianna, and her daughter had survived, she couldn't think of someone she would rather have raising her than Naomi.

"I second that."

They both turned to see Sam watching them. "Dinner's ready."

"Let's eat," Naomi said. "I'm starving."

"You're always starving." Sam rolled his eyes.

"Hey, I'm eating for two." Naomi punched him lightly in the arm.

As they all went to the table, Rylla realized she was feeling better. The pain of loss in her heart never left her, but her job and her friends helped her to heal. And who knew, maybe one day she would meet someone that she could envision spending her life with and have another child. Whether she did or didn't have other children she would always treasure those four months with Elianna as the most precious of her life.

～

8:16 P.M.

Nate sat and stared at his TV, completely unaware of what was playing.

Evenings were the worst. Unless he was working, he just sat around his quiet, empty house, all alone. Days he had work to keep his mind occupied, and nights he could sleep, well assuming he was able to fall asleep, but evenings he just sat here, doing nothing. Nothing but think.

He really hated thinking.

Why was it he never thought about anything good?

All he did was rehash his mistakes over and over again until he came up with a million different scenarios of how he should have handled things. It was so easy to be smart after the fact when emotions weren't running high, and you weren't in the heat of the moment.

Too bad there was no such thing as a do-over.

Like he did every night about this time, he picked up his cell phone, opened his contact and stared at the number.

Some days he called, some he backed out.

He hated making the call. Every day he battled the decision that it was time to let it go. Nothing was going to change. There was nothing he could do about it. It was what it was. He should accept it and move on.

But he couldn't.

How could he?

Was tonight a call night or a give up night?

Call.

He'd backed out the last few nights in a row. Tonight he had to call, he had to try, he never gave up hope that one night he would actually get through.

He dialed and waited. The phone rang and rang and rang. Eventually it clicked through to the message service.

"Rach, it's Nate. Again. Call me back, please. We have to talk. You can't do this, you know you can't. I never agreed to it. It's not fair, to any of us. Call me."

He hung up and stared at his phone.

Then tossed it across the room where it landed with a thud on the carpet.

Rachel had no right to do what she did, but it hadn't stopped her from doing it. If he'd been paying attention he might have known what she was planning on doing and found a way to stop her. But he hadn't.

He had been too wrapped up in work. Too busy with his friends. He had already known that things with Rachel were over even if neither one of them had wanted to admit it.

He might have known it was over, but he hadn't expected her to flee the country the way she had.

Nate stood and stretched until he heard his back crack. He might have called Sam to see if he wanted to go for a workout, but his friend had already told him that Rylla was coming over for dinner. As much as he loved any chance he could get to see her, he just wasn't in the mood tonight, calling Rachel did that to him.

He could call Nick Sleigh, he'd joined the team at Sam's company a couple of years ago and in that time they'd become good friends. But between his wife Aggie recently finding out she was pregnant with their first child, and Nick's brother Luke's upcoming wedding, he didn't have time for much else these days.

It seemed everyone was busy with family except him.

Because he had no family. Well, he had parents, and siblings, but it wasn't the same. He wanted a family of his own. By thirty-three he should have one. He shouldn't be spending his nights home alone watching but not really watching TV.

What was he going to do once all his friends had kids?

It was just going to highlight that they were all successful at life and he was a loser that continued to mess things up. The consequence of all those mistakes seemed to be that he would spend his life alone watching everyone else find happiness.

No way was he getting any sleep now. His brain was buzzing on overdrive and adrenaline was coursing through his body. He was going to have to work off some of this energy if he was to have any hope of catching a few hours sleep.

He may as well go for a run.

Alone.

Nate may as well get used to spending a lot of time on his own. His friends were all moving on with their lives, and while he knew they would always include him in their families, how much time could he spend watching them enjoy the very things he had lost?

He honestly didn't know the answer to that.

He was already dressed in sweats, so he slipped on some trainers, and headed out into the night, hopefully to let the mindlessness of running clear his cluttered head.

~

10:50 P.M.

She had a plan.

Was it the best plan? She wasn't sure.

Would it work? She wasn't sure of that either.

Georgia just knew she had to do something, and this was the best she had been able to come up with.

She knew she couldn't stay here. She couldn't submit to Leo's rules. She couldn't be the person he wanted her to be. She was going to get punished over and over again. She was going to end up making him so angry that he would kill her.

So, she had to escape or die trying.

Her plan was pretty basic. Arm herself with a weapon, then attack him when he came through the door. Hope she managed to hurt him enough that she could get out the door, close it behind her if there was time, then run for help.

Finding a weapon had been difficult, there wasn't much inside her fancy prison. The furniture was heavy and there was nothing she could really do with it to incapacitate him. He had taken the utensils he'd brought for her to eat lunch and then dinner with. He'd left her with a stack of books that she was supposed to read and study and presumably learn something from, but they weren't an effective weapon either.

Georgia had to be careful when searching for something to use to try to take down Leo because she didn't know how many cameras he had hidden in here and which parts of the room they were aimed at. For all she knew, he had them covering every inch of this place, including the bathroom.

Along with his list of rules on what she was and was not permitted to say and do, had been a list of rules about her appearance. She must dress nicely at all times, she must have her makeup on at all times, her hair must always be styled, and she must make sure her underarms and legs were shaved every second day.

That meant there were razors.

The blades were small, but they were better than nothing and the best she had to work with right now. Before preparing herself for bed, she had made a show of pretending to follow the rules and shaving, then in case he was watching her she had slipped the shaver head into her pocket then put on a nightgown and gone to bed. Under the cover of her blankets and the dark room she had worked on removing the blades.

Now she had them free, but she wasn't sure of the best way to use them. She had sliced up her fingertips working the blades out, she could try and find something to put them in and make a knife of sorts, or she could keep them as they were and try to slice Leo while he was unaware she even had them on her. But she wasn't sure how effective that would be, she needed to hurt him enough that she could get away.

Hurt him or kill him.

Never in her life would Georgia have thought that she would even contemplate taking a life, but now, if it was the only way she could survive she would kill Leo. Kill him without a second thought or an ounce of regret.

She *hated* Leo.

She didn't know how she had thought that she was in love with him. She didn't even know him. Everything he had told her was a lie. He had played her. He told her everything that she wanted to hear so that she would agree to meet him, and he could take her. None of it had been real. All she knew about him was that he was violent, insane, and wanted a woman who was an obedient slave.

How could she have been so stupid?

Georgia had never felt so humiliated in all her life. And being spanked as punishment by Leo was the icing on the cake.

She couldn't stay here.

She literally would rather die. And it was inevitable anyway. He was going to kill her, she knew that. It was only a matter of time and then he would kill her just like he had killed the other woman in the limousine.

This escape plan had to work, it was her only chance.

Her plan had one problem. Well probably it had several problems and there was a good chance it wasn't even going to work, but the major problem that she foresaw was how to get him in here. It was late, she didn't have a watch or a clock, apparently that was not permissible, but she knew it had to be late, Leo could have gone to bed already, he might not be watching her.

But what if he was?

She could wait till morning, try to get his attention then. Or she could just wait until he came back in, she assumed that he would bring her breakfast.

Although she *could* wait, she didn't want to.

Georgia didn't think she could take another second in this room. She was going to lose her mind. She needed to be out. Now.

It didn't hurt to try. She could attempt to draw Leo's attention, and if it didn't work then she could get a couple of hours sleep and be ready to pounce on him in the morning.

There were no rules about sleeping, going to bed at a certain hour, or how long she had to sleep, or whether or not she was allowed to get back up. At least there were no rules that he'd told her about yet. She climbed out of bed and went and switched on the light. There was only one switch, but it illuminated all twenty of the globes in the room, bathing it in light. Instead of returning to the bed where the tapestry curtains might obscure Leo's view of her if he was indeed watching, she went instead to the sitting area and draped herself out on the couch.

Then she drew in a breath.

The only way she could think of to draw Leo into the room was to cut herself. Just because she thought it was her only option didn't mean she was thrilled about. She was going to have to be careful, she didn't want to cut too deeply and cause herself an injury that was going to inhibit her ability to escape. She also needed to make sure that she did cut herself deep enough to draw enough blood to scare Leo enough that he would come in.

It was now or never. Before she could dwell on it or anticipate the pain, Georgia ran the blade along her wrist.

Immediately a line of blood appeared, oozing between the cut edges of her skin and dripping down onto her stark white nightgown.

For a moment she just stared at the bright red circle, mesmerized.

Another drop joined it, and another.

The door hadn't opened.

Leo hadn't come.

So much adrenaline was pumping through her body that she didn't feel any pain.

She lifted the blade and sliced herself again.

"What are you doing?" Leo roared, throwing the door open and storming toward her.

When Leo grabbed the hand that held the blade, Georgia swung her other hand at him. As she had hoped, he hadn't even thought about her having more than one weapon, and didn't predict her swinging the other blade at him.

She was aiming for his face, in particular his eye, but at the last moment he flung up his arms and instead she connected with the back of his hand.

His eyes blazed fire at her and his expression was pure furious malice.

Georgia scrambled to her feet. She had to try and make a run for it. She didn't think she was going to get very far but she certainly wasn't going to just lay there and wait for him to kill her.

She made it about four feet when he tackled her.

She landed heavily, his weight crushing into her back shoved the air out of her lungs.

He flipped her over and sat on her stomach, his hands pinning her arms above her head.

"You think you can trick me?" he growled.

Georgia fought not to cower, she didn't want to give him the satisfaction of knowing how afraid of him she was. He already thought he was superior, that he was stronger, that he was the one in control. Maybe he was the one in control, and he may be physically stronger than her, but she was mentally and emotionally stronger, and he was superior to no one.

"No woman tricks me." He released one of her hands and began to pry open her other hand which still clutched the razor in a tight fist. "So, you want to cut yourself to get my attention do you? Well, you've got my attention now."

Leo managed to get hold of the blade and held it just above the skin under her right eye, this time Georgia couldn't help but whimper. She knew he was about to kill her, and she also knew instinctively that it wasn't going to be a quick death.

Her gamble hadn't paid off.

She had chosen trying to escape over playing along and hoping someone found her, and now she was about to die. Just days ago, she had been so excited to have a first date with her Prince Charming, and now he was about to kill her.

"You want to be cut, I can happily accommodate your wishes."

He took one of her hands and put it under his knee so he could hold it in place, then gripped her other hand in one of his. With his free hand he pressed the razor into her cheek and dragged it down to her jaw.

An ugly smile warped his face as he watched her blood flow. He leaned in close and whispered in her ear, "Princesses don't try to trick their prince. I gave you everything. A beautiful place to live, exquisite clothes, I would have taken care of you. All I asked in return was that you follow the rules. You are the most ungrateful whore I've ever met. You think you can use your womanly assets to beguile men but that won't work with me. I want a pure woman. A good woman. A woman who understands her place. I was wrong about you."

How ironic was that? He thought he was wrong about her, but she couldn't have been more wrong about him.

"You're just like all the others." He moved the razor blade to her breast and sliced through it. "You think you can use these. And this," he put the razor between her legs, "to bewitch men into giving up their rightful position as leaders over women. Well not me."

Leo cut her again and she cried out, not so much in pain but in anguish. She didn't want to die like this.

"I will not be tricked," he shouted as he sliced at her manically. Her legs, her arms, her face, he didn't stop.

She was sobbing, and thrashing, trying pointlessly to maneuver his sizeable weight off her body. She couldn't give up though. If she was going to die, if he was going to kill her, then he would have to look her in the eye while he did it. She wanted to make sure that for the rest of his miserable, pathetic life he would remember the look in her eyes as her life ebbed away.

Georgia fixed her gaze on Leo's.

Apparently, that angered him. He released his grip on her wrist and instead held onto her face so hard she squawked in protest. "I told you that you don't look me in the eye. If you won't learn to submit, then I'll make you learn."

Two quick slices and her vision was gone.

A slice to her neck, and a moment later the world dissolved into nothingness.

CHAPTER
Four

July 26th
4:24 A.M.

The first thing she noticed was the hole.

It seemed to glow in the light of their torches.

Rylla shuddered, it was creepy. She didn't want to look at it a second longer. Instead, she focused her gaze on the face. Not that that was a whole lot better.

"He really did a number on her," Matthew said quietly.

"More than the others," she agreed. Other than the faint restraint marks on Tillie Schueman's wrists, he had killed her cleanly with the heel of the glass slipper through the eye. The only marks on Jeannie Jones were from the bears who had mauled her to death. So far, the killer hadn't been hands on.

Until now.

Georgia Lars' body was covered in gashes. Quite literally. They were everywhere. And she could see that they were everywhere because unlike with his previous victims the killer hadn't left Georgia dressed in a beautiful old fashioned ball gown. He had left her naked.

"Something was different about her," Rylla said.

"He only kept her for two days. That's a *lot* shorter than either of the previous women."

"He kept Tillie for a shorter period of time than he kept Jeannie, perhaps he's just escalating," she suggested.

Her partner shook his head. "This feels different than him just escalating."

Rylla agreed, she just didn't like it. It was obvious from the scene before them that Georgia had been different. Her body read like a map of the killer's rage. He wasn't getting what he wanted from the women he was abducting and each time he failed he got angrier. He was becoming more dangerous. The only upside to that was that the angrier he became the more reckless he would become, that would lead to mistakes, and mistakes would help them find him.

"He killed her because she did something to antagonize him," she said.

"The blade he used was small," Tracey inserted.

"How many cuts are there?" Matthew asked.

Skimming Georgia's body, Tracey replied, "two on her stomach, one on her left arm, three on her right, eleven on her breasts, nine on her face plus the ones on her eyes. Then what is almost certainly the fatal wound to her neck."

The killed had slashed both of Georgia's eyes, cutting right through the eyeballs and leaving them a bloody, gaping mess. That he had focused the majority of his anger on her face and breasts told them a lot about him. "He wanted to destroy her identity," she said. "Take away who she was by destroying her face."

"And what made her a woman," Matthew added. "Her breasts are a mangled mess. Tracey, did he cut her around her genitalia?"

With a grim look on her face, the medical examiner spread Georgia's legs. "Yes, he did. I see probably seven or eight cuts but it's hard to tell, things are a bit of a mess down there."

Rylla sighed and closed her eyes for a moment to gather herself. It wasn't surprising. Tracey had found signs that both Tillie and Jeannie had been sexually assaulted during the time that they were held prisoner. And given the level of rage the killer had displayed in his attack on Georgia it made sense that he would want to destroy what made her a woman. It looked like he was after a perfect princess, and if Georgia had done something to not fulfill those wishes and to make him angry, she could see how he might feel compelled to obliterate the very things that he felt she had failed in.

"Are there any other injuries?" Matthew asked.

Carefully Tracey rolled Georgia over onto her side so she could see her back. "There's a small welt on her bottom. Looks like he hit her with something."

"Do you know what?" Rylla asked.

"I see handprints, and probably a belt," the medical examiner replied.

"Any defensive wounds?" Matthew asked tightly.

Tracey picked up Georgia's left hand and examined it. "I see bruises here," she pointed to the back of the hand. "Looks like he might have held it down, possible with his knee or something while he attacked her." Setting her left hand down, Tracey picked up Georgia's right. "Bruises around her wrist, looks like fingertips, he restrained her." Turning her attention to Georgia's stomach. "Bruises here too. He sat on her. Explains why there are no cuts on her legs."

"So, she does something that makes him so angry that he broke with his usual MO and viciously attacked her then killed her only forty-eight hours in. Then he cleaned her, he's never done that before. With Tillie he redressed her, but he didn't worry about trying to clean anything up, something was different with Georgia," Rylla said.

"He was worried we might find something on her if he didn't clean her up," Matthew said.

"She got him." Rylla moved closer to the body and knelt down so she could see Georgia's hands. "There are small cuts on her fingertips. She found something she could use as a weapon and armed herself."

"Legs have been recently shaved," Tracey inserted.

"She got the blades out of a shaver, then she tries to attack him, she must have got him, only he managed to overpower her and cut her up before killing her. That's why he was so angry at her, he didn't expect a woman—a princess—to try and attack him. He couldn't take it, he couldn't control himself, he gave up on her, on his mission to teach her to be what he wanted, and just killed her."

Rylla felt a rush of pride for the woman lying dead at her feet. Georgia Lars hadn't given up. She had tried to escape at the warehouse, then she had kept her wits about her and formulated a plan of attack, she had executed it, and even though she had failed, she had been willing to risk him killing her to make a go at escaping. It was exactly how she herself would have played it. She would rather have died trying to get away than submit and be this man's plaything.

"He cleaned her thoroughly, I don't see a speck of blood," Tracey observed. "I'll check more carefully back at the morgue, but here in this light I don't see anything."

"So, he cleaned her after she was already dead. But did he do it before or after he did that?" Matthew pointed at the hole in Georgia's chest.

Unwillingly Rylla felt her eyes moving toward the hole. The hole that the killer had cut into her chest so that he could remove her heart.

It was grotesque.

That huge dark opening in Georgia's pale white chest—made even paler in the dark illuminated only by the torches and floodlights set up —looked so out of place.

But in the killer's princess game Georgia was Snow White, and even though in the fairytale the huntsman hadn't been able to cut out Snow White's heart, their killer had obviously had no trouble following through with Georgia.

"He cut out her heart before he cleaned her, I see a puddle of water inside her chest cavity," Tracey replied.

"But she was dead when he cut out her heart, right?" Rylla asked.

"There's no way to know at the moment. But I would assume so, otherwise there wouldn't have been much point in slitting her throat. The cut on her neck is deeper than any of the others on her body, so it was obviously intended to sever her arteries and make her bleed out. If she was already dead because he'd cut out her heart, then why would he do that? I think we can safely assume that she was indeed dead before he did it."

Taking a little comfort from that, she said, "He didn't stage this scene like he did with Tillie's. With that one he took his time laying her out and posing her just so, with Georgia he just parked his car, tossed her out, threw the heart out too, then sped off."

"911 caller said he didn't even get out of the car," Matthew said. "Just pulled up at the side of the road and then flung her out."

"The heart landed several feet away from the body," Rylla said. "He didn't even worry about them being together."

"Did the caller get a license plate?" Tracey asked.

"No, he just saw what looked like a body roll out of a car and then the car sped off. All he said was it was a dark color, black or maybe dark grey or blue," she replied.

"He was so angry with Georgia he couldn't even stand to have her in his presence any longer than was necessary."

"Maybe he killed her not long after he took her, but only just got around to dumping her," she contradicted.

Tracey shook her head. "No, she hadn't been dead more than a few hours, probably around midnight."

"Killing her this soon wasn't part of his plan. He took Tillie the same day he killed Jeannie. And he took Georgia the same day he killed Tillie. But this time around he might not be so prepared. He probably has more victims picked out, but he might not have them groomed enough that they're ready to meet right away. We might actually have some time to get ahead of him before he snatches his next victim," Rylla said, and desperately hoped it was true.

~

6:45 A.M.

Mila stretched, yawned, and rolled over in bed. Even though it had been eight months since she had separated with her husband, she still wasn't used to sleeping alone, and tended to stay on one side of the bed. Eventually she would adjust, or maybe she wouldn't even have too.

There was a guy.

A special guy.

Possibly the sweetest, kindest, most thoughtful, gentlemanly man she had ever met in her entire life.

She had met him on the internet. When she finally realized her marriage was crumbling into a state of disrepair and could never be rebuilt, nor did she want it to be, she had started hanging out on dating websites. Not really because she was interested in finding a partner, she had been looking forward to spending some time alone, to really figure out who she was and what she wanted out of life, but because she had just wanted to meet some new friends.

Then she had stumbled upon the Happily Ever After Club. The whole premise of finding a Prince Charming had appealed to her. Her soon-to-be ex-husband was not even close to Prince Charming, although she supposed back when they'd met, she had thought he was pretty dreamy and the fulfiller of all her desires. Thirteen years and two kids later, she no longer saw him that way. Now she saw all his flaws, and all the things that should have stopped her from marrying him in the first place. It wasn't really that he was a bad guy they just weren't compatible.

Unlike Sinbad Charise.

He was exactly what she had been looking for. In fact, he was a lot of things she hadn't even known she was looking for. For the first time in a long time, she was actually excited about her future. It was so nice not to just be going through the motions, stuck in a relationship that sucked the life out of her.

Her alarm buzzed, and simultaneously her phone chimed.

A message.

She knew who it was even before she reached over and picked up her phone from the nightstand.

It was SC.

She was smiling—grinning like a lovesick puppy—as she read his message. That grin managed to grow even bigger when she saw what it said.

He wanted to meet.

Tonight.

Butterflies fluttered in her stomach.

Meeting in person.

They had talked about it a little in the two and a half months they had been corresponding on the internet, but they hadn't talked anything definite. Was she ready to meet him? It would make everything so much more real. She loved talking to him, it was one of the bright spots of her day, but she wasn't even divorced yet, and she had two kids to think about. Bringing a man into their lives was something she would only do if she was completely serious about that man.

So was she?

Was she completely serious about SC?

Was she confident that he could be someone that she would end up marrying?

Mila knew what answer was in her heart, but she had to make sure that the same answer was in her head. She couldn't make another heart choice like she had with her ex. With him, she had let herself get swept up in the moment, let the passion and excitement overwhelm her to the point where she hadn't thought of anything else.

Now she was older and wiser. She had to be smart. This time her head and her heart were in agreement. SC was exactly what she wanted. He was exactly the kind of man she would want to help her raise her children.

Giddy with excitement, she typed back that she would be thrilled to meet him tonight.

He texted back immediately to tell her to expect a package some time this afternoon, and that a limousine would arrive to pick her up at eight.

After wishing each other a fabulous day, Mila climbed out of bed feeling so energized she wanted to go running through the house screaming and yelling for joy. Instead, she kept her cool and headed down to the kitchen. There her kids were already dressed for school, and making themselves breakfast, they were such morning people. Totally unlike herself, if she could, she would sleep till midday then stay up half the night.

Emmy and Mac were the lights of her life. Although she often had major doubts about her abilities as a mother, somehow her kids had turned out great. Emmy was twelve, and it was hard to believe she would soon be the parent of a teenager. Her daughter was a straight A student, and an accomplished swimmer. Mac was nine and was already following in his sister's footsteps with amazing grades and athletic abilities. Besides that, her kids were polite, caring, and well behaved.

"Hey, Mom." Emmy smiled at her and brought over a plate of waffles. "I made these for breakfast."

Could her daughter be more amazing? "Thanks, hon." She took the plate and the three of them moved to the table. "So, how do you guys feel about spending the night at Dad's tonight?"

Her daughter's keen eyes met hers squarely. "Do you have a date?"

Surprised at Emmy's perception but trying to hide it, Mila debated whether to tell the truth or fib. She had never lied to her kids before, well, besides the usual stuff about Santa Clause, the Easter Bunny, and the Tooth Fairy. "Yes, I do."

"I thought so," Mac spoke up.

Mila couldn't help but laugh at that. "You thought so? What made you think that?"

"You're always on the computer talking to that man," her son replied.

She'd thought she'd been so careful to hide her online chat sessions, but apparently she hadn't. "How did you two know about that?"

"Mom." Emmy rolled her eyes.

"Okay, okay, you guys are internet whizzes." She chuckled, then sobered. "So, Dad's tonight?"

"Is it serious?" Emmy asked.

As of right now it was, but she hadn't met SC in person yet, so there was a chance that once they had their date, she would find out that they weren't compatible after all. Again though she owed her kids the truth because this affected them too. "I think it could be."

Emmy and Mac exchanged glances, and Mila was hit by the fact that her kids were growing up. They weren't babies anymore. They knew that things were over between her and their dad. They knew that the divorce would soon be finalized. They knew that in all likelihood soon both her and her ex would move on to other relationships.

She wasn't sure how her kids would take her dating someone other than their father. They had been obviously upset when she and her ex had sat them down and explained that he would be moving out and that they were going to be getting divorced, but on the whole, they had held up well. But this was taking things to the next level. She would never do anything to hurt her kids, and if they needed her to take things slowly with SC because they weren't ready yet then she would do that.

"Dad's tonight," Emmy and Mac said simultaneously.

Letting out a breath she hadn't even known she was holding, Mila relaxed, her kids were the best kids ever. "I love you guys."

"Love you too, Mom," Emmy said, picking up her phone, ready to turn her attention back to her friends.

"Love you, Mom. Can I take my PlayStation to Dad's?"

Her son's priorities were the same as always. Great kids, a great guy who liked her and wanted to be with her, and spoil her, and make her feel like a princess, her life was going great.

9:03 A.M.

"What progress have we made?" Heidi asked as she and Matthew entered their boss' office.

"Tracey ran tox screens on Tillie Schueman," Rylla told Heidi. "There were traces of sleeping pills in her blood, so the killer didn't really have to worry about restraining her when he stabbed her."

"It also means she probably wasn't really aware of what was happening," Matthew added.

"Was that important to him?" Heidi asked. "He drugged Jeannie Jones before he threw her to the bears. Maybe it's not important to him that they suffer, he just has to kill them because since they've seen him and spent time with him he can't let them go."

"I don't think killing them is his goal," Rylla said. "I think he wants them, what exactly he wants from them I don't know, but I think he only kills them because they fail him."

"Except with Georgia," her partner said.

"But Georgia was different. We believe she fought back in a way he wasn't expecting. Tracey found a wound on her wrist that was self inflicted," she informed their boss. "Georgia had to have gotten hold of a blade, she wanted to get him in the room so she could attempt to escape. We believe that she managed to cut him and that's why he washed her down when he didn't bother to do that with the others. Her attempt at escape obviously infuriated him and he lost it, he cut her over thirty times, that's a lot of rage."

"He meets the women on a dating website where people are specifically looking for the whole fairytale package, princesses, prince charmings, and happily ever afters. He manages to charm them, tells them what they want to hear, and convinces them to agree to meet him in person. Alone. There were signs that he had punished Georgia, we assume for not being what he wanted. I think what he's looking for is the perfect woman," Matthew said.

"Only no such thing exists," she said.

"Right," her partner agreed.

"So, he's going to keep killing them. And his tolerance for failure is diminishing. He kept Tillie for less time than he kept Jeannie, and he only kept Georgia two days. Since he has abducted a new victim on the same day as he killed his previous victim, he obviously has several women lined up ready to go, he could be ready to take his next victim today." Although she wanted to believe that they had some time, the killer's MO said he was probably already contacting the next woman, if he hadn't already, to meet tonight for a date.

"As of right now, we don't have any forensics, but we can probably work out a profile that might help us narrow down which profiles on the website are worth flagging," Matthew suggested.

"Can't we just look for any profiles that use a name that means Prince Charming?"

"If we could, we would, but the only way to access every single user of the website is to get a warrant for their records," Matthew replied.

"There are two ways to set up your account," Rylla elaborated. "You can have it set to public where it shows your name, and whatever information about yourself you choose to share. What your job is, have you been married before, do you have kids, hobbies, interests, likes and dislikes, favorite foods, favorite sports, and anything else you want to tell prospective dating partners. Even if you choose to have your profile public that doesn't mean you have to display your name, you can do full name, just first name, initials, just one initial, or a nickname of your choosing. Or you can have your profile set to private, so no one sees anything about you."

"Why would you set it to private?" Heidi looked confused. "Isn't the whole point of the website to meet people? If it's set to private, how would people even know you're there?"

"If you have your profile set to private other people can't see you but you can still see other people. So, you're free to look through profiles and contact anyone that you're interested in, and it means you don't attract the attention of anyone who you don't choose to, which is perfect for our killer. Two public profiles can meet up, one public and one private profile can meet up, but two private profiles can't. Jeannie, Tillie, and Georgia all had public profiles, we're assuming the killer had his set to private," Rylla said.

"Although we are still monitoring any names we have found that mean either prince or charming and taking note of who the person interacts with," Matthew added.

"Even if we could find the killer's profile, some interactions only happen in private. Once you contact someone and they check you out and reply back you can keep your communications on the website or take things to whatever other media you choose. Emails, texts, social media, whatever they choose, so there's no way for us to monitor conversations. With our victims, it looks like they took things to email first, presumably because the women felt safer with that option, then they moved to texting. Keeping things away from the website makes it even harder for us to find him."

"And we can't track him through his account?" Heidi asked. "We would have a record of the account because we went through the women's, so we would know who contacted them."

"He deleted the account as soon as he made contact and they took things to email," Matthew answered.

"And he's obviously good with computers because we weren't able to do anything about backtracking and finding anything out about his account," Rylla said.

"So, computer savvy, that's one thing we know about him for sure. Do we think anything in the stories he told the women was true?" Heidi asked.

"In all the stories he's told he has parents who come from the United Kingdom, so that might possibly be true. Or it might not, and it might just have to do with the names he chose. Otherwise, everything else is different. He listed different schools he went to, different hobbies he's interested in, different number of siblings, different places where he grew up, he seems to tailor each story for the woman he's interacting with," Matthew said. "We are going through everything he told Jeannie Jones extremely carefully. Given that she was his first victim, we thought he might have been more honest with her as he tweaked his strategies of luring the women."

"Although just because he took Jeannie first doesn't mean she was the first woman he spoke with, he obviously has multiple women he's corresponding with at a time," Rylla added.

"Which implies he expects the women to fail," Matthew said thoughtfully. "He has a woman he's abducted but at the same time he's talking to other women who he might want to abduct in the future. It's like although he's searching for something at the same time he doesn't seem to think it exists."

"What *is* he searching for? The perfect woman? If he knows that doesn't exist, then why is he bothering?" Heidi picked up a stress ball in the shape of a teddy bear and began to squeeze it between her fingers.

"He thinks he can train them. He chooses them for certain qualities then believes he can punish them into behaving in the way he wants, then when that fails, he kills them. Assuming he does have his profile set to private on the website, we won't be able to find him on there, we should focus on trying to figure out which women he might target," she said.

"What similarities do they have?" Heidi asked.

"Similar ages," Matthew said. "He's not after anyone too young, or too old, Tillie was the youngest so far at twenty-nine, Jeannie was thirty-one, and Georgia the oldest at thirty-four, that probably puts his age at mid to late thirties."

"Different features but all the women were Caucasian. Jeannie was a brunette with brown eyes, Tillie was a blue eyed blonde, and Georgia had black hair and brown eyes, so obviously hair and eye color aren't important to him. They all had different jobs, Jeannie was a middle school science teacher, Tillie was a dentist, and Georgia worked in finance. Jeannie was a widow, Tillie had been engaged but the wedding fell through at the last minute, and Georgia had never been married or engaged," Rylla summarized.

"That's a lot of differences," Heidi said.

"There are a lot of similarities too," Rylla assured her. "All three women indicated they enjoyed cooking, all expressed an interest in art and literature. All wanted to find a husband who was loving, attentive, and supportive. All wanted kids and to give them a stable home, and their preference was to be able to stay at home with the children for the first years of their lives. All three of them enjoyed eating out at fancy restaurants, liked expensive clothes and shoes, liked traveling and staying in five-star hotels."

"So that's what he's looking for," Heidi said. "That's his picture of an ideal wife. Cultured, will take care of him, will take care of their children, and who enjoys being spoiled."

"And then when the women don't appreciate what he's given them and what he wants to do for them, and they don't want to stay there and take care of him and have children with him, he kills them."

∽

1:17 P.M.

"I wrapped up the Brewster case last night," Nate told Sam as he entered his friend's house. "Turns out he *was* planning on taking the kids and fleeing the country."

"I can't imagine someone taking my child away from me," Sam said. "I don't even like to let Naomi out of my sight because I'm scared something is going to happen to her and the baby. But for someone to take them away, I can't even comprehend how I would cope with that."

Unfortunately, Nate knew exactly what it felt like to have the most important person in your life taken away from you. Six years later and it hadn't gotten any easier. Some days it was hard to believe that he hadn't seen his son in six years. He didn't even know what Andrew looked like, Rachel refused to send him pictures, or to let him talk to him on the phone.

At first, he'd called daily—nearly hourly those first few days and weeks—but over time he had lost hope. He didn't know his son, Rachel was never going to bring him back to the country, and even when he'd flown to Australia to see him, she had refused and called the cops on him.

His own son didn't even know who he was. Andrew had been just a toddler when Rachel had snatched him and fled the country. His two-year-old little brain had forgotten all about him, and Andrew thought that Rachel's new husband was his father.

It killed him to know that his gorgeous little boy was growing up without him.

And what made it worse was knowing it was his own fault he had lost his son.

"Thinking about Andrew?"

Sam, of course, knew about his son, although they didn't talk about him much. Some days Nate wondered if it was time to let his boy go, maybe it would be better for Andrew if he didn't make waves in his life. But he didn't know how to let go of his child. He loved him.

"I should have handled the Brewster case and not left it to you." Sam looked apologetic.

"No, it's fine. It's not like I don't think about him all the time anyway."

"Let's bring another lawyer in, see what we can do."

"I signed over full custody to her, she was free to take Andrew anyplace she wanted." Although if he had of known what Rachel was planning, he would never have given her full custody. At the time, it had seemed like the best option for Andrew. He was in the military, and he had expected that they would work out a visitation schedule that allowed him to co-parent their child when he was in the country.

"You didn't know she was going to take him to another country and cut you out of his life."

"He doesn't even remember me. I haven't spoken to him since he was two years old. He's eight now, he's spent most of his life without me in it."

"Do you want to give up on him?"

"No." He didn't even have to think about it. One day his son would become an adult and then there was nothing Rachel could do to keep them apart. When that time came, Nate wanted Andrew to know that he had never given up on him.

"Then let's find another lawyer, it can't hurt."

In a way it could hurt. If he got his hopes up again only to be told once more there was nothing he could legally do to force his ex-wife to let him see their son, he would be crushed. But Andrew needed him to keep fighting, so he would keep fighting.

"Oh, Nate, I didn't know you were here," Naomi said as she walked into the living room.

"Came for lunch and to update your husband on work since he doesn't want to leave you alone in case you ..." he trailed off when he saw Rylla Franklin walk in behind Naomi.

He and Sam had decided that Luke Sleigh and Summer Height's wedding would be the perfect place for him to try to connect with her again, after all, the last time they'd been at a wedding she'd asked him out. But she was here now, and he needed a distraction.

When her gaze fell on him, Rylla's big green eyes shuttered, and a small frown creased her face.

"I better head back to work," Rylla said to Naomi.

"But you just got here," Naomi protested.

"I know, but I really should be going through the website, looking for women that the killer may be targeting." Rylla steadfastly turned away from him and kept her eyes on Naomi.

Nate knew Rylla and her partner Matthew were working the Fairytale Killer case. The case was all over the media with the melodramatic fairytale themed murders. "Maybe we could help out? Have our computer people run your profiles through their system?" he offered. Sam's company had consulted with the cops before.

"We have people working on it, but thank you," Rylla said formally, borderline icily. "I really should go."

"Stay for a while, please," Naomi begged. "I'm bored, Sam won't let me work, I need some company."

Rylla's gaze darted quickly in his direction then skittered away again. It was clear from the look on her face that she didn't want to stay. Because of him. He had to explain to her why he'd said no when she asked him out. Explain that he'd been scared. That his ex-wife running and taking their son with her had made him afraid of getting involved with someone else. But he knew Rylla was different, she'd never do what Rachel had done. Maybe if he explained it to her, she'd forgive him and give him another chance.

"I'll just grab a quick sandwich and then I'll go," Rylla finally said.

"Great." Naomi beamed. "Sam and I will go whip something up."

Sam rolled his eyes at Naomi but followed her into the kitchen. Rylla glared, and Sam fought back a snort. Naomi loved any opportunity to put him and Rylla in the same room together. He'd known her almost as long as he had known Sam, she was like a sister, and he was just as guilty of trying to set her and Sam up as she was of trying to set him and Rylla up. Although Sam and Naomi had known each other since they were children, it hadn't been until a couple of years ago when someone started stalking Naomi that they had finally gotten together. As much as he wanted Rylla, he hoped it didn't take something that dramatic for them to get together.

Alone, he stared at Rylla, he didn't even know where to start trying to explain Rachel and Andrew. "Did you buy a new dress for Luke and Summer's wedding?" he asked. He knew it was lame, but it was the best he could come up with.

She glared.

"I loved the dress you wore for Sam and Naomi's wedding, the green matched your eyes so beautifully," he tried again.

Her glare deepened. "I can't believe you're bringing that up."

"Rylla, I want to explain why I said no," Nate said earnestly.

"I don't care why," she said haughtily.

He couldn't blame her for not wanting to hear him out, he knew how he would have felt if their positions had been reversed. He'd be embarrassed and angry. He wouldn't want to hear excuses, he would just want to forget it had ever happened and move on, he suspected Rylla felt the same way. But Rylla hadn't moved on. It had been fifteen months and she hadn't dated anyone else, that had to mean he still had a shot. He hoped.

"It's not what you think," he tried again. "I wanted to say yes, but ..."

"I. Don't. Care," she over enunciated each word. "Look, we have to see each other, it's inevitable, Sam's your best friend and Naomi's mine, but that's it. I don't want to talk to you, I don't want to see you, I don't want to listen to anything you have to say. I don't care why you said no, I don't care about you at all. Tell Naomi I'm sorry but I had to go."

With that she turned and stalked out of the room.

Nate watched her go then stared at the empty doorway.

Okay, so that had been a disaster. Getting Rylla to listen to him was going to be harder than he thought. But Rylla wouldn't be this angry if she hadn't felt something for him. He didn't know why his rejection had hurt her so badly, but he intended to find out. He liked her, he thought they could be happy together, he thought he could love her, he wasn't walking away from her just like he wasn't walking away from his son.

7:58 P.M.

He was still furious.

Fuming.

So angry it was a wonder he was able to function at all.

He was beginning to think that the woman he was looking for didn't exist. He'd had three failures now. Three women he thought were the answer to his prayers and all three had not lived up to his expectations.

Jeannie Jones. Fail.

Tillie Schueman. Fail.

Georgia Lars. Fail.

Fail.

Fail.

Fail.

He was sick of failing.

It was *not* going to happen again. He wouldn't let it. He couldn't. He had to find the one. She had to exist. She was out there somewhere. She had to be. She *had* to be. He just couldn't take it not working out again.

He couldn't figure out why things kept turning into a disaster.

What was he doing wrong?

He was choosing women who were smart, with university degrees and good jobs. Who were interested in culture and would appreciate night outs at the opera, the ballet, the theatre, or an art exhibition. Who wanted to work in the home taking care of him and their future children. Who were sweet, kind, and thoughtful women. Who said they were looking for a Prince Charming who would take care of them and provide them with a beautiful home and life.

Well, he was doing just that.

He was providing them with a gorgeous home, where they didn't have to worry about anything, and all he was asking in return was that they follow a few simple rules. Don't speak unless spoken to, know their place as the woman in the relationship, and make fulfilling his needs their top priority.

That was it. That was all he wanted. So why couldn't he get it?

These women acted like he was doing something horrible to them. In reality, he had wooed them, he had asked them out and they had said yes, he had acted like the perfect gentleman. Okay he had needed to discipline them, but that was what you did when you cared about someone.

He had done everything right and what had they done? They had been ungrateful witches. He'd had no choice but to get rid of them and try again.

Georgia was the worst.

Pretending to hurt herself to get him in the room, then trying to attack him.

Unbelievable.

He touched the white bandage on his hand. Georgia had managed to get in a cut, he had been terrified that his blood had gotten on her, that when the cops found her body they would find it and then him. But he thought he'd been thorough enough with his clean. He had scrubbed her for hours, working his way methodically over every inch of her body. Not just focusing on the area where he thought the blood might have fallen but every single part of her. It was better to be safe than sorry.

Even thinking about what she had done made his blood boil. He had been in bed, watching the monitor, and touching himself as he fantasized about the first time he and Georgia would make love. He had been so sure she was the one. She was so smart, so strong, he had thought she would relish having someone who thought she was the most beautiful woman he had ever laid eyes on. He had wanted to treat her like the princess he believed her to be.

But she had fooled him. She wasn't a princess. She wasn't even close. She was a wicked witch who had deserved everything she'd gotten.

Although Georgia had deserved it, and he wasn't sorry about what he had done to her, he was going to have to be more careful. He couldn't let his emotions take over like that again. He had to remain in control. He couldn't expect his women to act like a princess if he wasn't acting like a prince. And a prince never behaved that way. A prince was always in control, guiding, rebuking, caring for his subjects.

If he didn't do his part, how could he ever expect to find happiness?

He'd thought he'd found it. Thought that his life was complete, that he had everything he wanted. But then, in one instant, it was gone.

Just like that.

She was gone.

It was over.

He was alone.

He didn't want to be alone. He wanted to find his soul mate, his other half, his princess, but he kept striking out. Jeannie did nothing but hide in a corner, jumping like a terrified mouse every time he entered the room. Tillie did nothing but sob and cry and weep until he couldn't think straight because of the incessant noise. And Georgia had tried to escape.

Three strikes.

But he wasn't out yet.

Tonight he had a date. With a beautiful red head called Mila. He had decided to do something different this time. Mila was a mother. None of the other women had been. Maybe that was what he was missing. Maybe that was why things hadn't worked out.

A mother was different. She knew what it was to put others before herself.

Mila was the one.

He knew it. He *felt* it. She was going to be the one to make him happy. She was different than the others. He had to approach this differently too. Maybe not reveal himself to her right away. Maybe just give her the rules and let her learn them, then let her know who he was and why he had brought her here. Then once everything was worked out and they were happy together he would bring her children back to her. Then they would be happy too.

He pulled the limousine to a stop outside Mila's house. Just a little late, enough to make sure she was anxious and off-guard. Grabbing the bag of rose petals, he climbed out of the vehicle, and sprinkled a trail up to the front door. It was a nice romantic touch that the women seemed to enjoy, and it gave him time to get ready.

He rang the doorbell and then hurried back to the limousine. He climbed into the driver's seat and watched and waited. A moment later the door swung open, and Mila stepped out.

She took his breath away.

She was a vision of beauty.

He had sent her a gorgeous pink dress, his favorite of all the dresses he'd given to his prospective princesses. He had worried that the pink might clash with her beautiful red locks but seeing her now, standing at her open front door, with her hair swept up on top of her head, and her milky white skin glowing in the last of the sunlight, he knew he needn't have worried. She was gorgeous, and even from here her green eyes glowed like emeralds.

She was literally breathtaking.

Confusion marred her pretty face when she saw that no one was at the door waiting for her. Then she noticed the rose petals and a smile transformed her from beautiful to something he couldn't ever put into words. She stooped and scooped a few off the ground, bringing them to her nose and breathing in the sweet fragrance.

Then she stood and looked down the front path. He could tell the exact second she spotted the limousine and realized it was waiting for her. It was like she looked right through the one-way glass and saw him. Their eyes met and he felt that connection. He'd been right. Mila was the one.

She hurried down the path toward the limousine and threw open the door. He heard her small exclamation of surprise when she found it empty. He had a camera in the back and watched on the small screen as she saw the box of chocolates and the glass of champagne waiting for her.

She slid onto the leather seat and closed the door, and he let out a breath. She was in. She was his. She ate a couple of the chocolates, drank half the glass of champagne, and picked up the envelope addressed to her. She was just sliding the card out when the glass dropped from her hand.

The sedatives he'd laced the chocolate and her drink with were strong and fast acting.

Realizing something was wrong with her, her features became concerned, her smile vanished, all sense of intrigue and curiosity gone. Mila turned to the door but found that there were no doorhandles on the inside.

She was trapped.

Well not trapped, that had such negative connotations. She was safe, protected, secure until he could get her to her new home.

Mila thumped a weak hand on the window, then slumped down against the seat, the card fluttered to the floor. A moment later, she was unconscious.

He couldn't take his eyes off her as she lay on the seat of the limousine. She was so pretty, his sleeping beauty. He had to touch her.

He quickly climbed out of the car and moved into the back, reverently he reached out a hand and touched her cheek. Her skin was so soft, so delicate, so smooth beneath his fingertips.

She was perfect, and she was his.

CHAPTER
Five

July 27th
6:23 A.M.

Rylla lay in bed staring at the ceiling. She hadn't slept well last night. Well, that wasn't one hundred percent true. The real problem was that she had slept *too* well. Her deep sleep had been filled with dreams. Erotic dreams. Erotic dreams of Nate Oakland.

Why did she have to see him yesterday? Usually, she avoided him as best she could. Sometimes she had to see him since they had mutual friends, but that was usually more of a group gathering where she could just make sure she kept herself occupied with other people, but yesterday it had just been Sam, Naomi, Nate, and herself. She'd had no choice but to talk to him, especially since Naomi had made sure they ended up alone in the room together.

She felt a teensy bit bad about just walking out on him.

No, more than a teensy big.

She'd been rude. She hadn't done it consciously, she just couldn't be around him.

Nate had been the first man since her husband's death that she had been seriously interested in. She'd known him for several years, and the attraction had been almost instantaneous. Back then, her loss had been too fresh, and her emotions too raw, and she hadn't done anything about it.

That attraction had never diminished. In fact, it had only grown stronger. But she had been afraid, it was hard to think about stepping into a new relationship when you had lost the man of your dreams. Her love for Josh didn't die with him, and it felt like a betrayal of sorts to move on and be with someone else. She knew that Nate was interested in her and they sort of danced around each other, neither of them willing to make the first move. Rylla knew about Nate's ex and his son, although she didn't know the details, and she had assumed that just as she wasn't ready to try dating, he wasn't either.

Then her best friend's wedding had come along.

She fully admitted to getting caught up in the magic of Naomi and Sam's wedding. The dress, flowers, lights, and the happiness on her friend's face. As much as it had reminded her of Josh and their wedding and everything she had lost, it had also filled her with longing. She missed being married, she missed coming home to someone each night, and just sitting around talking about their days or chilling and watching TV. She knew she could never replace her husband, and he would always be her first love, but she had been ready to open her heart up to someone else.

So, she had asked Nate out.

And he had said no.

She had never felt so humiliated in all her life. She'd been young when she and Josh got together, *very* young, so she hadn't dated much, and she had never asked anyone out. The few guys she had dated since her husband died had been nothing serious, more like hanging out with a friend, but she had felt something for Nate, and she'd thought he felt the something for her. To find out he didn't made her feel so stupid, and completely turned her off the whole dating thing. Maybe you only got one real chance at love in a lifetime, and she had already had hers.

Now she couldn't even look at Nate without feel mortified and stupid—but still oh so attracted to him—so the easier option was just to ignore him and ...

The chiming of her doorbell pulled her out of her thoughts.

It was early, who would be here?

Rylla climbed out of bed and threw on an oversized t-shirt over the tank top and panties she slept in. She debated grabbing her gun but decided again it, if it was someone who wanted to hurt her, they wouldn't ring the doorbell.

The sense of foreboding that often foreshadowed bad news descended on her, but she brushed it away. What bad news could she get? Her husband and daughter were already dead. What else was there for her to lose?

Nonetheless that feeling grew when she opened her door to find Matthew, and Jonathon Dawson and Allina Bennett standing there. Three cops on her doorstep before seven in the morning, that couldn't be a good thing.

"What's up?" she asked, wondering if there had been a break in the Fairytale Killer case and she had slept through a phone call.

"Can we come in?" Matthew asked.

The look on her partner's face had her stomach dropping, but she pasted on a smile and shoved all bad feelings away. There was no news she could receive that would be worse than officers turning up at her door to tell her that her family had been killed in a car accident.

"Sure." She held the door open and led everyone to the living room. As much as she wanted to ask what was going on, she kept her mouth shut. If she didn't acknowledge the somber presence in the room then maybe it didn't really exist.

Jonathon was Naomi's brother-in-law, and he was steadfastly refusing to meet her gaze, as was her partner. Allina was looking at her but the look in her eyes was even more non-reassuring than the guys' refusals to look at her.

Since it seemed none of them were going to start the conversation she asked, "What's going on?"

"It's your sister." Matthew finally looked her way.

"Mila?" Panic shot through her. What had happened to her sister?

Car accident? Home invasion? Fire? Had her niece and nephew been hurt too? "What happened to her?"

"She's missing," Jonathon blurted out.

That took a moment to sink in. "Missing?"

"After a date," Allina added.

A date? Her sister was dating? She and Mila hadn't been close since they were in high school. After her older sister and brother had left home some really bad stuff had happened and it had divided the family and torn them apart. She and Mila talked, but not regularly, and when they did it was more of a quick catch up because they both felt obligated to keep the relationship going. She knew that her sister was in the process of getting divorced, but she hadn't known she was dating.

"With someone she met on a website," Allina said gently.

Rylla felt her stomach drop. It was clear where this was headed but she clung to denial.

"The Happily Ever After Club. I'm sorry, Rylla." Allina looked devastated.

That couldn't be true. Why would her sister be looking for men in an online dating community when she was looking forward to getting divorced and spending some time figuring out her own life?

"There were rose petals on the front path, and she received a package earlier that day. A dress. I'm really sorry," Allina said again.

"No," she said firmly. "The Fairytale Killer didn't take Mila. She's going through a messy divorce. She and her almost ex have been fighting over custody of Emmy and Mac. You need to look into Beau Drake. That's her husband. I don't like him. I never did. I told Mila he was no good. He must have done something to her so that he could get the house and the kids and everything else."

"How would he know about the killer's MO, Ry?" Matthew asked.

She shrugged, then stood and began to move restlessly around the room. "I don't know, but I do know that my sister wouldn't be looking for men online. And she's smart. Even if she was hanging out in some dating chat room, she wouldn't fall for whatever stupid story the Fairytale Killer would have made up. She has kids, she wouldn't agree to meet some guy she didn't even know on her own, she would meet in a public place where she'd be safe, she always puts Emmy and Mac first. She just wouldn't do it. She wouldn't," she argued against her friends' stubborn silence. "You don't know her like I do. Beau must have done something to her. He must have. My sister is not a victim of the Fairytale Killer."

"Okay, okay," Matthew soothed. He'd followed her when she began to pace and now grabbed hold of her shoulders, stilling her. "You know we're going to look into everything. Everything, Rylla. We will find whoever took your sister."

How?

How would they find her?

If Beau had done something to Mila then they might never find her. He could have thrown her into a lake or a river tied to a rock so her body was never found. He could have buried her somewhere in a shallow grave. He could have burned her body till it was nothing but a pile of ash. He could have done anything to her. Literally anything. He wanted his kids and everything he and Mila had accumulated during their marriage, and getting Mila out of the picture certainly accomplished that.

And if the Fairytale Killer had her sister, Rylla didn't even want to think about that.

She knew what the killer was capable of, and she knew they had no solid leads.

If it was the Fairytale Killer who had taken Mila, then she knew she would never see her sister alive again.

∼

8:16 A.M.

Matthew hadn't wanted to leave Rylla alone, so he'd called Naomi and Sam and asked them to go and check up on her. She had wanted to come with him, but she couldn't be part of this case now that her sister was a victim. And even if his partner couldn't accept it yet they all knew that Mila was the Fairytale Killer's next victim.

It was hard to believe this was happening. How had Rylla's sister ended up on the killer's hit list? So far, he hadn't gone after anyone with children, and Mila wasn't even divorced yet, did the killer know that? It didn't seem like the kind of woman he would be interested in. If he was really after the perfect woman, wouldn't that mean someone who was a good mother? And if he wanted a good mother then why would he take her and leave her children without their mother?

The killer was getting so desperate he wasn't thinking straight anymore. That could be a good or a bad thing. It made him more dangerous as he was likely to be less tolerant to the women failing and not meet his expectations. The flip side was hopefully the more desperate he got the more mistakes he would make, and one big mistake could be all it took to lead them straight to him.

"Naomi just texted to say she and Sam are at Rylla's," Jonathon announced.

"Good, I'm glad she's not alone," Matthew said. He'd wanted to stay at Rylla's until Naomi and Sam arrived, but his partner had insisted she needed some time alone to try to wrap her head around the news.

"Mila Drake doesn't seem to fit the killer's profile," Jonathon said.

Hopefully they would find out more about why the killer may have targeted her inside the house they had pulled up in front of.

"Do they know?" Allina asked.

"Yes, they were the ones who called it in. When Mila didn't call her kids to say goodnight, they were worried and insisted on getting their dad to take them around to their mom's house to check on her. At the house they saw rose petals on the front path and no sign of Mila. The press had reported on the flower petal thing, so they immediately called the cops," Matthew replied.

He knocked on the door and a moment later it was flung open by Mila's soon to be ex-husband, Beau Drake.

"Do you know anything yet?" the man demanded immediately.

"No, nothing yet," Matthew answered. "May we come in?"

Beau hesitated, his dark eyes uncertain. "Can we do this later?"

"No, we can't," he said, gently but firmly. "We need to get as much information as we can as quickly as we can so that we can find Mila." Although he didn't want to say it, Matthew didn't hold out much hope that they would find Mila Drake alive. They didn't know enough about the killer yet, and he'd kept Georgia Lars for only two days. He was devolving quickly and anything Mila did that angered him would likely lead to him killing her in a rage. Right now, her family didn't need to know that.

"I need to do what's best for my kids," Beau said.

"Isn't what's best for your kids that we do whatever we can to find their mother?" Jonathon asked quietly.

"They're upset, they're scared, they haven't slept, maybe it would be better if you came back tomorrow," Beau persisted, edging the door closed a little.

Matthew was surprised by the man's attitude. While he didn't agree with Rylla's theory that her sister's almost ex was responsible for whatever happened to her—they knew it was the Fairytale Killer—Beau Drake certainly didn't seem particularly concerned about his wife's fate. Whether their relationship was over or not, they had been married for over a decade and had two children together, but instead of being worried he seemed almost pleased to have Mila out of the way.

Before he could say again that time was of the essence if they wanted to have a hope of finding his children's mother alive, a figure appeared in the hall behind Beau.

"It's okay, Dad. We want to talk to them. We want to do anything we can to help them find Mom."

Twelve-year-old Emmy Drake came up behind her father. The girl was tall and thin, with long dark hair that hung to her waist and dark soulful eyes. She looked just like her father, only unlike her father her expression was worried, and her eyes were red rimmed with dark circles underneath.

"You don't have to talk to them, honey." Beau put an arm around her shoulders.

"But I want to," Emmy said firmly.

"Okay," Beau relented and opened the door for them.

The townhouse was small, just one open room. A couch was by the door facing a TV, a kitchen was at the far end, and a four-seater dining table sat between the sitting area and the kitchen. A young boy sat at the table, a plate with a piece of toast sat in front of him but he wasn't touching it, he was watching them with big scared green eyes. While Emmy took after her father, nine-year-old Mac took after his mother, he had Mila—and Rylla's—curly red hair, freckles, and green eyes.

"Is it true that a serial killer took Mom?" Emmy asked, her pale face serious but composed.

Seeing no reason to lie, Matthew nodded. "At the moment that is what we believe."

"Did you guys know your mom was dating someone?" Allina asked.

The children exchanged glances then looked to their father. It was clear they were uncomfortable discussing their mother's love life when their parents were in the middle of a divorce.

"It was someone she met online," Emmy finally said.

"Do you know his name?" Matthew asked.

The girl shook her head. "It was something weird."

That the children didn't know was no big deal, they would look through Mila's computer and find the name the killer had used for his persona with her.

"Mom talked to you about her boyfriend?" Beau looked angry at the prospect.

Both kids shook their heads. "We saw stuff on Mom's computer," Mac said quietly.

"Do you know where your mom met him?" Matthew wanted to keep the children focused on him and his questions and not on their dad and his feelings.

"A chat room I think, one of those dating ones," Emmy replied.

"Do you remember anything he told your mom about himself?"

"Not really," Emmy said slowly. "I didn't really pay much attention. When I used Mom's computer it was usually for school stuff."

Sensing she had picked up the odd thing about her mom's online boyfriend, Matthew pushed her. "Anything at all that you remember could be really helpful, Emmy."

"I did see a couple of things," the girl said cautiously.

"Tell them, honey," Beau prompted, looking interested for the first time. Perhaps he wanted to know what kind of man his wife had been dating so quickly after they separated.

"He said he was from Europe, but that he came here as a kid. Then moved back there when he got married, but his wife had recently divorced him, so he'd come back here again. I didn't mean to be nosy, I was just curious." She eyed them all imploringly.

"It's okay, honey," Beau said, his tone seemed false and patronizingly placating.

The story Emmy had told them fitted in with the rest of the victims. The Europe connection again, and he had tailored his story to fit with what Mila was currently going through. "Did your mom talk about him at all?"

"No," Mac said.

"She didn't even know we knew about him until yesterday when she asked us if we would spend the night at Dad's," Emmy added.

Maybe Mila had chosen yesterday to mention her new boyfriend to her kids because he had asked her to meet in person. He had moved up his schedule with her because he had expected to keep Georgia for a lot longer. Obviously, on some level, he never expected to find the woman of his dreams because if he did there would be no need to have a whole lot of women lined up, cultivated, and ready to go.

"Has anything unusual happened lately?" Jonathon asked the kids.

Again, they exchanged glances. "There was something," Emmy said.

"A man in our house about a week ago," Mac added.

That sounded promising. "A man?"

"We came home early. We were at a friend's house, swimming in their pool, but their grandmother got rushed to the hospital. It was only a couple of hours till Mom would be home from work, so she said it was okay for us to go home and hang out there. When we got home a man was inside, he said he was an electrician that Mom had called to do some work. He said he was done, and he left," Emmy trailed off nervously.

"Did he come back?" Matthew asked. "Did he do something to either of you?" If it was the Fairytale Killer that the children had seen then it didn't fit his MO that he would harm either of them, but just because he hadn't done it so far—that they knew of—didn't mean he wouldn't do it.

"No," Emmy replied quickly. "But Mom was angry when we told her. She said everything was fine, but we heard her on the phone with someone later that night. She said she never called an electrician and she thought the man was ..." again she trailed off and shot her father an anxious glance.

"Who did she think it was, Emmy," he prodded.

"She thought Dad hired a private investigator to try and find something on her that he could use in the divorce so he'd get us, and the house, and everything else," Emmy finished.

"I wouldn't do that, Emmy," Beau said quickly.

The girl turned scared eyes to them. "Do you think we saw the man who took our mom?"

"You very well could have," Matthew answered. "Do you remember what he looked like?"

"He was old," Mac said immediately.

Old to a kid and actually old were two different things. "How old?" Matthew asked. "My age, your dad's age, older?"

"About dad's age," Emmy said.

That would put him in his late thirties, the age they believed the killer to be. "What did he look like?"

"He was tall, and he had blonde hair, and brown eyes," Emmy replied quickly.

"Do you think if we asked you to work with someone who draws faces that you two could help him draw one that looked like the man you saw?" Jonathon asked.

Both children nodded solemnly.

"Are you going to find our mom?" Emmy asked.

"Yes," he answered honestly.

"Alive?" the girl asked.

That was still up in the air. He wanted to promise her that they would find her mother alive and bring her home, but he couldn't do it. He couldn't lie just to give her false hope. Although he didn't want to lie to the twelve-year-old the words stuck in his throat and wouldn't come out.

Apparently, he didn't need to say the words. The look on his face was answer enough.

Emmy's composure finally cracked, her face crumpled, her dark eyes filled with tears that quickly overflowed down her cheeks, and she flung herself into her father's arms. When his sister fell apart, Mac quickly followed. Beau gathered both of his crying children into his arms, but the smug look on his face set Matthew's teeth on edge. Beau Drake may not be the killer, but he was still a rotten human being.

~

11:06 A.M.

Mila was frantic about her kids.

She had to get to them. They'd be worried about her. They'd be scared and hurting. They couldn't lose their mother. She couldn't die here, she couldn't do that to her children. She had to get out of here. Mila just didn't know how.

How could she have been so stupid?

Falling for some ridiculous story from a stranger. She knew better than that. She had spent many hours talking at length with her twelve-year-old about keeping herself safe online. They had talked about predators, that some people were out to hook victims and would tell them anything they wanted to hear. They had talked about being cautions and remembering that the photo the person showed you wasn't necessarily them, and that you could never know if what they were telling you was true or not.

All this time she had been so worried about her almost teenage daughter falling victim to a sexual predator, and yet she hadn't heeded her own warning and now she was the victim.

Was this her punishment for dating someone while she was still married? Sure, she and Beau were separated and were in the process of getting divorced, but technically she was still married so technically she had been planning on committing adultery.

She had to get out of this room. Mila had been trying to work the screws out of the door pretty much since she woke up here.

He had drugged her. The chocolates and champagne waiting for her in the limousine had been laced with sleeping pills or something. When she woke up, she had been here. In this room reminiscent of a medieval castle. He had changed her out of the pink dress he'd had sent to her house for their supposed first date and into a long white cotton night-gown. Her first thought had been that he'd raped her while she was unconscious, but she didn't think he had.

The second thought she'd had upon waking was how she was going to get out of here. During her frenetic search to try to find a way out she had found the food he left for her alongside a detailed list of rules she was to learn.

She couldn't care less about his rules.

All she wanted was to get out of here.

She wouldn't allow herself to die here, alone, and leave her children without a mother. So, she had been working on the door. Logically she knew it made no sense. With her bare hands she would never remove the screws from the door hinges, but she couldn't stop. No matter how slim the chances of escaping were, she couldn't stop. She couldn't give up. If she never made it home to Emmy and Mac, she at least had to die knowing she did everything she could.

Mila was so engrossed in her task that when the door suddenly swung open, she jumped to her feet, thinking she had succeeded, and ran right into a man.

"Enough." He grasped her shoulders and shook her. "Stop trying to escape, you're hurting yourself."

Stunned by the man she had known as SC suddenly being here in front of her, Mila just stood there. By the time she snapped out of her shocked haze, he had closed the door and was locking it behind him. She wanted to fight him for the key that he put on a chain around his neck, but she sensed that fighting him would make him angry. Possibly angry enough to kill her, and she couldn't do that to her children. So, she bit her lip to keep quiet and just stood there, unsure what to do. What *did* one say when alone in a room with their kidnapper?

"I thought you would stop," he said.

He thought she would stop? Had he been watching her? Were there cameras in here? The thought made her shiver.

"I'll bandage your hands."

Her hands? Mila looked down at them and saw that they were covered in blood, and most of her nails were ragged and partially ripped off. She hadn't even realized she'd hurt them. She had no time to worry about that, her sole focus was getting away from here alive.

"Come. Sit." He took her arm and led her toward the sitting area.

Unable to fight against it any longer, Mila pulled back and tugged herself free from his grip. "Don't touch me," she spat.

She couldn't see his face because he was wearing a black ski mask, but she could feel the anger rolling off him. He didn't like her talking back to him. Well, that was too bad, he could take her against her will and lock her up here, but he couldn't control how she felt about it.

"Didn't you read the rules?" he asked tightly.

She stared defiantly at him and shook her head. She didn't care about his rules, she didn't care about what he wanted from her, she just wanted to go home. His arm twitched like he wanted to hit her, and she tried not to flinch.

"You will read the rules while I tend to your hands," he instructed.

The way he said it like it was a foregone conclusion angered her. He thought he could break her down and make her become his ideal woman, but she wasn't playing that game. She just didn't know how far to push him, and gauging it was harder because she couldn't see his face.

"Go and sit down." He pointed to the armchairs by the fireplace.

He was testing her, seeing how compliant she was going to be. The sensible part of her brain said to do as she was told, but the part that hadn't allowed another adult to order her around since she had become an adult herself screamed at her to resist. "Let me go, please. I have two children, they need me. Please, I want to go home."

"If you had bothered to read the rules I left for you then you'd know that you don't speak unless spoken to, and if I tell you to do something you do it."

No longer thinking whether the choices she was making were smart or not, desperation descended on her and she threw herself at him. "Let me go, please. Why are you doing this? Why did you lie to me? Why did you pretend to be someone who wanted to date me? I don't understand. I thought you liked me. I liked you, I thought we could have been happy together. I don't understand why you kidnapped me, I don't understand why you brought me here, I don't understand any of this. Let me go, please, let me go, let me go, let me go." She began to sob and sank down to the floor. She couldn't take any more of this.

"Stop it." He grabbed her roughly and dragged her to her feet. "This ridiculous behavior is unacceptable."

He bent her over his arm and delivered a hard blow to her backside. Mila yelped in surprise and tried to wiggle out of his arms. The man tightened his hold on her and delivered several more blows. Then he released her, and she crumpled to the floor.

There were plenty of times in her marriage where her husband had made her feel like less than nothing, but she had never felt like *this* in her life. The fear, the humiliation of being spanked, she wanted to curl up and die. Only she didn't. She wanted to live. She wanted to go home to her children.

"You *will* learn to obey me." He put his hands under her arms and carried her over to the sitting area and deposited her into an armchair.

Mila didn't fight back.

The fight had temporarily drained from her.

Was he right?

Would she really learn to obey him if it was the only way to stay alive?

Staying alive had to be her number one priority. The police would find her. Rylla would do whatever it took to get her home. She had to believe that. No matter how repulsive the idea of submitting to this masked man was, if it was the only thing that guaranteed she remained alive then she might have to do it.

3:34 P.M.

"Did we get the interview?" Matthew asked Jonathon and Allina. Now that Rylla had become personally involved in the case their boss was taking her off it, Jonathon and Allina were going to be replacing her.

"Yes, we did," Jonathon replied. "First thing tomorrow we're meeting with Joynelle and Jaden Kite."

The Kites were the owners of the Happily Ever After Club. So far, they had refused to speak with them, saying that there was no proof that they had done anything wrong or that the murders were related to their business. One case and that might be true, back then they had been looking at someone with a personal grudge against Jeannie Jones. Two cases and they had started looking for connections between Jeannie and Tillie Schueman, the only one they had been able to find was the internet dating company. Three cases and it was no longer just a coincidence that the victims had all gone missing from dates with someone they met on the website.

And now there were four cases.

There was no doubt that the link was the Happily Ever After Club. Whether that meant it was a user or one of the owners was still up for debate.

Jaden Kite was thirty-seven, he and his wife had recently filed for divorce, he had a history of drinking and becoming violent, and he matched the description the Drake kids had given them. At the moment he was their prime suspect, hopefully when they interviewed him, they would be able to figure out if there was more than circumstantial evidence that pointed to him.

"We also have another avenue," Jonathon pulled out a photo. "This is Hendrick Mint."

Matthew took the photo, an angry, brown-eyed man with shortly cropped blonde hair and a scowl stared back at him. "Who is he?"

"He's Georgia Lars gardener," Allina replied.

"Why is he a suspect?"

"He used to work at the same school where Jeannie worked," Allina answered.

"Why didn't we know about him earlier?"

"His name just came up. We're still going through backgrounds of all the women looking for connections. Apparently, Hendrick was fired from the school after several complaints about him," Jonathon said.

"What kind of complains?"

"He was a little too interested in some of the moms," Allina told him. "There were at least four women who claimed he would come up to them and try to strike up a conversation. He would pepper them with questions about themselves, and then get angry when his interest wasn't reciprocated. He would then harass the women every morning when they dropped their kids off at school. When the women reported him to the principal, he was given a talk and told not to speak with the parents. He didn't listen. In the end the school fired him, and he went to work for a company that does residential garden work, mowing lawns, trimming trees, mulching flower or vegetable garden beds, that kind of thing."

"Did he ever interact with either Jeannie or Georgia?"

"Teachers at the school said they never saw Jeannie talk to him, but he was often seen watching the female teachers. Georgia's roommate said no, Hendrick was just the contractor the company sent out," Matthew replied.

"They remembered him though?"

"He was good-looking, but he couldn't seem to interact well with people," Allina said. "If he's our guy it could be why he moved to internet dating, easier to make a good first impression."

"Any connections yet to Tillie and Mila?"

"Nothing yet but we'll keep looking," Jonathon said.

"We need to try and set up an interview."

"We're still trying to track him down. He lost his apartment when he lost his job at the school, he's been staying with friends but moving around a bit," Allina told him.

Matthew was about to say they should call family and friends of Tillie Schueman and Mila Drake and see if anyone recognized the gardener when he spotted Rylla enter the room. Jonathon and Allina saw her too.

"She shouldn't be here," Allina said quietly.

"No, she shouldn't." He stood and went to his partner, stopping her before she could see the sketch her niece and nephew had given them, and the picture of their potential suspects. "Go home, Ry."

"I don't want to go home," she snapped. "I need to work."

"You can't work this case anymore," he reminded her gently.

"Why?" she demanded, her green eyes shooting arrows at him. "We don't know for sure what happened to my sister."

"Go home, Rylla," Matthew repeated. He didn't take his partner's anger personally, she was upset and lashing out.

She brushed past him and zeroed in on the photo of Hendrick Mint. "Is that him?"

"Rylla, go and be with your family."

"I can't go and see those kids now, not until I can bring their mother home to them." She looked aghast at the prospect of seeing her niece and nephew under any other circumstances.

"You are not working this case, take a couple of days, we're doing everything we can to find her."

Rylla deflated right in front of him. "We haven't been close since we were little girls, I was angry that she didn't believe me, that she never came looking for me those years I was gone, but now I don't care, I just want her back."

He had no idea what she was talking about, but it didn't matter, he put his arms around his partner and felt her shudder. "We'll find her, Rylla."

"She's stubborn, she might make him angry like Georgia did," she whispered. "It's our fault. We couldn't find him. We didn't stop him. And now he has my sister."

～

9:12 P.M.

She felt so guilty.

Rylla was no stranger to guilt.

She had felt guilty about what had happened to her parents. If only she'd paid more attention to what was going on at home, if only she hadn't been so wrapped up in her friends and the boys she liked, then maybe it wouldn't have happened.

And she felt guilty that Josh had taken Elianna out that afternoon because she had forgotten the flour for the cake she'd been planning on baking for a party with some of their friends that weekend. If she hadn't forgotten then they wouldn't have been in the car, and if they hadn't been in the car they would never have been in the accident, and if they had never been in the accident then they wouldn't have died. She should have been the one to go to the supermarket. Then if the accident had still occurred, she would have been the one to die, and not her precious husband and daughter.

Now, because she and Matthew had failed at their job, her sister might die. Her niece and nephew might grow up without a mother.

The guilt was crushing her.

"Rylla, you should eat something," Naomi said for probably the hundredth time.

"I can't, my stomach is churning," she replied, chewing on her already ripped and tattered fingernails.

"You shouldn't bite your nails anymore, you're going to make them bleed." Naomi tried to tug her hand away from her mouth.

Shaking her friend's hand off, she snapped, "*You're* going to reprimand me for how I deal with guilt and stress? Really? Aren't you the person that allowed herself to get kidnapped because she felt guilty about what her stalker had done?"

Rylla regretted saying that as soon as the words were out of her mouth.

Naomi's eyes dropped and she lifted her hand and pressed it to her chest, just below her left breast where Rylla knew there was a scar from the bullet wound that had almost killed her. She knew Naomi still had nightmares about the stalker and bringing it up served no purpose other than making them both feel bad. She hated making her friend feel bad. Why did she keep lashing out? Naomi had been here all day with her, helping to distract her, and how did she repay her friend? By being mean.

"I'm sorry, Naomi."

"It's okay."

"No, it's not, I'm being mean for no good reason. Thanks for being here today, I really appreciate it." If she'd been alone today, she would have lost it. She wanted to work. She wanted to keep so busy that she didn't have time to dwell on her sister's abduction and her guilt about not finding the killer quickly enough. She hated that Matthew had made her leave, and that Jonathon and Allina and Heidi had backed him up. She didn't want to take time off from work, work would help keep her sane.

"Naomi, it's time to go home," Sam announced.

"We can't go, I don't want Rylla to be alone," Naomi protested.

"I'll be fine on my own," Rylla said immediately, although the prospect of being alone with her thoughts was a daunting one, but Naomi looked tired and she needed sleep.

"She won't be on her own," Sam said.

Rylla wondered who was coming. Matthew maybe?

"Who's coming?" Naomi asked.

"Me."

They all turned as Nate walked into her kitchen.

"Sam, I don't think this is the time for matchmaking." Naomi shot her husband a reprimanding look.

"I'm not trying to, this is just about being practical. They know each other, Rylla won't be alone, and I can take you home so you can get some rest."

"I can stay here with Rylla, I'm not that tired, and I can sleep here," Naomi said.

"No," Sam said bluntly. "I'm taking you home to go to bed, that's not up for debate. I know you won't sleep if you're worried about Rylla, if Nate stays here then you won't have to worry."

"Rylla is going to send him away the second we drive off down the street," Naomi protested.

"I won't," she assured her friend. She didn't want Nate to stay, she'd rather be alone than have him here in her home, but Sam was right. Naomi would lie awake all night worrying if she didn't let Nate stay. And so as not to have just lied to her best friend she'd let Nate stay for an hour or so and then send him on his way.

"You promise?" Naomi asked.

"Yes." *I hope*, she added to herself.

"Okay." Her friend sighed. "But you'll call if you need me, right?"

"Of course."

Naomi moved to stand, but Sam preempted her by scooping her into his arms. Naomi slipped her arm around his shoulders and relaxed into him. They looked so at ease with one another. Rylla missed that so much, that comfortableness around another person. She had loved it when Josh had swung her up into his arms and carried her around like she weighed nothing at all.

Her eyes misted but she faked a smile. "I'll call you in the morning," she told Naomi.

"Try to sleep," Naomi told her.

"I will."

Uncomfortable alone with Nate, Rylla stood and made herself a cup of tea. She didn't want him here in her home. Although she supposed it *was* a distraction. His presence had pushed thoughts of her sister to the back of her mind, which made her feel guilty all over again. She should not be thinking about men, even men she had no intention of ever dating, when her sister was suffering.

"It's not necessary for you to stay. I don't know why Naomi is making such a fuss, I am fine to be on my own but thank you for your concern," she said formally. She might not be thrilled about being alone with her thoughts, but it was still preferable to spending the evening with Nate Oakland.

"You just found out your sister has been abducted by a serial killer. You shouldn't be on your own right now. No one should. You're stuck with me." Nate's brown eyes were calm and he appeared unfazed by her orders to leave.

Why did he have to be so delectably hot?

If she wasn't physically attracted to him then rebuffing him would be so much easier. Whatever. It didn't matter. He obviously wasn't interested in her. He'd said no when she asked him out.

She turned to the counter, keeping her back firmly to Nate, and fiddled with the canisters. "Thank you for the offer, and I appreciate you being here to ease Naomi and Sam's concerns, but I'm not your concern, so you can leave."

"I'm not here for Naomi and Sam."

Large hands covered her shoulders, spun her around, and then he kissed her.

Stunned, for a moment she just stood there before leaning into him and kissing him back. Before she even realized it, her hands were running up his stomach and winding around his neck. For one moment she didn't think of anything other than that she was kissing Nate, that his hands were around her waist, pulling her up against his hard, lean body.

Too soon he pulled away. His breathing was ragged, his eyes swirling with a mess of emotions. "I shouldn't have done that. I'm sorry."

"I'm not," she said softly.

His eyes widened like he hadn't expected her to say that. "I guess it was a good distraction," he said cautiously.

Rylla nodded slowly. "It was, but that wasn't what I meant."

Hope lit up his face. "Rylla, when I said no it wasn't because I didn't want to go out with you, it was ..."

"No." She pressed a finger to his lips and held it there. "I can't do this now. We can talk later, but not now." She believed him when he said that he had wanted to say yes, she'd felt it when they kissed, and if she was honest with herself, she had known it all along. But staying angry with him and blaming him for them not being a couple was easier than letting go of the fear that came with opening up her heart again. They would talk, but now wasn't the time for a conversation about it. Right now she had to focus on her sister and finding her and bringing her home to her children.

Nate nodded and gently removed her finger from his lips, turning it around and examining the torn and bloody nail. "You bite your nails," he noted. "Come, sit, I'll give you a manicure."

That was the last thing she had expected him to say, and she couldn't help but laugh. "You're going to give me a manicure?"

He smiled, which made him look pretty darn adorable. "My mom owned a salon, I practically grew up there, and I have four sisters, I know how to do a manicure. You have things I can use?"

"Upstairs bathroom," she answered.

"Meet you back here in a moment." He grinned then dashed up the stairs.

Rylla was still smiling as she took a seat at the table, Nate was just full of surprises. She had never had a manicure, she'd always been too ashamed of her chewed nails to go and get one. Between her and Mila her sister had always been the girly one. As a kid, Rylla had preferred climbing trees, and playing sports, and doing stunts on her bike. Mila had loved the whole makeup and hair and clothes thing. Jeans and sweaters and sneakers had been Rylla's outfits of choice. So many times Mila had rebuked her about her dress sense and told her that more boys would ask her out, but Rylla had been happy with her guy friends and had never bothered to girly herself up.

"Try not to think about it."

Her eyes were watery when she looked up at Nate. "How?"

"I don't know," he said as he sat and picked up her hand, beginning to file her nails with an emery board.

"He could be hurting her." Pictures of what the Fairytale Killer could be doing to Mila right at this very second kept playing through her mind on a loop.

"Thinking that doesn't help. It doesn't help you, and it doesn't help your sister. You have to try to keep positive. You have to try not to keep thinking about it."

"I don't know how to do that."

"We'll talk, about whatever you want, whatever it takes so you don't dwell." Nate set her left hand in a small dish of warm water and picked up her other hand.

"Nate?"

"Yeah?" He glanced up from his task.

"Thank you."

He shot her another winning smile. "Any time."

CHAPTER
Six

July 28th
8:54 A.M.

"Thank you for meeting with us today," Matthew addressed the Kites as he and Allina settled themselves in chairs in the interview room, Jonathon was observing the interview from outside. They had thought it was best to do the interview here at the precinct rather than at the Kites offices.

"Are we under arrest?" Jaden asked. He already had a belligerent face on and they hadn't even started yet.

"No, definitely not," Matthew answered. They didn't even have enough to force the couple to meet with them. They were hoping this interview would tell them whether or not they should pursue Jaden as a suspect while they continued to work on getting a warrant for the Happily Ever After Club user profiles.

"Then why are we here?" the man whined.

"Because three women are dead and a fourth is missing," Allina answered.

"That has nothing to do with us." His sulkiness was already annoying, and they'd only been in the room a minute.

"All of those women went missing after going on dates with someone they met on the online dating website you run," Allina reminded him.

"That's probably just a coincidence," Joynelle spoke up, but she looked uncertain.

"Two victims perhaps," he agreed. "But four? That is not a coincidence. We can't deny the connection."

"We can't hand over access to people's personal information without a warrant," Jaden said.

"We're working on one," Matthew assured him. "Are you sure you wouldn't prefer to have a lawyer with you?"

"You said we weren't under arrest."

"You're not."

"Then we don't need one, we didn't do anything wrong."

"Can you think on anyone who might want to hurt either of you?" Allina asked.

Joynelle's blue eyes grew wide. "You think someone might be doing this to hurt us?"

"We can't rule it out as a possibility," Allina replied.

Joynelle trembled at the thought. She was a petite woman, a little over five feet tall, and barely one hundred pounds. She had shoulder-length light blonde hair, and her large blue eyes seemed too large for her narrow face. Despite the already hot day she was dressed in jeans and a long-sleeved shirt, and Matthew had noticed the way she cradled her left wrist, and favored her right side. She was hurt, and he suspected he knew how she had sustained those injuries.

"Can you think of anyone who would want to hurt you?" he asked.

"No." Joynelle dropped her gaze to the table and let her hair fall in a curtain around her face.

Jaden just shrugged indifferently.

"We understand you have a bit of a temper, Mr. Kite." Matthew turned his attention to the other man.

"Who says?" Jaden scowled.

"You have a couple of DUI charges, and the arresting officers say you were belligerent and argumentative."

"So what? Are you implying that I'm a suspect?" Jaden looked more angry than scared about the prospect.

"We have to look into every possibility," Matthew said. "All four victims are connected to your website. We would be remiss if we didn't look into you and your wife."

"I own fourteen businesses, I make millions every year, I own three houses, I drive a Porsche," Jaden snapped.

None of those things excluded him from being the killer. In fact, in this particular case, given the dresses the women had been found in and the prince charming and princess theme to the crimes, it only added further evidence against him.

"One of your businesses is a limousine company, correct?" Allina asked.

For the first time Jaden looked confused and a little wary. "Correct."

"How many people have access to the vehicles?"

"I own five, so I have five drivers, a mechanic, and someone who takes care of the bookings and the finances. Why?" Some of the wind had been taken out of his sails as though it was sinking in that they might actually think he did this.

"We believe that the killer drove a limousine to the victims' houses to pick them up for their dates. I presume you also have access to the vehicles?" Allina asked.

"I've never driven those cars," Jaden said firmly. "I might have a bit of a drinking problem but I'm not violent."

Matthew arched a brow. "There are several complaints about you at your favorite bar. There have been half a dozen police call outs for disturbances of the peace."

"I was never violent with anyone," Jaden snapped.

Even if that was true, and Matthew didn't believe it was, that didn't count him out as a suspect. The Fairytale Killer wasn't violent per se, he killed the women when he realized they could never be what he wanted, and the frenzied assault on Georgia Lars was almost definitely spurred by an outburst of anger. Matthew believed that Jaden was prone to such violent bursts of anger.

"Where were you on the night of the 26th?" Allina asked.

The sudden change of topic threw him for a moment. "Home."

"Can anyone verify that?"

"No."

"What about the night of the 23rd?"

"Home. Alone."

"And the ..."

"Whatever day you're going to ask me about I was home alone. I'm always home alone since *she* left me." He threw a look of disgust Joynelle's way.

"Do you know a Mila Drake?" Matthew asked.

"Doesn't sound familiar."

"What about Georgia Lars?"

"Nope."

"Tillie Schueman? Jeannie Jones?"

"Look, I'm not interested in other women," Jaden sulked.

That was interesting, perhaps when Joynelle had filed for divorce he had decided to try and find someone who would never leave him. Who would replace her, who would be the woman he felt he deserved.

"Perhaps you met them at a bar?" Allina suggested. If they could find something that definitively linked him to one of the women, they might be able to get a warrant to search his house and hopefully find something incriminating.

"No. I told you, I'm not interested in other women," Jaden repeated.

The clear implication being he was still interested in his wife. They would have to talk to Joynelle alone because Matthew was concerned about her safety. "And you can't think of anyone who would want to hurt you by destroying your business?"

"I don't think so. No one springs to mind. I have a few rivals but no one who would kill just to cause me trouble." Jaden was looking bored now.

"Mrs. Kite, may I see your wrist," Matthew asked.

Joynelle's terrified blue eyes darted up to meet his. "Wh-what?" she stammered.

"I'd like to take a look at your wrist."

She was visibly trembling as she held out her right arm.

"Your left wrist, Mrs. Kite," he said gently.

Clamping her bottom lip between her teeth, Joynelle tentatively lifted her left arm and held it just above the tabletop.

"May I?" he asked.

When she nodded, Matthew carefully took her hand and eased the shirt sleeve up. Dark black and purple bruises circled her wrist. Fingertip bruises. If he didn't think it might lead to a sexual harassment claim, Matthew would have asked to see her chest, which he thought he would find just as bruised and swollen as her arm. "Who hurt you, Mrs. Kite?"

Her eyes darted all around the room and he could feel the fear rolling off her.

"Mrs. Kite, who did this to you?" he repeated patiently.

Slowly she turned her head to look at Jaden, who had suddenly gone very quiet and very pale, and was looking a little queasy. Her lips parted, her tongue darted out to wet them, then she snapped them closed again. "I-I fell down the stairs," she said softly, keeping her gaze averted.

"These bruises are from a hand," he contradicted. "Someone put their hands on you and that is not okay."

"It-it was ..."

"If you say anything, I'll kill you." Jaden leapt to his feet and launched himself at his wife, slamming her up against the wall and holding his forearm against her throat.

Joynelle clawed at his arm as it cut off her air supply, while Matthew lunged at Jaden, tackling the other man and bringing him down to the floor, where he pressed his knee into his back and pulled out a pair of handcuffs and snapped them on.

Jonathon and two other cops rushed into the room and hauled Jaden to his feet. "I didn't do anything. I never killed anybody."

"You beat up your wife," Matthew said, disgusted. Nothing revolted him more than a man who put his hands on a woman or child.

"My wife," he screamed. "Mine. She belongs to me. She can't just walk away. It doesn't work that way. You won't ever leave me, Joy," he continued to shriek as he was dragged from the room. "I'd rather kill you than let you leave."

Allina held a sobbing Joynelle Kite, and Matthew hoped the woman would give them a statement. They could arrest Jaden for domestic violence, and hopefully find something that would indicate his involvement in the Fairytale murders. He was a dangerous man. He believed women were his property to do with as he wished. But they needed to move quickly, Jaden was rich and would have no problem posting bail. They needed to find something to keep him locked up indefinitely or he was never going to stop killing.

～

10:39 A.M.

Rylla pressed play again.

Elianna's chubby little face filled the screen. And then a moment later her husband's voice.

"You ready?" Josh asked.

"Ready," she replied.

"Here you go, Elianna," Josh leaned closer to the baby and popped onto the screen. In his hand he held a stuffed bumblebee. "Buzzzzz," he said as he tickled Elianna's tummy.

The baby gave a gurgley laugh.

In the video she and Josh laughed too.

"She's really doing it," she said. "She's really laughing, that's a real laugh. Do it again."

"Okay, Mommy," Josh giggled. "Buzzzzz," he said again, and once again Elianna began to laugh.

"I love that sound, I could listen to it forever," she sighed happily.

"You can listen to it forever." Josh turned to the camera and smiled at her, then he picked up their little girl and tickled her tummy. "Laugh for Mommy, Elianna."

"I want to get in on some of that perfectly pudgy little tummy," she said.

The screen went black.

She had filmed the video just six days before the accident.

They had all been so happy, thinking they had the rest of their lives to enjoy each other. If she had known that in less than a week her family would be gone, she would have grabbed hold of them and never let them go.

As devastating as the loss had been she obviously hadn't learned from it.

It hadn't spurred her to fix things with her sister or her brother. She and Elliot spoke maybe once or twice a year, usually around Christmas when they got together for their yearly family gathering. Rylla had skipped the last two because she just couldn't take the tension.

Elliot and Mila hadn't believed her, and she hadn't been able to forgive them for it.

When she was fifteen her mother had suffered a psychotic break and poisoned her father. Her dad had survived but the damage to their family had been irreparable. Eighteen and twenty-one, Mila and Elliot, had already been out of the house by then. But she had been there. She had been the one to find their mom cowering in a corner screaming about birds trying to peck out her eyes, and her dad lying unresponsive and barely breathing on the floor.

Her mom had been committed to a psychiatric hospital and with just her and her dad left in the home things began to change. Her dad began to change. He wasn't the same easy-going, sports loving, outdoor loving, fun man she had always known. He became paranoid, and depressed, rarely leaving the house and making up rules.

So many rules.

She and Mila were the spitting image of their mother, and her dad had been afraid that she was going to turn out like her mom. He had forbidden her from going out with friends, he'd wanted to stop her from playing sports, he'd wanted to control the way she dressed, and what she ate. He wanted to control everything about her.

The control issues were one thing, but it had been the threats that really started scaring her. The punishment for every perceived infraction of the rules was threats that if she didn't start complying, he was going to have her committed. He started watching her constantly, many nights she would wake up to find him standing in her room, above her bed, staring at her.

Rylla had been scared, terrified. She didn't want to be committed but living in that house was like being a prisoner. She hadn't known how far her father intended to take things. The night she woke up to find him in a room with a knife in his hand had been the final straw. That day she had packed her bags and fled.

She had told her siblings what was going on, but they hadn't believed her. They'd thought it was just the trauma of their mom's murder attempt, and had told her to be patient and things would settle down. But how could she be patient when every night she went to bed afraid that she would never wake up again because her father would kill her?

Six months after her mother was committed, she ran.

As hard as it had been living on the streets at just sixteen years old if everything with her parents hadn't happened, she would never have met Josh and had Elianna, so it was hard to regret it all.

It hurt that Mila and Elliot hadn't believed her, she'd reached out for help and they had rebuffed her. Because she hadn't been able to let go of it, she had never mended fences with her sister, and now she might never get a chance.

Rylla stared at her phone, she didn't want to lose her sister like she had lost her husband and daughter.

She didn't want to lose Nate either.

He was a good guy and if they both set their fears aside then maybe they could be happy together. She had to accept that being happy, that still living her life, didn't mean that she had stopped loving Josh and Elianna, and it didn't mean that she would forget them. It just meant that she was still alive, and she was lonely, and wanted someone to share the rest of her life with. That person really could be Nate.

Last night he had talked with her for hours, then slept on her couch because she had insisted she couldn't go to bed and wanted to watch movies instead. Even though she had been ignoring him for fifteen months, things between them had been so comfortable. That hurt and humiliation that she had been clinging to had been washed away in that first kiss. She knew he meant it when he said that saying no when she asked him out didn't have anything to do with her. He had been trying to apologize and explain for months and she had been the one to keep shutting him down. Yet he hadn't stopped, he'd fought for her. And last night when she really needed someone, he had been there.

As if he could read her thoughts, there was a knock at her bedroom door and a moment later he appeared.

"You awake?" he whispered loudly.

"Mmmhmm."

Nate came in and perched on the edge of her bed, one large hand resting on her hip. She liked the feel of it there. It was heavy and reassuring and gave her something to tether her. "How're you doing?"

She just stared up at him. She was *so* tired. She felt completely drained, utterly exhausted. Not just right now, but always. Most days she came home so worn out that she ate dinner then collapsed into bed immediately after that. It wasn't her demanding and sometimes emotionally draining job, or her vigorous exercise regime, but because of the immense effort it took to portray the person she wanted others to see her as.

"You don't have to pretend with me, Rylla." Nate's understanding eyes assessed her.

Maybe she didn't have to, but it was habit. She knew that Naomi saw through her act but that didn't stop her from putting it on every day. But maybe, possibly, with Nate could be a safe place where she could let down her guard. She reached for his hand and squeezed it because right now, her throat was too tight to talk.

Nate squeezed back then lifted her hand to his lips and pressed a kiss to it. "Matthew is here," he told her.

She bolted upright. "Bad news?"

"He didn't say that it was."

"Good news?"

"He didn't say that either. I think he just stopped by to give you an update."

Like he promised he would. Her partner really was a great guy. She was already dressed so she gently tugged her hand from Nate's and climbed out of bed. As soon as she was on her feet, he reclaimed her hand. It was sweet and intimate, and it had been so long since she had just held hands, that her eyes misted again. So he wouldn't see that she was almost crying, Rylla kept her head down as they walked downstairs.

"It's okay to cry, Rylla."

That tugged the corners of her lips up into a small smile. "You're a mind reader now, huh?"

"Yep," Nate agreed shooting her a crooked grin. He really was pretty adorable, on top of being unearthly level hot.

As soon as she saw Matthew, her mind snapped back into cop mode. "Do you know something?"

"We have someone in custody," her partner told her.

For a moment her heart soared with relief. "You have him?"

"Maybe. It's Jaden Kite, but we don't know for sure it's him."

"He hadn't admitted anything?"

"No. And I don't see a confession in his near future."

"But you have him in custody?"

"For domestic violence. But if we don't find something to prove he's the Fairytale Killer then he'll make bail and be back on the streets."

"Are you sure it's him?"

"No, we have another suspect we're interviewing this afternoon."

"Do you *think* it's Jaden?"

Matthew paused and considered this. "I'm more sure than not."

"If you have him in custody then Mila's all alone. What if it is him and he won't tell you where he has her? What will happen to her? If she's all alone and there's no one to bring her food and water, she could die."

Even if Jaden Kite was the Fairytale Killer, and they had him in custody, that still didn't mean that her sister would make it out of this alive.

2:12 P.M.

"Hendrick Mint?"

The man straightened from the pile of leaves he had been raking and turned in their direction. It was apparent that he immediately pegged them as cops. He hesitated for barely a second before he flung the rake on the ground and bolted.

Matthew sighed.

He was *not* in the mood to go chasing after their second suspect in the fairytale murders.

"I'll go around the back, you take the front," Jonathon said, already taking off at a sprint after the man.

Annoyed, Matthew also took off in a sprint after the man, heading in the other direction so he could circle around to the front of the house. As he rounded the corner, he saw Hendrick Mint darting across the street. He was in good shape, and he quickly caught up with the man, tackling him to the ground.

He was just snapping on handcuffs when Jonathon came running up to join them. "You got him."

"He's not very fast."

Matthew rolled Hendrick onto his back. The man was panting, his face beaded in sweat, his eyes darting nervously around as though he thought someone might suddenly come and snatch him away from this mess he had found himself in. Hendrick was surprisingly good looking, with a tall, lean body, he shouldn't have had any trouble attracting women, and yet he had resorted to harassing single mothers at the school.

"Why did you run, Hendrick?" Matthew asked, dragging the man to his feet.

"Rick," he mumbled.

"What?"

"No one calls me Hendrick, my name is Rick," the man muttered again.

"Why did you run, Rick," Matthew repeated.

Rick shrugged.

"You don't run from the cops if you haven't done anything wrong," Jonathon said.

"I haven't done nothing," Rick sulked.

Resisting the urge to correct his grammar and inform him that his sentence meant that he *had* done something, he asked, "Then why did you run?"

"You were going to blame me for something. Cops are *always* blaming me for stuff I didn't do."

"*Have* you done something we'd be interested in?" Jonathon asked.

"No."

"You know a Jeannie Jones?" Matthew asked as they led him back toward their car.

"No," he answered quickly. A little too quickly.

"You're a gardener, correct, Rick?"

"Yes," he replied hesitantly as though he expected them to trick him, but he wasn't quite sure how.

"And you work on people's gardens?"

"Yes."

"Before that you worked at a school, right?"

Rick didn't answer but they felt him tense.

"A middle school, wasn't it? I think you were pretty interested in the parents. Well, the moms anyway," Matthew said.

Again, Rick remained silent.

"You ever been married, Rick?" Jonathon asked.

"No."

"But you were engaged, right?"

"Yes."

"She left you at the altar. You dated for three years. Were engaged for almost another two. She planned a lavish wedding, spared no expense, left you in debt when she just ran out on you." Matthew couldn't imagine standing at the alter on what was supposed to be the happiest day of your life only to have the woman you were about to marry never turn up.

Rick just growled.

"You would have thought that might have soured you on women and relationships," Matthew said conversationally. "But it didn't. You were *very* interested in finding a woman to date. From what we heard that was all you were interested in."

"So, I used to talk to the moms, so what?" Rick snapped. "Not like it went anywhere."

"Because they wouldn't reciprocate," Jonathon said.

Rick nodded slowly. "I was just talking to them, wanted to find out about them, find out what kind of women they were. But they blew it out of proportion, acted like I was stalking them or something."

"You used to watch the teachers too."

"Teachers make good wives."

"You want a good wife, Rick?"

He shrugged. "Don't we all?"

"Jeannie Jones, I bet she would have made a great wife. She loved kids, she loved to cook, she loved art and visiting galleries, she loved to travel, she was sweet, kind, pretty."

"I ... uh ... don't know a Jeannie Jones," Rick said nervously.

"Oh." Matthew feigned surprise. "We were told when you worked at the school you used to watch her."

Rick gave a violent shake of his head.

"You know someone killed her," Matthew said quietly. "Someone like you who wanted to find a princess to marry, only then he decided Jeannie didn't live up to his standards so he killed her. Did you kill her, Rick?"

His brown eyes fixed firmly on the ground. "I never killed anybody."

"When she didn't work out you tried again. Tillie Schueman. Then Georgia Lars, you do know Georgia, right?"

"I do her garden," the man muttered.

"You liked her, thought she might be the one, so you hooked up with her online."

"I don't own no computer."

They knew for a fact he did. One of the friends who had opened up his home to Hendrick had filed a report claiming that Rick had stolen several things from him when he left, including a laptop. Rick claimed the things were gifts.

"You broke into her house," Jonathon said.

"No. No, I didn't."

"Georgia's roommate said someone had broken in. It was you. You wanted to find out things about Georgia you could use to con her, to get her comfortable enough with you to agree to meet you in person. You wanted her dress size so you could have a dress made for her for your date."

"No." Rick finally lifted his gaze to look at them. "I wasn't interested in Georgia. It was Whitney."

Exchanging glances with Jonathon. "You were really after Whitney Leroy?"

"Yes. No. I wasn't *after* her, I was *interested* in her. She was pretty. Sometimes when I was there, she would talk to me. She was sweet. She would bring me homemade lemonade. I wanted to ask her out, but I thought she'd say no. I just wanted something. Something to remind me of her."

The glassy look in the man's eyes bordered on creepily possessive. Whitney hadn't mentioned any of this when they'd asked her about the gardener, so Matthew wasn't sure how much of what Rick was saying actually happened and how much he had imagined. "What did you take when you broke into the house?"

His face turned beet red. "A pair of her panties," he mumbled half under his breath.

Could Rick really have been after Georgia's roommate Whitney? The relationship had developed over the internet, just like the women hadn't really known who the man on the other end of the computer was, so their killer couldn't really know who was on the other end of his computer. Perhaps Hendrick Mint had thought that he was building a relationship with Whitney, it could explain why Georgia hadn't lasted very long. The others he had kept for weeks, Georgia was dead two days later.

"You're under arrest," Matthew informed the man as he opened the backdoor of their car.

"For what?"

"Multiple counts of murder."

"Not breaking and entering?" Rick looked confused.

"Breaking and entering is the least of your concerns."

~

4:50 P.M.

. . .

"Jaden Kite is out on bail."

"Already?" Allina asked, dismayed.

"Called in his fancy lawyer," Heidi replied.

"Is Joynelle safe?" she asked. Once they had dragged her husband away earlier the woman had given her statement.

Her story read like so many others. Jaden had seemed like the perfect boyfriend, almost too good to be true, but that all changed shortly after the honeymoon. He started becoming suspicious of her, demanding to know where she was and who she was spending her time with. Checking her phone and email, insisting she tell him her plans for the day and calling her regularly to see if she was where she told him she would be. Then he became controlling. They had joint bank accounts, but he wouldn't let her have access to her cards, instead keeping them in his possession. He gave her a weekly cash allowance and demanded receipts to prove where she spent her money. Although she was smart and well educated, he told her she didn't need to work, that he and his businesses could support them, then isolating her further by distancing her from her friends until all she had in her life was him.

After that came the physical abuse. At first it was just the occasional slap or shove when they were arguing, and he was drunk. Then the violence escalated. He would punch and hit her in the chest or abdomen so that the bruises wouldn't show when he paraded his pretty wife around in public. Their sex life also grew rougher. Jaden wanted to tie her up and paddle and whip her.

Eventually, after one particularly violent night a neighbor came to her the following day. It had been summer and a window had been open, the neighbor heard what had happened and offered Joynelle help in leaving her husband. Like a lot of battered women Joynelle had refused, insisted everything was fine, implied she deserved what her husband did to her, and begged the other woman not to go to the cops. The neighbor was persistent and after a couple of months she managed to convince Joynelle to leave her husband for good.

Allina had no doubt that the neighbor had saved Joynelle Kite's life.

"She's staying with her sister and brother-in-law. He's a former Navy SEAL. She should be safe there," Heidi explained. "So we have two suspects, are we leaning in either direction?"

"Jaden Kite is definitely the more violent of the two. So far although we know Hendrick Mint has a temper, we haven't had reports from anyone that he has gotten physical with his anger," Matthew replied. "The Kites have been married for almost seven years, and over that time Jaden had grown progressively violent. It's not a huge leap to go from beating his wife to murdering women who he had hoped would take his wife's place but failed."

"And the Fairytale Killer punished his victims by spanking them. Georgia had marks and welts on her backside," Allina said. "Jaden enjoyed paddling and whipping his wife on her backside."

"He's also wealthy," Jonathon said. "So he could quite easily have a quiet place to lock the women away where no one would find them. And one of his businesses is a limousine company, that would be the perfect vehicle to use in the abductions. The women would be comfortable getting inside one because they think they're about to have their dream date with their Prince Charming. And it's large enough for him to be able to easily transport an unconscious victim, assuming that he knocks them out once he gets them in the car so that he can safely take them to wherever he's holding them. There's also the added benefit that most limousines have tinted glass so no one is going to see that there's a passed-out woman in there."

"Okay, what reasons are there to think it's not him?" Heidi asked.

"So far, we don't have anything to link him to any of the women. Doesn't mean he didn't meet them somewhere, or that he didn't just randomly choose them on the website. Which is absolutely how things could have played out since we know that's where the relationships were founded. But at some point, he knew who they were, and we believe he broke into their homes to get information on them and to learn their clothing size to surprise them with the dresses for the date," Allina said.

"He also claims he's not interested in other women," Matthew said. "And when we interviewed him, he certainly seemed like his focus was more on his wife than other women. I think his ego can't take that she walked away from him and not the other way around. He wants a woman that won't leave him, that wants to serve him, that wants to accept him as her master. But whether he would find other women to take that place or try to force his wife to be what he thinks a woman should be is still up in the air."

Allina wasn't sure that Jaden would go looking elsewhere. He was a control freak, he had spent years dominating his wife. Sure, he would be angry that his hold on her had been broken and he had lost her, but she felt like he would be more likely to kill Joynelle, or abduct her and hold her against her will, than find other women. She might not be convinced, but she couldn't rule him out either. He was violent and he wanted to find a submissive woman, both fitted with their killer.

"Hendrick Mint is the complete opposite," Jonathon said. "He's interested in pretty much any woman he comes across. When he was working at the school he didn't target and zero in on one particular woman."

"Although it's possible that the killer came across the women for the first time in the Happily Ever After Club, it's also possible that he knew them somewhere else as well which is why he focused on those specific women in the club," Matthew said. "And so far, we have Rick linked to three of the victims."

"Three?" Heidi asked. "I thought we could only link him to Jeannie Jones from the school and Georgia Lars because he worked at her house."

"Once we knew about the school we checked to see if Mila Drake's twelve-year-old daughter goes there. She does. She's in the seventh grade so she would have been there while Hendrick was still working there," Allina explained.

"Nothing to suggest they ever interacted," Matthew added, "but it's another link. It's certainly possible that when he joined the dating website and then realized he actually knew some of the women on there, that's why he chose them and not someone else."

"Rick claims that he was really interested in Georgia Lars' room-mate, Whitney, though," Jonathon said. "He even admitted to commit-ting the break in that Whitney mentioned. He says he took a pair of Whitney's underwear. That could be a cover though. Maybe he's just telling us it's Whitney he likes so we don't think he'd have a reason to abduct Georgia. If he was in the house then he could have been in both women's rooms, so he could have gotten Georgia's clothing size while he was there, and Whitney never mentioned a missing pair of underwear."

"Although he hasn't been violent as far as we know, personality wise, he's the more likely of our two suspects to be wanting to play Prince Charming. He just wants someone to love him. Background for Rick, he grew up without a father, mother was constantly remarrying, men were in an out of her and her kids' lives on an almost yearly basis. He doesn't want that. He wants a woman who's going to worship him," Allina said.

"So two suspects, reasons for and against both of them. Who do we like for these murders?" Heidi asked.

"Jaden Kite," she replied. "He's violent. He has a very low opinion of women. He has the means to commit the physicalities of the crimes, the abduction and detaining of the women. And he's smart, certainly able to work the computer side of things so that we couldn't track him."

"Hendrick Mint," Jonathon said. "We can link him to several of the women. He has admitted to breaking and entering at one of the women's houses, and we believe that's something the killer does. He is on a quest to find love. He wants someone who's going to love him, he wants the whole fairytale package, and judging from the conversations we've read between the killer and the victims that seems to be what our killer is after."

"Matthew?" Heidi asked.

"I don't know," he said slowly. "I'm not sure Jaden has the patience to play games with the women online. I can't see him looking up names that mean Prince Charming or making up stories about who he is to try and woo the women. But I can't see Hendrick having the skills to hide his tracks on the computer or having bursts of such violent anger that he would commit the level of violence shown on Georgia's body. For all we know it's neither of them."

While they all knew that could certainly be true, they had nothing definitive on either suspect, Allina knew they were all praying that they were getting closer to finding this killer because none of them wanted to have to tell Rylla that her sister was dead.

∾

6:39 P.M.

She didn't know what to do.

Mila had never felt so helpless in her entire life. She wanted to keep trying to fight her way out of the room, but she couldn't. After he had bandaged her hands and left her alone, she had resumed trying to claw her way through the door. Her brain knew it would never happen, but she couldn't stop her body from trying anyway.

Her hands hurt so badly, each time she tried to pry a screw loose it would rip off more of her skin and cause another rivulet of blood to trickle down her fingers. She kept telling herself to stop. That she wasn't achieving anything. That she was only going to make the man angry. But she just couldn't stop.

Eventually, he had stopped her himself.

Mila didn't know how long she spent on her knees working desperately to get through the door, but eventually it had burst open once more and the man had stormed in. He hadn't spoken a word, but he had been almost vibrating with anger. She had thought he was going to spank her again, and her bloody hands had subconsciously moved to cover her still sore bottom.

He hadn't wanted to spank her though.

Instead, he had wrapped a thick arm around her waist, yanked her up against a hard chest, grabbed one of her hands, and shoved it inside a mitt. The mitt was black and made from a dense, heavy material. It had a large Velcro strap around the wrist which he secured tightly. Almost too tightly.

Realizing he meant to physically restrain her now instead of letting her roam freely around the room had her flipping out. Claustrophobia was already suffocating her, the thought of not been able to move was incomprehensible.

She began to struggle frantically.

Fighting against the arms that held her, she scratched at him with her free hand, and swung her legs, managing to connect squarely with one of his shins causing him to grunt in pain.

He had taken hold of her by the shoulders and shook her so

violently her head snapped backward and forward and her neck burned with pain at the sharp movements.

She was going to get herself killed.

Why couldn't she stop fighting him?

Why couldn't she play things smart?

Mila knew that her sister would do anything to find her. She and Rylla may have their problems, but her sister was a good cop and a good person, and she would work non-stop to find her.

While she was still stunned, he had shoved her other hand inside a matching mitt then snapped on a pair of handcuffs. He had added a belt around her waist and secured her already bound wrists to it. Then he had dragged her over to one of the corners where a small metal ring had been set into the stone wall and attached the belt to it so that she was forced to stand on her tiptoes, with her nose pushed up against the cold wall.

That had been hours ago.

He hadn't been back since.

She knew there were cameras in here so he was probably watching her, but he had kept his distance.

She was still standing in that same awkward position, unable to move more than an inch or so to either side. Her calf muscles ached from being perched on her toes for so long. Inside the mitts, her hands stung from all the cuts and bruises she had given herself.

How long did he intend to leave her here?

Indefinitely?

She wasn't sure how much longer she could stand it.

She wished that the man would come back and yet at the same time she desperately prayed he wouldn't.

Was this how Rylla had felt as a teenager about their father?

Before this, she had never believed her little sister. Had thought that Rylla's claims about their father were simply fueled by shock over their mother's actions, grief about their destroyed family, and typical teenage unhappiness about parental rules and limitations.

But what if Rylla had been telling the truth?

What if she really *had* been afraid that their father would physically harm her?

After all, Rylla had fled and chosen to live on the streets rather than return home. Why would she do that if she hadn't truly feared for her life? Back then, Mila had been busy with her own life, and after her mom attempted to kill her dad, she had distanced herself from her family, embarrassed for her new college friends to find out what had happened. She hadn't wanted to listen to Rylla's claims, she hadn't wanted to be bothered figuring out if they were true or not. And then Rylla had moved on, gotten married, had a child, become a cop, and everything had seemed to work out okay, so she had brushed aside the guilt that niggled at her about possibly abandoning her sister when she needed her.

Now she was deeply ashamed of her actions. Her sister had needed her, and she hadn't been there.

Tears streamed down her face.

Was this her punishment?

If their father really had gone off the deep end and been afraid that Rylla would try to kill him just like his wife had, then he very well might have murdered her while she slept. And Rylla had been all alone, just fifteen years of age, with no one there to protect her.

Now *she* was here all alone with no one to protect her.

If Rylla treated her the same way Mila had treated her then she could very well die here.

But her sister wouldn't do that. Rylla wasn't selfish, no matter what their problems were Mila knew without a shadow of a doubt that her sister would find her. The only questions was if she would find her alive or dead.

Her foot and leg began to cramp so badly she felt nauseous. Although she tried to hold it in, tried to breathe through the pain and pretend she was someplace else, it didn't do any good. Her stomach heaved and she vomited. She retched again and again until she was dry heaving, her empty stomach having nothing left to expel.

"Have you learned your lesson yet?"

She knew the rules.

The man had insisted that she read them while he tended to her hands, so she knew what was expected of her. He didn't want her to speak to him unless he gave her permission. He didn't want her to look at him unless he gave her permission. He didn't want her to do *anything* without his permission.

So, ignoring the spasms of pure agony in her legs, she clamped her lips together and focused her eyes on the floor.

"You may speak." He came closer and stood beside her. His tone was pleased, proud even, and Mila felt a little flush of pleasure at having pleased him. She quickly stopped herself. Following the rules to keep herself alive was one thing, but she couldn't let him break her. She didn't want him to be pleased with her, she didn't care how he felt about her one way or the other, she just wanted to keep him from hurting her.

"I have learned my lesson," she whispered.

"And you will stop trying to escape?"

"Yes. Please unlock me, my legs hurt so badly," she whimpered.

"Are you telling me what to do?" he demanded, his tone reverting to angry.

"No," she answered quickly. How angry with her was he? Was he leaving her here longer? She didn't think she could take that, either physically or mentally. "I'm sorry," she begged. "I'm sorry."

"Okay," he said gently, his hand smoothing her hair in comfort. "It's okay."

She heard him take out a key and she breathed out a sigh of relief. He was going to unlock her binds. Her legs quivered, and she had to fight to remain standing.

"I will give you a bath," he informed her as he unlocked the cuff securing her to the wall.

Mila wanted to protest that she could bathe on her own, but she was afraid that would upset him. As the tension keeping her on her feet disappeared, she pitched forward, straight into the man's arms, which he wrapped around her. Her muscles still cramped, and she couldn't stand, leaving her with no choice but to remain in the arms of her captor. Balancing her, he unlocked and removed the handcuffs and the mitts, then gathered her into his arms and carried her to the bathroom.

When he set her down on the closed toilet seat, Mila had to fight the urge to clamber away from him as quickly as her aching body could manage. That would make him angry. He wanted someone who was subservient, obedient, completely compliant. If she wanted to live she had to take on that role.

The man drew her a bath, and once he had adjusted the temperature, he pulled off his shirt—now smeared with her vomit—while he waited for it to fill.

Her brow furrowed. That chest was familiar. She had seen it somewhere before. Did she know this man? Not SC who she had thought she was falling in love with, but whoever this man really was.

With the bath full, he turned toward her, taking hold of the hem of her dress and lifting it up and over her head and off her body. Although she tried not to resist, afraid it would anger him, Mila couldn't help but lift her hands to cover her now bare breasts. She didn't want this man looking at her. He looked at her as if he owned her, as if she was his possession.

Picking her up he set her down in the bath. It scared her how easily he could pick her up and move her about. He was so big, so strong, how could she fight against that?

The warm bath water did soothe her aching leg muscles, and for a moment she almost didn't notice the man pouring shampoo into the palm of his hand, but when his hands moved to her head, and he began to wash her hair every molecule in her body focused in on that one spot.

Keeping her gaze fixed on the wall, she spoke softly, "My sister is a cop. She'll be looking for me. She might be angry with you when she finds me." Maybe if she phrased it in such a way that made it sound like her fears were for him and not that she wanted to get away from him, she could keep him from being too angry but also put the idea in his head that maybe it was better to just let her go.

Although she feared his tone would be sharp with a reprimand when he spoke, his voice was calm. "She won't find us, you're safe here."

"She's a very good cop. She's smart, and strong, and determined. She takes her job very seriously. She loves to help people. She won't stop looking for me. Ever." Her sister really was such a great person, why hadn't she worked harder to bridge the gap between them?

"Don't fear, I won't let anyone take you from me. Not even your sister." The man's voice grew husky as his hands drifted from massaging her scalp down to her shoulders. He kneaded them briefly before moving to her chest where his hands found her breasts. In her sex life, Mila had always loved when a man paid attention to her breasts, it was usually enough to make her come without him having to even touch her anywhere else. But this, this was the most revolting feeling she had ever had. She didn't want this man's hands on her body.

She wanted to swat him away, to scream at him that she wasn't his and she never would be. It was only the fear that he would shove her head under the water and keep it there until water flooded her lungs and she drowned that kept her mouth shut.

His hands didn't play with her breasts for long. They traveled down her stomach, then glided up her back to her neck. His fingers were long and strong, and he was clearly well-versed with a woman's body, he knew just how much pressure to apply and all the right places to hit. If this was a date and not an abduction she would be reveling in every single move of his talented hands. He picked up each foot and washed it, then slowly made his way up her legs. She knew it was coming. In her head she counted the seconds. When his hands finally dipped between her legs her whole body clenched involuntarily.

Rylla, where are you? Mila silently asked herself. *Please come soon. Please.*

∽

8:41 P.M.

"Naomi, you look tired," Nate said as Naomi yawned for about the hundredth time in the last five minutes.

"I'm fine," she said, immediately straightening in her chair.

"You don't look fine," Rylla said. "You look like you should be home in bed."

"Sam doesn't want me to be home alone. The Fairytale Killer has him all freaked out, I think it brings back bad memories from my stalker."

"Why don't you go lie down upstairs for a while," Rylla said.

"Or down here on the couch," Nate suggested. When Sam had gone to work this morning, he had dropped Naomi off at Rylla's and insisted that Nate not let her out of his sight. He understood his friend's fears. Sam had almost lost Naomi three times in twelve months, and now she was pregnant. Now if anything happened to her, he didn't just lose the woman he loved but his child as well.

"Yeah, maybe, okay," Naomi agreed.

Her acquiescence immediately concerned him. Naomi *never* agreed to voluntarily stay still. She was usually a whirlwind who constantly spun in circles. "Are you okay?"

She shot him a tired smile. "Just tired."

She was pale too. Rylla obviously agreed because she pressed the back of her hand to Naomi's cheek. "Are you sure you're feeling okay?"

"I'm sure. Just tired. That's it."

"You want me to call Sam?" Nate asked.

"No, he'll worry, and I'm really okay, I just haven't been sleeping." Naomi yawned again.

"Yeah, I remember those days." Rylla gave a sad smile. "You're so big every position you lie in is uncomfortable."

Nate remembered those days too. He had been home during the last month of his wife's pregnancy, leaving again when Andrew was three months old. He remembered Rachel had complained that no matter where or how she laid in the bed she was still uncomfortable.

"All right, let's get you settled on the couch." Rylla took Naomi's arm and helped her stand. Nate too stood and took Naomi's other elbow.

"I can walk on my own," Naomi said but made no move to tug herself free from their grasp, and Nate's concerns about her went up a notch.

"Here you go," he said, helping her onto the couch. "I'll grab your feet." He lifted them up onto the couch and he and Rylla helped her wiggle herself into a comfortable position. "Call out if you need us," he told his friend as he spread out a blanket over her.

"I will." Naomi yawned, her eyes already falling closed. She was asleep by the time he and Rylla sat back down at the dining table.

Getting Naomi to sleep hadn't just been because she looked like she needed the rest, there was also the added bonus of some alone time with

Rylla. As much as he wanted to be alone with her, he was glad Naomi had come to spend the day with them. She had done a fabulous job of keeping Rylla busy and distracted. Despite being eight and a half months pregnant she refused to stop working. Sam wouldn't let her do anything outside the office, but she still researched cases, ran background checks, and helped in any other way she could.

"You should get some rest too," he told Rylla. She hadn't slept last night and now there were dark circles under her eyes. "I can stay up and answer any calls."

"You didn't sleep last night either," Rylla reminded him. "If you want to go upstairs and take a nap, go ahead."

"Are you sleeping?"

"I can't."

"Then I'm staying right here with you."

"I appreciate it, but you don't have to stay with me, I'll be fine on my own for a bit and you'll only be upstairs."

Nate reached across the table and grasped Rylla's hands. "I'm not leaving you."

"Thank you." The gratitude in her green eyes made the lack of sleep more than worth it.

"Besides, I promised Sam I wouldn't let Naomi out of my sight," he joked.

"He's so over-protective of her," Rylla said a little wistfully.

"It's Naomi, can you blame him?" Naomi was one of those people who seemed to attract trouble.

She gave a small chuckle. "No, I can't. And he loves her so much."

A shadow of doubt flickered inside him. Rylla was a widow, she and her husband hadn't broken up, they hadn't gotten divorced, they hadn't drifted apart. He had been taken from her. In one horrible moment she had lost him. But what about her feelings? Nate knew they hadn't gone away, she still loved Joshua. The question was, was there any space left in her heart for him?

Rachel had taken his heart, ripped it out of his chest, and shredded it into millions of tiny pieces when she had taken his son away. Trusting his heart with another woman was a terrifying prospect. Even if that woman was Rylla.

Could he risk his heart to her only to let her break it?

Doubts were beginning to bubble up.

What if they started dating only for him to discover that she was still in love with her deceased husband and she couldn't love him the same way?

What if they had children and she just walked out on him?

Mentally and emotionally he backed up a little. Rylla hadn't spoken to him in over a year, he had tried apologizing before and she had refused to even listen. Now all of a sudden, she was listening to him, and talking to him, and kissing him, and letting him offer comfort. Now. When her sister had been abducted and she was scared. Was that all this sudden closeness between them was?

He had told her he was here for her, and he was, but maybe sticking with friendship was the better option.

It was certainly the safer one.

As hard as it was to accept, if Rylla's husband hadn't died then he wouldn't be sitting here with her right now. He had to keep that in mind. He couldn't let himself get carried away. Rylla needed comfort right now, she needed reassurance, she needed someone to help keep her mind off what might be happening to her sister. That could just as easily be any one of her friends as it could him.

"You really should go get some sleep." He released her hands and stretched back in his chair.

Her brow furrowed at the sudden change in his tone and demeanor. "I don't think I can. Every time I close my eyes I picture Mila, and the bodies of the Fairytale Killer's victims."

Nate ached to reach out to her, to pull her into his arms, to cradle her, to kiss her, to make love to her, to do whatever it took to soothe her even if momentarily. But he couldn't. He couldn't be with someone who was only with him because she needed a distraction. He couldn't set himself up for disappointment and get his heart broken all over again. It hurt, but he had to do the right thing. For both of them.

"I'm going to doze in the chair for a bit," he said, standing to dismiss her.

"You could come upstairs." Rylla paused, drew in a deep breath, "And lie down with me for a while."

His heart stuttered, and he wanted to throw caution to the wind and fall asleep with Rylla curled up in his arms. But needing comfort and falling in love were two different things. He was falling in love with Rylla, he had been for years now, she just needed someone to lean on while she battled her way through this hell she had been tossed into. Still, he didn't want to hurt her, so he threw her a smile—albeit a false one—and said, "I need to stay down here so I can keep an eye on Naomi."

"Oh." Rylla's face fell, her cheeks pinked, and she flashed him a fake smile of her own. "Right. Okay. I guess I'll see you in the morning?" She looked at him questioningly.

Clinging to every bit of self-restraint he possessed, Nate kept his smile in place. "Yeah, maybe, otherwise Sam and Naomi will be here."

Her eyes grew watery, and she gave him a single nod, then turned and hurried up the stairs to her bedroom.

He'd made her cry.

While she was petrified her sister was about to be brutally murdered, he had made things worse by sending her mixed messages. Because he was afraid to get his heart broken, he had just crushed hers.

He was an idiot.

He should go to her. Explain. Hold her while she slept and keep her bad dreams at bay.

But he didn't.

He went and settled into the recliner beside the couch and watched Naomi sleep. She and Sam were so happy together, they loved each other so much, the kind of love that overcame everything else, that blasted away any obstacles that got in its path. He wanted that. He wanted it with Rylla. But he still had so many doubts.

How could she ever love him the way he loved her when part of her heart still belonged to her husband?

How could he love her the way she deserved when he had let his own son walk out of his life?

How could he apologize for making this difficult time that much more difficult by kissing her one day and then pushing her away the next?

CHAPTER
Seven

July 29th
9:36 A.M.

"Good morning, Ms. Leroy," Matthew said as they opened the door to the interview room where she was waiting for them. They had asked her to come in to see what she could tell them about Hendrick Mint. Although she hadn't mentioned much about him when they'd asked her about the gardener, perhaps now that they knew he was obsessed with her they could ask some more specific questions and hopefully get something more useful out of her.

"I don't have anything else to tell you," Whitney said. Her eyes and her voice were dull, and her long blonde hair hung limply around her shoulders. She obviously wasn't coping with her friend's death, or the guilt she felt for being the one to suggest that Georgia try online dating.

"We wanted to talk to you about Hendrick," he told her as he took a seat. He was doing this interview solo as he, Allina, and Jonathon had split up the family members of the victims to re-interview with a focus on their two suspects.

For a moment Whitney's face was confused, then she said, "The gardener? Do you think it's him?"

"We're looking into him," he acknowledged.

Whitney paled. So dramatically that he was afraid she was about to pass out. She knew something. Something she hadn't told them. Whether because she hadn't known it was important or because she was deliberately keeping it from him, he didn't know, but he intended to find out. "You said that he and Georgia never interacted but what about you and him?"

"*Me* and him?" she repeated, her voice shrill with panic. "Why are you asking about me? If he's the killer, it's Georgia who he killed."

"Hendrick was the man who broke into your home, only he wasn't interested in Georgia, he was interested in you." He tried to break the news gently, wondering if she already knew this.

From the look on Whitney's face and the shock in her blue eyes she hadn't known that. She opened her mouth, but no words came out.

"He took a pair of your underwear," he told her, watching her carefully for her reactions, he needed to know what she knew.

She shook her head in denial, her whole body began to tremble. "Are you saying he was really after me?"

"I don't know. Could that be a possibility?"

"It was Georgia he was talking to online. He knew it was her and not me, he saw pictures of her. This has nothing to do with me."

Matthew might have believed her had it not been for the look of wild panic in her eyes. "Did you know Hendrick Mint was interested in you, Ms. Leroy?"

Whitney shook her head again, but this time her eyes dropped to stare at her hands, which she had clamped tightly together in her lap.

"Do you know him, Ms. Leroy?"

"I didn't know it was him," she whispered so softly he barely heard her.

"You'd met him before?"

"A little over a year ago I found out my husband was cheating on me. I should have known, he was cheating on his second wife with me when I first met him. I was devastated. I loved him so much. I wanted to spend the rest of my life with him. He broke my heart into a million pieces when I came home and found him in our bed with his twenty-two-year-old secretary. I didn't know what to do so I just left. I walked and walked for hours and ended up in the park. It was dark, I couldn't walk anymore so I just sat down under a tree and cried. I don't know how long I sat there crying, but the next I remember was a man. He came and sat beside me, asked me what was wrong, and I told him everything."

"The man was Hendrick Mint."

"Yes." Whitney finally lifted her eyes to meet his. "But I never knew his name. I never even knew what he looked like. It was late—dark—I never saw the man's face, but the first time I heard him talk I knew it was him. I thought it was a sign. I thought he might ask me out, but he never said anything, so I assumed he either didn't recognize me or that night really didn't mean anything to him."

"What happened that night?"

"I was upset, I've never done anything like that before, but he seemed so sweet, he listened to me, told me I was too special to allow anyone to treat me that way, it just happened," Whitney said in a rush.

"You had sex with him."

"After I felt guilty. I was still married, and no matter what my husband did I had promised to love him and forsake all others. I wanted to make my marriage work, but my husband told me he wanted a divorce."

"Did Hendrick talk to you at all that night?"

"He told me the woman who he had been with for the last five years had left him at the altar, and left him with debt he wasn't sure he could ever repay. I don't know how it happened. One moment we were sitting there talking about our messed-up love lives, and the next we were ripping off each other's clothes and making love right there in the park."

"Do you remember anything specific that he said?"

Whitney paused, considered, then said, "Right before he entered me, he said that he wasn't good enough for me, that I was beautiful like a princess, and he was nothing. I told him that inside every man lives some girl's Prince Charming."

"Did you think he was your Prince Charming? Did you look for him?"

"For weeks I went back to that park every night, but I never saw him again. He'd been working as Georgia's gardener for a couple of months before I realized it was him. One day it was hot, and I was bored and lonely, I took him some homemade lemonade, when he thanked me I knew. I could never forget that voice. But I didn't know. I didn't know he was a killer, I didn't know. Do you really think it's him? Is this my fault? Did Georgia die because of me?"

Matthew wondered if that night had been the inspiration for the whole Prince Charming, princess, fairytale theme the killer had chosen. If indeed Hendrick Mint was the killer, and he still wasn't convinced either way. An argument could be made that either Rick or Jaden was the killer. And an argument could be made that either Rick or Jaden *weren't* the killer. What he did know was that none of this was Whitney's fault.

"Georgia died because someone made a choice to kidnap her and kill her. Those choices were not made because of anything you did or said," he assured her. Whitney didn't look like she believed him. "Do you have someone you can stay with for a while?"

"I have a brother," she said softly. Her eyes had taken on a glassy sheen, he didn't think he would get anything else useful out of her today.

"I'm going to call him and ask him to come and pick you up, perhaps you could stay with him for a few days."

"Okay," she whispered in a small, childlike voice.

Leaving Whitney in the care of an officer, Matthew headed downstairs. He'd asked Beau Drake to bring in Emmy and Mac so he could show them pictures of Hendrick Mint and Jaden Kite to see if they could identify either as the man they saw in their house. Beau had been reluctant to bring the children by. Reluctant was quite the understatement. He had been extremely uncooperative, refusing to let the children come, claiming he was trying to do what was in their best interests, but really it seemed like he was only interested in doing what was in his own best interest. His children wanted their mother found alive, but from his point of view, having Mila out of the picture meant he could have his children all to himself and didn't have to worry about the divorce or the custody case. It was hard to comprehend someone being co cruel and callous, but Beau certainly didn't seem upset about the mother of his children being abducted.

"We can't stay long," Beau said as soon as he saw Matthew.

"That's fine, Mr. Drake. I just need to show the kids a couple of pictures."

"What kind of pictures?" Beau asked suspiciously.

"Just photos of our suspects. I want to see if you guys recognize either of these men as the one you saw in your house," he turned to address Emmy and Mac.

"Do you know for sure it's one of these men?" Emmy asked, her eyes way too old for a twelve-year-old. She had grown up a lot the last couple of days.

"No, but you two can help me narrow things down," he told them honestly.

"Are the pictures scary?" Mac asked, his face serious.

"No, they're just photos of the men, kind of like you get when you get your school pictures taken. Are you ready?"

Emmy and Mac both nodded solemnly.

Matthew held out the photos of Hendrick and Jaden for the children to see. They immediately pointed at a photo. Or rather they immediately pointed at the opposite photos.

"It's him," Emmy said, pointing to Hendrick.

"Him." Mac pointed at Jaden.

The children looked at each other, and then helplessly at him. Matthew felt just as helpless. They were no closer to discovering which man was the killer, and they had no definitive proof it was either of them anyway. His partner's sister was running out of time.

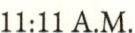

11:11 A.M.

"You got the profiles set up?" Matthew asked as he entered the room.

"We're just finalizing them," Jonathon replied.

"We're going with two?"

"Yes," he nodded. "One for each of them."

They were setting up decoy profiles on the Happily Ever After Club dating website in the hopes of luring the killer. They had to assume that until they found him, he was going to keep getting disappointed with the women he abducted and need to keep looking for more. Although he almost certainly already had a number of women lined up who he had been grooming and communicating with, he was likely to be killing them quicker than he could build relationships.

So, they would help him a little.

If they could just hook him, then they could reel him in as quickly as possible and get him off the streets before anyone else was killed. Jonathon wanted to believe they could find the killer before Rylla's sister wound up dead. He'd known Rylla for several years, since they worked out of the same precinct, and gotten to know her even better since he'd married her best friend's sister. His wife Clara was close with her sisters, so he spent a lot of time with both Aggie and Naomi. And since Naomi was close with Rylla, he spent a lot of time with her too. He considered her a part of his extended family and he didn't want her to have to go through losing her sister in such a horrible manner on top of the other losses she had suffered.

"We're assuming that Jaden Kite's ideal woman is as similar to his wife as he can find. So, we've named the profile aimed at him Elle. She's thirty-five, we've made her a widow with no children. She has a degree in graphic design and plays several musical instruments. We've made her quiet, not a lot of friends, preferring quiet evenings at home than going out to parties and events. Hopefully the quieter side to her will appeal to his controlling nature and he'll pick her out as someone who would be easy to isolate and dominate," Allina said.

"Since Hendrick Mint appears to have an obsession with Whitney Leroy, we've modeled the profile aimed at him on her. We've named her Wendy, she's had a husband cheat on her and she's divorced. She doesn't work, she wants kids—that seemed important to him since he hit on a lot of mothers at the school—and she loves long walks in the park," he added.

"We've also listed all the same interests and hobbies as the victims had listed on their profiles," Allina added.

"Who are we using for the pictures?" Matthew asked.

Jonathon didn't like this part. It was inevitable that they had to put a face to the profiles. And it was also inevitable that it was going to wind up being a cop because assuming they could get the Fairytale Killer to develop an interest in either or both of the profiles, they needed someone who could do the meet when they set it up. But that didn't mean he liked the idea of his partner playing bait.

"Me," Allina answered. "Keeping the curls for one and straightening my hair for the other. It should make me look different enough in the photos that if the killer likes both profiles then he won't realize I'm the same person. It makes sense for me to do it because I'm already working the case, so it means we don't have to bring someone else in and brief them."

Matthew didn't seem to like the idea of Allina making herself bait either. No doubt it had something to do with Allina's sister-in-law being abducted six and a half years ago. He wasn't sure the Bennett family could take another hit it anything should happen to Allina.

"You sure you want to do this?" Matthew asked.

"This is my job, and none of us can deny that it makes sense to use me. Besides, when we do attract his attention and we set up a date it's not like I'm going to go alone, I'll have backup."

"I guess," Matthew said slowly. "I don't like it, but you're right, it does make sense to use you."

Sometimes making sense sucked. "We should make sure we keep an eye on both Whitney and Joynelle," Jonathon said. "Either of them could be the killer's end game. These other women could be substitutes for the woman he really wants. He's trying to find a better more perfect version of the woman he already loves. When he realizes that he can't, he could come for one of them and decided he'll have better luck taking them and making them what he wants."

"We have regular patrols on their streets. We've told them to not go anywhere alone, and to call if they notice anything at all suspicious. We've done the best we can right now to keep them safe, if we can figure out which one of the men is the Fairytale Killer then we can look at bringing that woman in and putting her in a safehouse or something," Allina said.

"Or using her as bait," he said slowly. It would be risky, but it could work if they could set it up in a public place where the killer didn't know they were there watching him, ready to arrest him as soon as he arrived.

"Only if they agreed," Matthew said. "And hopefully it won't come to that. Hopefully he's attracted to one of the fake profiles we set up. Once we get him talking a little bit, we can suggest a meet in person. He should go for it because he's desperate. Then we just wait for him to turn up in the limousine for the date and arrest him. Easy and quick, and no one gets hurt."

"The kids couldn't come to an agreement of who they thought the man they'd seen in their house was?" he asked.

"No, they were both only reasonably sure that the man they had picked was the man they'd seen. But were both sure that the man the other had picked wasn't him," Matthew replied. "So, it's either get him with the fake profiles, or find some forensics that tells us who he is. Both Jaden and Hendrick are out on bail, which means they're still a threat, to all the women on that website, Joynelle and Whitney, and Mila Drake."

～

5:55 P.M.

He watched her on the monitor as he made dinner.

Mila sat in the chair, right where he'd left her after he'd bathed her. That was almost twenty-four hours ago. He was trying to keep his distance from her, for a number of reasons. One of them being that the more she was alone the more he believed she would learn. And she was certainly learning to become more obedient. Her punishment seemed to have done the trick and after standing in the corner for several hours she had not returned to her ridiculous task of trying to unscrew the door with her bare hands.

He should be pleased with her progress, with her obedience, with her new willingness to follow the rules. He should be but he wasn't.

He wasn't altogether sure why that was. He wanted an obedient woman. One who knew her place and accepted it with grace and elegance. He wanted a woman who wanted to be with him, who wanted him, who woke up each morning feeling complete because she was by his side.

But he needed more.

There had been something missing in all the other women.

Strength.

Not bull-headed strength like Georgia who had tried to attack him and escape, and not stupid strength like Mila who thought she could brute force her way out of this room, but the kind of strength that would make the woman a true mate. The kind of partner who was always there beside you, who lifted you up, who made you better than you would be on your own.

He had avoided looking for women who were too strong because he had thought it would be too much work to break them down and teach them just what place a woman should possess in life, but maybe that had been his mistake. He had purposefully chosen women who lack self-confidence, who were eager to please, who he believed he could easily persuade to meet him and then once he had them here in his little castle he could dominate without fuss.

What if he tried something different?

So far, he had four failures. In his mind he had already discounted Mila Drake as the woman he was searching for.

He wanted a challenge. He wanted to take a woman he knew was strong enough to be his other half, then mold her into the perfect wife. It was now so clear to him, if the woman wasn't strong enough then all he would end up with was a shell. A woman who might outwardly do as she was told, but inside was crumbling away into nothingness. He didn't want to wake up one morning and find that the woman he had groomed so carefully was nothing but a useless pile of flesh.

For the first time he realized he needed more. He needed someone who would never break. They must be teachable, but they must also be resilient, so that in forty years from now when he was old and grey, that woman remained by his side.

He already had an inkling who this woman was.

Mila had babbled almost non-stop about her sister. A cop. Never in a million years would he have ever dreamed that he would consider bringing a police office here. But he had been looking at things all wrong.

A cop would be kind, caring, and compassionate. They wanted to help people and were willing to risk themselves in the process. They were strong, and they were also obedient, used to following orders, taking their place in the chain of command.

A potentially perfect combination.

Mila's sister could be just the woman he had been looking for.

He was excited. He wanted to run and grab her immediately, but he couldn't. If he was seriously going to contemplate bringing a police officer here, then he was going to have to play this smart. Smart and different from the others. The sister wouldn't be on the dating website, he wouldn't be able to lure her with a story that appealed to her personality and a name that meant Prince Charming.

If he was seriously going to bring the woman here, he was going to have to straight up abduct her.

Abducting a cop would be no easy feat. She would probably be armed, she would know self-defense tactics, and she would likely be more aware of her surroundings and the people in them than the average person. It would be difficult but not impossible. Especially if she was distracted.

What better distraction than a dead sister.

He had no more use for Mila anyway. She wasn't what he wanted, looking back on it now, she never had been. There was no point in keeping her here any longer, working with her, trying to see if she could fulfill his expectations. She was a failure. Although he supposed not a complete failure since she had managed to help illuminate to him what he was really wanting in his woman.

May as well go and get things over with, there was no point dragging them out. The quicker he got Mila disposed of, the quicker he could make a move on getting the sister. And the quicker he got the sister here, the quicker he could begin her training. And the quicker he began her training, the quicker he got what he wanted.

Abandoning dinner, he grabbed his black mask and put it on then headed for Mila's room. Her head snapped up when she heard the door open and the book she had held clutched in her hands tumbled to the floor.

She started to rise but then stopped midway up, her face full of fear and uncertainty. She didn't want to make him angry by breaking the rules, but she still wasn't sure what was expected of her in every situation. He liked her eagerness to please, it was too bad things weren't going to work out between them, but he had given it his best shot.

"You may stand," he gave his permission.

Mila straightened quickly, wincing a little at the movement, her muscles must still be aching from her punishment.

"Remove your clothing," he instructed as he locked the door behind him, he didn't really think Mila would make a run for it, but he felt better knowing it was safely locked.

She hesitated, a little burst of fire lighting in her green eyes. She didn't want to do as he told her. She wanted to fight him, but her common sense told her not to. She probably believed that if she played along and did as he wanted then she would stay alive until her sister got here, and she would be rescued and reunited with her children.

But she was wrong.

On so many levels.

She wouldn't be alive in just a few minutes from now. And although her sister *would* be coming here it wouldn't be to rescue her, it would be to take her place.

"I said remove your clothing." He took a threatening step toward her.

She hesitated again but then quickly slipped out of the green dress he had put on her earlier and let it drop to the floor.

As he stood there looking at her naked body, her long legs, her flat stomach, all that white skin that he knew was every bit as soft as it looked, he felt his body stirring with desire.

Now it was his turn to hesitate. He wanted her. He wanted to touch her and taste her and come inside her.

He took a deep breath and controlled his desires. Being the perfect husband was just as much about controlling himself as it was about being in control of his woman.

Hopefully it wouldn't be long. Hopefully Mila's sister was the one. And hopefully her body was just as amazing as Mila's. He couldn't wait to find out.

"Walk to the bathroom," he told Mila.

Although she shuddered, she turned and walked there without complaint or argument. He followed her and turned on the tap for the bath. For a moment, they both stood in silence watching as the water slowly filled the bathtub.

"My sister will find you," Mila said, her voice desperate as though she knew what was coming.

"She won't have to. I intend to find her first."

Mila's big green eyes grew bigger as realization sunk in. "Stay away from her."

"But you made her sound so appealing."

She shook her head, eyed the door, then him. Weighed her options then ran.

He was on her before she reached the door.

He wrapped an arm around her chest, pinning her arms to her sides, and carried her to the bathtub. She fought him. As best she could anyway.

The bath was full enough, so he plunged her into it, shoving her head under the water and holding it there.

Mila thrashed, her hands trying to claw at his hand on the back of her head, her body trying to climb out of the tub.

Bubbles filled the tub from the still running tap, from Mila's frantic movements, from the air as her lungs finally commanded her to try to breathe.

Eventually she went limp.

It took longer to drown someone than he'd thought.

CHAPTER
Eight

July 30th
3:47 A.M.

This was the last place on earth he wanted to be right now.

Matthew felt his feet dragging as he walked toward the light and the bustle of activity. He'd been in bed asleep when he'd gotten the call he'd been dreading. By the time he'd gotten dressed, gotten in his car, and driven here, the crime scene unit had already arrived. They would thoroughly search the dump site as well as carefully examine the body, but he didn't believe they would find anything. The killer was too meticulous to leave behind any physical evidence that would point them straight in his direction.

No one was speaking when he reached the scene.

He didn't even need to ask for confirmation that it was who they thought it was. The mass of red curls and green eyes. If he hadn't known better, he would have thought he was staring at his partner's lifeless corpse. There was no one else this could be but Rylla's sister, Mila Drake.

"He only kept her three days," he said softly. Matthew had hoped they would have had more time to find Mila.

"Doesn't look like she made him angry like Georgia did," Tracey said.

"What wounds does she have?" he asked the medical examiner.

"A few faint marks on her bottom," Tracey replied.

"He punished her," Matthew said for no other reason than that he felt like he had to say something.

"Not badly," Tracey consoled.

"Cause of death, Trace?" Matthew asked, his gaze fixed unwaveringly on Mila's face.

"I'm not sure. No major injuries—stab wounds or gunshots—there's petechiae present so maybe he smothered her. I don't see any trauma to the mouth or nose though, maybe he drowned her." Tracey gently lifted Mila's head and tilted it to the side, "I see some bruising on the back of her neck, possible he held her head under water and drowned her. I'll do the autopsy as soon as I get her back to the morgue."

"What about her hands?" He pointed to Mila's hands which were bruised and bloody with torn nails.

Releasing her head, Tracey picked up one of Mila's hands and examined it. "Looks like she tried to claw through something. Most of the damage is to her fingertips. It looks like someone tried to tend to the wounds, they're clean and already starting to heal."

"So, the killer tends to her injuries but then kills her, he makes no sense. He kept Mila a day longer than he kept Georgia, but he killed Georgia in a rage, I think he intended to keep her for longer. But there's no signs he lost his temper with Mila, it's like he just changed his mind and decided she wasn't what he's looking for. He's moved on, he has another target in mind."

"Do you have any idea who she might be?" Tracey asked.

"No. There are too many women on the website for us to make contact with them all, and all we can warn them of anyway is to be careful and not agree to meet anyone they met on there alone. We set up two profiles hoping to lure him, but so far, we don't have any hits from someone we think is the killer."

"Is it ...?" Jonathon asked as he and Allina came up behind him.

"It's Rylla's sister," he answered.

Just like he had done, for a long moment Jonathon and Allina just stood and stared at the body as though trying to force their brains to comprehend what their eyes were seeing.

"Does she know yet?" Allina asked. Her face was pained, she knew what it was like to be in Rylla's position, having someone you loved snatched away from you. Waiting every second for the phone to ring with the news you were dreading with every fiber of your being.

"Not yet," he answered. "When we're done here I'll go and break the news." He was dreading having to do it. Rylla was going to be both devastated and guilt ridden.

"We'll come," Jonathon said immediately.

"Thank you." He appreciated the support even if it wouldn't make having to say those words to his partner any easier.

"Who found the body?" Allina asked.

"A patrol unit," Matthew told her. "They saw the body, and when they saw that she was dressed up like that they assumed she was the Fairytale Killer's next victim." Mila had been left in a beautiful pink dress, and with the red hair, and Tracey's suspicions that she had potentially been drowned, he was assuming she was the killer's version of The Little Mermaid.

"Did they see anyone?"

"No. They just saw the body and stopped to check it out."

"Do we have a cause of death?" Jonathon asked.

"Possible drowning," Tracey replied.

"So, he didn't kill her here," Jonathon said.

"He probably killed her wherever he was keeping her then dumped her body here," Matthew said.

"Different than the others," Allina said. "Jeannie was killed where she was found, Tillie was killed where she was found, Georgia was killed and dumped but it seemed like her murder was more spur of the moment rather than planned out. But this time he decided to kill her, then came and dumped her."

"He has another victim lined up, one he thinks is going to give him what he wants," he said.

"Any women reported missing last night?"

"None so far but we should be on the lookout for one," Matthew said. "He usually has his next victim lined up and ready. Even with Georgia, whose murder was committed in a rage, he was ready to go with Mila the next day. For him to decide Mila wasn't going to fulfill his wishes this quickly means he must be excited about his next prospect. Is he going after Joynelle or Whitney? Either of the decoy profiles we set up? Someone we don't know about?" There were too many options, and that he had no direction to turn in left him feeling so helpless.

~

8:04 A.M.

"What do you want for breakfast?"

Rylla curled her nose up at the entire kitchen as though it were one great big disgusting pit of stomach-churning revulsion. She had no interest in eating whatsoever.

"Don't even think about saying you're not hungry," Sam warned. "We're eating breakfast. All of us," he added with a stern look that included both her and Naomi.

Naomi looked as unenthusiastic about the prospect of breakfast as Rylla knew she herself did, but since she knew Sam was going to insist, she said, "I'll have cereal."

Sam nodded approvingly. "Naomi?"

"Cereal too I guess," she replied.

While Sam organized the food, Rylla took a seat at the table. She was pleased and yet not pleased that Nate was sitting across from her.

She was so confused about him. She'd thought that something was developing between them, he'd kissed her, she'd let go of her anger toward him, she had resolved to set aside her fear, they had spent the night talking, she had drawn strength and comfort from him. Then all of a sudden, he had backed away.

It was like a switch had been turned.

They had been talking about Sam and Naomi, about how much

Sam loved and worried about Naomi and their unborn baby. She had been thinking of Nate and wondering if maybe someday there could be that kind of love between them. But when she had looked at him something had been different.

Gone was the softness in his face, the longing in his eyes, the closeness she felt with him. In its place was distance. Almost coldness.

She didn't know why he had pulled away, or why he was sending her mixed signals.

When she had asked if he wanted to come upstairs and lie down with her, she had expected him to say yes, but he hadn't, he had turned her down. Again. Not even willing to commit to still being there in the morning.

Rylla had gone upstairs, curled up in bed, and cried. Sobbed might be a better word. She had sobbed so hard and for so long that her chest had ached, and her eyes burned. She didn't cry much. When Josh and Elianna had died of course, and when she'd thought Naomi was going to die, and a few other times, but on the whole she wasn't a crier. But she had felt so stupid. She'd gotten up the courage to ask Nate out, he'd turned her down. Then she had forgiven him and gotten up the courage to let it all go and see if she and Nate could have something, then he'd turned her down again.

So exhausted from lack of sleep and torrential tears, she had finally passed out into a deep, dreamless sleep. When she had gotten up the next morning, she had expected Nate to be gone. She wasn't even sure if she'd ever see him again or if he was gone for good.

But he'd still been there. And he'd stayed all day yesterday. Then here he was again this morning, he'd obviously been here all night.

He was sending her all sorts of mixed messages, and it wasn't fair. She was dealing with enough right now. He could either stay here with her if he wanted to, but he was also free to walk away, she didn't want him to play games.

Feeling eyes on her, she looked up and Nate quickly glanced away. Why was he watching her? If he didn't want to date her that was up to him, but then why stay here? He'd said that fear had him saying no when she'd asked him out at the wedding, was fear holding him back now too?

Sam was just setting down bowls of cereal when her doorbell rang.

"I'll get it," Sam immediately offered.

Rylla shook her head and stood slowly. "No, I'll go." She couldn't take another second of sitting there with Nate watching her but pretending he wasn't. She understood being afraid, but Nate had to make the decision of whether it was worth risking being hurt and setting his fears aside. Until he made his choice, he should keep his distance. It was too hard having him here but not really having him.

"Matthew." A bad feeling washed over her when she opened the door to see her partner standing there. She shoved those feelings away, her partner had just come by to give her another update on the case.

"Morning, Rylla," Matthew said, "may we come in?" His tone was off, and that bad feeling was quickly upgrading to a cold knot of dread that set itself firmly in her stomach.

"Sure." She stood back so Matthew, Jonathon, and Allina could enter. Why were the others here? She knew they were working the case with Matthew since she had been removed from it, but usually her partner came by on his own to give her updates. The last time the three of them had arrived at her house they'd been here to tell her that Mila had been abducted.

She led them into the living room, where Sam, Naomi, and Nate appeared in the kitchen doorway. Rylla wanted to ask what was going on, but at the same time the cold knot of dread warned her not to ask.

So they all just stood there.

Her brain knew what was coming but she was fighting against it.

"Rylla," Matthew began, his brown eyes full of sympathy. "I'm so sorry."

"Sorry? Why?" She still clung to denial. Memories were flashing through her mind. The knock on her door, opening it to find two somber faced young police officers, hearing the news that there had been an accident, learning Josh and Elianna were dead, the shock, the pain, the denial, the tears, the swirling in her head, her knees buckling, the cops attempting to offer comfort.

"Mila's body was found this morning," Matthew said in a rush.

The room seemed to spin around her.

"Rylla?"

She heard the voice, knew it belonged to her partner, and yet it sounded like it was very far away.

"Rylla?"

This time the voice was Naomi's, and her friend suddenly appeared in front of her, her face fading in and out of focus.

"Rylla."

Matthew again, and this time she snapped back into the moment. "Stop saying my name," she growled.

"I'm so sorry." Matthew looked devastated.

Grief and shock had anger flashing forward as a coping mechanism. "You should be sorry. You convinced Heidi to take me off this case and now Mila is dead."

Dead.

She still couldn't believe it.

How were Emmy and Mac going to cope with the news? They were just children and now they were going to have to grow up without their mother.

It wasn't fair.

Why did she keep losing people she loved?

First her mom, then her dad and siblings, then her husband and daughter, and now her sister. It was enough. She didn't want to lose anyone else.

"I'm sorry," her partner said again, looking at her helplessly.

"Stop saying that," she yelled.

"Rylla, I'm so sorry." Naomi tried to hug her, but she shoved her friend away, earning her a glare from Sam.

"Just go. All of you." In times of stress she always reverted to her default which was dealing with things on her own.

"I don't think you should be alone right now," Naomi said cautiously.

"Stop giving me advice," Rylla screamed. "What do you know? Pushing people away and dealing with everything yourself is your MO, you're the last person I should take advice from."

"That's enough, Rylla," Sam warned her.

Naomi's sad brown eyes just added to her guilt. It was the second time in the last few days that she had lashed out at her friend, and she knew Naomi didn't deserve it. She had been a good friend in the decade they'd known each other, but she just couldn't stop herself. "Go. Everyone out now. I mean it. Just get out." She knew she was freaking out but couldn't seem to do anything about it.

With a last guilty look in her direction, Matthew left with Jonathon and Allina. Sam took Naomi's arm and tried to guide her from the room.

"No, I don't want to go," Naomi protested.

"She wants space," Sam said quietly. "She's entitled to that. She'll call you if she needs you."

Reluctantly, Naomi let her husband take her away, leaving Rylla alone.

Or almost alone.

As she turned, she saw Nate still standing silently in the corner.

"Why are you still here?" she demanded, quietly now, the fight draining out of her, pain taking its place.

"I'm staying," Nate said, just as quietly.

"I don't want company right now."

He nodded solemnly. "I want to respect your wishes, but I can't. I'm not leaving you alone at a time like this."

Why was he being so nice to her all of a sudden? Especially after she'd just insulted both her partner and her best friend.

Rylla could feel her composure cracking.

Mila was really dead.

She'd never get a chance to work things out with her sister and be as close as they'd been when they were little.

She looked at Nate, tears blurring her vision. "She's gone. He killed her. I couldn't save her."

Nate didn't say anything, just came to her and wrapped his arms around her, holding her firmly against his chest. Completely surprising herself Rylla burst into tears and clung to Nate like he was her lifeline.

∽

5:12 P.M.

. . .

He was so excited.

It was hard to wait. Patience had never been a strong suit of his, but it was one he wanted to work on. It was equally as important to him that he be a good husband as it was that the woman he chose to be his wife be successful at it. As such, he knew that learning to be more patient was important. He had the feeling that teaching Detective Rylla Franklin how to be the perfect wife was going to be a great opportunity to work on his patience.

He knew things with Rylla would not be easy.

She would fight him. It was inevitable. Her inner strength would require her to do it even if her common sense told her she shouldn't. But the payoff once he had educated her and turned her into a quiet, obedient, submissive partner would be unlike anything he could even imagine.

Rylla was everything he had been looking for, he was sure of it.

Now he just had to wait for the perfect opportunity to grab her.

He had been watching her house ever since he'd dumped Mila's body in a parking lot outside a shopping center. He'd seen people arrive. Cops. He could tell that even from a distance.

They hadn't stayed long.

Just minutes after walking in the front door they walked back out. Shortly after a pregnant woman and a man also walked out.

He hadn't been sure if anyone else was in there, but two cars were parked in the driveway so he suspected that there might be. Although he wanted to go running—well sneaking—straight inside to take Rylla, he didn't. He played it smart. Just like he had with everything else so far, and it had paid off. So far, they had nothing on him. It was important that he kept that up.

Although it was hard, he had to stay here, keep watch on Rylla's house, and wait for the perfect time to make his move.

He wasn't quite sure yet if it would be better to break into her house to get her, perhaps wait until night and then get her while she was sleeping, or whether he should wait until she came out. Both had their pros and cons.

Given that Rylla was a cop, grabbing her while she was in bed asleep would certainly make things easier. He wouldn't have to worry about her pulling a weapon on him or managing to get out of his grasp if he tried to tackle her. He was a strong guy, but he wasn't proficient in self-defense so he didn't know what moves she might have up her sleeves.

On the other hand, if he took her in her house then she would have the home ground advantage. Sometimes that made all the difference. If he waited for her to come out, he could follow her and take her at the perfect moment. She had to know about her sister, he assumed that was why the cops had been there earlier, so she would be distracted, she might not even notice him coming up behind her until it was too late. Then he could tuck her safely away in his car and take her away to his castle and begin his training.

He couldn't wait to have her all to himself. From what he knew, Rylla was every bit as beautiful as Mila. It was hard to wait till he could run his hands over all that soft milky white skin, let his fingers glide through those red curls, press his lips to her plump ones.

He drew in a deep breath and made himself stay put. He had to keep focusing on the big picture, if he made a play for Rylla right now it might not work out, he could even wind up arrested.

With just a little patience he would have her.

Maybe he should take a little break. He had been here for a good twelve hours, he didn't want anyone to get suspicious. He should go and get some dinner, get some fresh air, relax and stretch his stiff muscles, then once he was refreshed he could come back here, ready to lie in wait for the perfect opportunity to take Rylla home with him.

～

8:47 P.M.

She needed space, fresh air. She needed to move. She needed to do something that was going to distract her mind from constantly replaying memories over and over again tormenting her relentlessly.

Rylla felt like she was suffocating. She couldn't spend another second trapped inside her house.

Well, she knew she wasn't really trapped but she just needed to get out.

Not that she didn't appreciated Nate being here with her because she did, she *really* did. He had let her cry all over him, he had stayed with her all day, he had made sure she ate, he had tried to keep her distracted and lift her spirits, he had been sensitive and compassionate and caring, he had comforted her, basically he had been perfect.

But now she needed some time to herself.

It wasn't personal. She wouldn't have gotten through the day without Nate, and she was hoping he intended to sleep in her spare room again, but right now, she just needed to be out of the stifling grief that filled her house.

She needed to run.

If Naomi hadn't been a couple of weeks away from giving birth, she would have called her friend and asked her to come and go running with her. Instead, she would have to settle for running on her own, which wasn't really such a horrible prospect.

Slipping quietly out of the house while Nate was busy talking on his phone since she didn't want to explain to him that she needed to be on her own for a while, and she didn't want to hurt his feelings, especially after how great he had been all day. The last of the day's light was just fading away, the sky was dark and clear and full of twinkling stars. She took a moment just to stare at it, to let the beauty and peacefulness of it seep into her.

She didn't want to think anymore. She just wanted to let her mind go blank as her body fell into a routine it knew so well.

Barely paying attention to where she was going, Rylla began to run.

With each step she felt the tension inside her easing. The grief was still there, but it was no longer choking her. She knew it would never go away, she would never stop missing her sister and all that could have been between them, just as she would never stop blaming herself for not stopping this killer before he got his hands on Mila.

As she ran she lost all track of time. Her mind blocked out everything else. Everything but placing one foot in front of the other. The monotonous rhythm made everything around her blur into nothingness. Her lungs were burning, her legs starting to go numb, but she pushed through it, continuing to run until her body physically gave out.

Rylla collapsed on the grass, breathing hard. Now that she was no longer moving her mind wandered again.

Had Mila known she was going to die?

Had she suffered?

Had she thought that someone would come and save her?

Had her last thoughts been of her children?

So many questions and she had no answers to any of them. She supposed she could call Matthew and ask how Mila had been killed, but she was embarrassed to talk to him after blaming him for not finding her sister in time. And she wasn't sure she wanted to know how Mila had died, that would just set her imagination into overdrive.

In the morning she would go and visit Emmy and Mac. She had wanted to give them and Beau some space, let them process the news. But she wanted to be there for them, they were her family, she had failed their mother, but she wasn't going to fail them too. She would be there for them no matter what, anything they needed, anything she could do to help she would do.

She didn't have a watch on her but at least an hour must have passed since she left, and Nate probably knew she was gone and would be worrying, she should go back home.

Rylla stood and was just about to start jogging when an arm wrapped around her chest, and something cold was pressed against her neck.

A knife.

"Hello, princess," a voice spoke in her ear, a warm breath whooshed across her cheek.

Instinctively, her self-defense training kicked in and had her automatically fighting back. She lifted her foot and stomped firmly on his. Then without pausing her hand thumped his groin, her elbow slammed into his ribs, then moved seamlessly up to connect with the bottom of his jaw.

The man yelped in surprise and pain and loosened his grip.

As she spun sideways out of his arms, she felt the knife slice through her neck. Warm, sticky blood oozed from the gash, but she didn't have time to worry about whether or not the wound was serious, she was already on the move.

She got only a couple of steps when the full force of the man's body tackled her. He landed on top of her as she crashed into the ground. The weight of him on top of her shoved the air from her lungs and pain exploded in her chest.

Again, she had no time to worry about what injuries he had caused her. Rylla knew the man was too big and too strong for her to throw him off her, but she wasn't out of options yet.

"Your sister told me all about you." His hot breath tickled the back of her neck.

Sister?

This was the Fairytale Killer?

Why was he after her?

Shaking off the whys for now, Rylla opened her mouth and sunk her teeth into the forearm that was trying to drag her up to her feet.

The man grunted and released her.

Without a pause, she darted up and toward the nearest house, screaming at the top of her lungs.

He recovered quickly and wrapped a hand around her ankle, yanking and knocking her off-balance. As she fell her leg twisted and she landed awkwardly. Pain flashed in her knee, spreading down to her ankle and up to her hip.

He was on his knees, attempting to pull her closer. With her free leg she delivered a well-placed kick to his face, connecting squarely with his nose, and he released her again.

All of a sudden a voice called out, "What's going on? Is everything okay over there?"

The man paused. His huge body frozen in place as he appeared to weigh his options.

"Call 911," she yelled to whoever had heard the scuffle and come to her aid.

"I'll be back," her attacker said, then darted to a nearby car.

For the first time fear took hold of her, and she sank back against the grass.

If that man hadn't chosen that moment to come out to see what was happening, the Fairytale Killer would have gotten her into his car. She'd fought him off twice, but he was bigger and stronger, and eventually he would have overpowered her. Adrenalin, training, and instinct had taken hold while she fought for her life, but now that the man was gone it was quickly draining out of her system leaving her shaking, hurting, and scared.

"I called 911, are you okay?" A man suddenly appeared above her.

Struggling into a sitting position, Rylla winced at the pain in her chest. "I'm fine."

"I think you're bleeding," the man sounded doubtful.

"Nothing serious." She hoped. "Do you have a phone I can borrow?" She would never again go running without her phone and her gun.

The man handed over his cell and she called in the attack, giving a brief rundown of what had happened, asked for CSU to come, and told them she'd be at home waiting to give her statement.

"Are you sure you shouldn't wait here for the ambulance?" the man asked when she handed him back her phone.

"I just live a few streets over," she assured him as she slowly staggered to her feet. She just wanted to go home.

Still looking doubtful, the man offered no more protests, and Rylla began the walk home. With her injured knee she couldn't go any faster than a slow limp, and what would normally have taken only a couple of minutes took almost fifteen.

At her back door she hesitated.

Nate was going to freak out when he saw her.

Taking a deep breath, she opened the door and hobbled into her kitchen.

"Where have you be—?" Nate broke off when he caught sight of her. And what a sight she must be. She knew her neck was bleeding, and she was probably dirty and pale as well.

"What happened?" his voice was strained with fear as he grabbed a towel, then her arm and pushed her down into a chair, holding the towel firmly against the cut on her neck.

"It was the Fairytale Killer," she whispered, meeting Nate's fearful gaze.

"He tried to attack you? Where else are you hurt?" He pulled his phone out of his pocket.

"I already called it in," she told him before he could make a call.

With a shaking hand he set the phone down. "Where are you hurt?"

"I'm fine," she told him.

"Where are you hurt?" he repeated again, his voice shook more than his hands.

There was no point in hiding it, an ambulance was no doubt already on its way here. "My ribs and my knee."

He lifted her hand to get her to keep pressure on her neck while he checked her other injuries, but she wrapped her fingers tightly around his and clung to them.

"Hold me," she whispered, tears welling up in her eyes.

She was strong, she was tough, she had fought back against the killer and gotten away alive, she didn't want to cry but she couldn't stop the tears from tumbling down her cheeks.

~

9:29 P.M.

He didn't need to be asked a second time to hold her.

Nate had been wanting to drag Rylla into his arms and cling to her since she'd stepped into her kitchen dirty and covered in blood. Actually, he'd wanted to keep holding her in his arms ever since she'd collapsed against him in tears after learning her sister had been killed.

Now he scooped her up with one arm while keeping pressure on her neck, and took her place in the chair, setting Rylla in his lap. He didn't think the wound on her neck was too serious, but every breath she took was strained and he hoped she hadn't broken any ribs. He hated to see her in pain just as he hated to see her cry.

Rylla reclaimed her grip on his hand, holding it so tightly he couldn't help wincing, not that he wanted her to let go. He had assumed she'd gone out for a run when he finished his phone call and couldn't find her anywhere. If he'd had even an inkling that she was in any physical danger he would have taken off after her, but there had been no indication whatsoever that the killer she and her partner had been hunting would come after her.

He still couldn't believe it.

The thought of Rylla in danger left him feeling sick to his stomach.

He was done with being afraid of his feelings for her.

He'd been over thinking things the other day. Convincing himself to walk away from Rylla because it was easier than risking getting hurt again. But he hadn't been able to walk out the door. He couldn't leave her. The feelings were there whether he wanted to pretend otherwise or not.

So he'd stayed.

And when Rylla had needed him today he'd been here. He'd held her and attempted to offer whatever comfort her could. She hadn't pushed him away, she'd wanted him to hold her, drawn strength from his presence. He had been wrong. She *could* love her husband and still have room in her heart to love him too.

He was going to have to find a way to be okay with that, to let go of the doubts, because the woman he held in his arms, he loved. It was as simple as that. The fear that stabbed his heart when he took in her bloody neck and thought she was about to collapse and die right in front of him confirmed that what he felt for her was real and it wasn't going anywhere.

Nate pressed his lips to the top of Rylla's head and held them there.

Sirens filled the air and Rylla stirred, attempting to get out of his arms and stand up.

"You're not going anywhere," he told her. "Hold the towel." When she pressed a hand to it, maintaining pressure on the still bleeding wound, he stood with her in his arms and carried her through to the living room, depositing her on the couch, then with another kiss to the top of her head, he went to the front door to let in the paramedics.

He couldn't focus on anything but Rylla as the medics examined her. He thought he used his manners and greeted them, but maybe he didn't. He stayed just far enough away from her to give the medics space to work, and stood there, arms crossed over his chest, body ridged, ready to pounce like a protective guard dog on anything that wanted to hurt her.

As they cleaned the gash on her neck and held the edges together with butterfly bandages, before taping a stark white bandage over the top, Nate couldn't tear his eyes away. If the killer's knife had cut just a little deeper, a little higher, then she would have bled out on the spot. He would never have gotten a chance to tell her he loved her, to tell her he was sorry, to make love to her, or even to say goodbye.

"Nate."

At the sound of Rylla's voice he snapped to attention. Was something wrong? Was she more seriously hurt than he'd thought? He should have rushed her to the hospital as soon as she got here rather than wait for the medics.

"What?" he asked tightly.

"They're going to check out my ribs, could you leave the room for a moment?"

"No." Hell would freeze over before he left her alone.

"Could you at least turn around then?"

"No." He wasn't taking his eyes off her. He had to keep her in sight to try to believe that she was really here and alive.

Rylla's eyes widened, then narrowed, but then she just shrugged, and nodded to the medic. She winced as the medic helped her take off her t-shirt, leaving her in only her sports bra and yoga pants. Usually, he would have found that arousing but right now sex was the furthest thing from his mind. Well maybe not the furthest, Rylla was toned all over with a pretty decent six pack that rivaled his own, and his body definitely responded. Her chest was already swollen and bruised, and the sight of her hurt had his body giving itself a metaphorical cold shower.

"Broken?" he asked when the paramedic finished probing the area.

"No, bruised or maybe cracked. They'll do an x-ray at the hospital."

"I'm not going to the hospital," Rylla said immediately.

The medic frowned at her and was no doubt about to give her a lecture when Matthew suddenly burst into the room.

"Rylla. Are you okay?"

"Yes," she answered firmly, reclaiming her t-shirt and managing to struggle back into it. "A little sore and a bit banged up but I'm fine."

"If you won't go to the hospital, then ice your ribs for the next seventy-two hours. Have someone check out your neck tomorrow, and see your doctor if you get worse," the medic told her.

"She will," Nate assured him, he'd make sure of it.

"I'm sorry," Rylla told her partner as soon as the paramedics had packed up their stuff and left. "I shouldn't have blamed you for Mila's death. It's not your fault, we did everything we could to find him. I'm sorry."

"It's fine," Matthew assured her as he sat beside her on the couch. "You were lashing out in grief."

"That doesn't make it okay, I'm really sorry, Matt."

He took her hand and squeezed it. "I forgive you."

Rylla relaxed a little, settling back against the couch cushions, her face was pinched, she was obviously in a lot of pain. "Could you grab some ice and painkillers?" he asked Matthew, who nodded and left the room.

Nate pulled over an ottoman and gently lifted Rylla's injured leg so it rested on the soft cushion. He put some pillows behind her and propped her against them, then slipped her shoes off and sat beside her. Rylla immediately leaned into him. Matthew returned and Rylla swallowed the pain pills without protest, while he positioned the ice against her injured ribs.

"You said it was the Fairytale Killer who attacked you. How do you know that?" Matthew asked as he pulled an armchair closer to the couch and perched on the edge of it.

"When he grabbed me, he said, 'Hello, princess'."

"Does anyone else call you that?"

"No one's ever called me princess. Rylla, Ry, when we were kids Elliot and Mila would sometimes call me crybaby because I went through that baby of the family stage of crying to get my way. Josh would call me honey or babe, but I've never been called princess before."

"Did he say anything else to you?"

"He told me that my sister told him a lot about me."

He wouldn't have felt the shiver that sliced through her if she hadn't been plastered against his side. He shivered too. The Fairytale Killer had chosen her as his next victim. Nate put his arm around

Rylla's shoulders and held her as tightly as he dared without aggravating her injuries.

"Did you get a look at him?"

"No, it was too dark."

"I'm going to stay here tonight," Matthew announced.

Although he appreciated that, Nate wanted Rylla all to himself right now. "I'm going to be staying, I'm a trained bodyguard, she'll be safe with me. And Sam has sent someone to watch the house."

Matthew looked like he wanted to argue but chose not to. "Anything else you can tell me about him?"

"It all happened so quickly," Rylla said softly. "He was big, and strong, I got away from him twice, but if that man hadn't come outside when he did, I think the killer would have gotten me in his car." Nate would forever be grateful to that man for saving Rylla's life.

"Okay," Matthew stood and patted Rylla's uninjured knee, "you should get some rest. Kane is coming to collect your clothes. I'm going to have a patrol car posted outside your house as well as whoever Sam is sending."

"He, uh, he said something else right before he ran off," Rylla said.

Nate stiffened, not liking her tone. "What?"

"He said he'd be back."

He had known the killer wouldn't walk away from Rylla if he had decided she was the woman he had been searching for, but hearing her confirm it made his blood turn to ice. He was *not* going to lose the woman he loved. He would kill that man if he tried to get to Rylla again. He would kill anyone who tried to hurt Rylla.

CHAPTER
Nine

July 31st
1:22 A.M.

The scream jolted him out of the light sleep he had been hovering in since taking Rylla up to bed after her partner had left.

Screams.

Rylla.

With his heart in his throat, Nate jumped out of the bed in Rylla's spare room and ran to the room across the hall.

Gun in hand, he threw open the door, expecting to see Rylla fighting with the killer.

Instead, the room was empty except for Rylla.

She lay in her bed, under a sheet, ramrod straight, her body wasn't moving at all as though whatever she was dreaming had her paralyzed in fear. Her face was pasty and beaded in sweat, a look of abject terror marred her features.

Another scream was ripped from her throat.

He ran to the bed and grabbed hold of her shoulders. Her bare skin was icy cold to the touch, and small tremors were rippling through her. He shook her. "Rylla."

She moaned. The most pitiful sound he had ever heard. His heart was hammering in his chest, he couldn't stand to see her suffering like this.

"Rylla." He shook her again. "Wake up. Come on." He gave her another shake, but she remained trapped within her nightmare. He wanted to shake her harder, but he was concerned about hurting her, the square white bandage taped to her throat was a stark reminder that she had almost been killed just a few hours ago. "Rylla," he begged, "wake up, please."

Nate gave her one more shake and her eyes finally popped open. They were wild and disoriented. She was awake but she wasn't.

He took her face in his hands and turned it, so she was looking at him. "Rylla," he said softly, "it's Nate. You were dreaming. Nightmares."

It took a moment but slowly her eyes cleared, and she drew in a shuddering breath. He wasn't ready to let go of her yet, so he sat on the edge of the bed and ran his hands down her shoulders, along her arms, and settled them on her hips.

"Are you okay?"

She nodded.

"Were you dreaming about being attacked?"

"No," her voice shook, he wasn't used to seeing Rylla like this, scared and vulnerable. "Well, yes, but not just that. Everything. My parents, Mila's death, someone going after her kids, what happened last night, Josh and Elianna."

Nate withdrew his hands. Doubts immediately creeping back in. It wasn't that he wanted to be thinking this way, but he knew that Rylla still loved her husband, there was a photo of the two of them with their baby daughter on the nightstand. Did she have room in her heart for him too?

Rylla sighed and struggled to sit up. "You have to stop doing that, Nate."

"Doing what?" he feigned innocence. Rylla should be resting, and he wasn't ready for this conversation yet. Right now, he wanted to focus on keeping her safe. They could talk once the Fairytale Killer was in custody or dead.

"Stop sending me mixed signals. I like you, I think I've made that clear. I think you like me too but you keep pulling back. Yesterday you were great. You were the reason I got through the day. But now as soon as I mention my husband you pull away. Josh is dead, it's not like I'm going to leave you to go back to him. So why? Why do you keep sending me mixed messages?"

He might not be ready to have this conversation, but it seemed like they were having it regardless. "I'm afraid."

"Of what?"

"My last marriage didn't end well."

Rylla settled herself against the headboard and reached for his hand. "I know that your ex took your son out of the country. I'm so sorry, I know what it feels like to lose a child," she said sympathetically.

Only Rylla had lost her daughter forever, he still had hope that one day he would have a relationship with Andrew.

"What happened?"

"You know I was in the military before I went to work with Sam. Rachel cheated on me while I was away on tour. When I came home, she told me about it, I didn't contest the divorce, and when she asked for full custody of our son I agreed. I was going to go away again, how could I parent a child from the other side of the world? He'd be spending all his time with his mother anyway, so it seemed logical. I thought we would work out a visitation schedule when I was home and I'd get to spend a lot of time with him, but it didn't turn out that way. Rachel left the country with her new boyfriend and Andrew. She never came back. That was six years ago, I haven't seen my son since."

"Oh, Nate, I'm so sorry." Rylla's eyes were full of empathy.

"I've done everything I can to try and get him back, but I have zero rights to him. Her new husband has adopted him. Rachel won't let me talk to him. She won't even send me pictures. I have no idea what he looks like now. I don't know what his hobbies are, I don't know how he does in school, he's a stranger to me. I never should have given her full custody. I *wouldn't* have if I'd known what she was going to do," he said that a little desperately. Rylla had had her child ripped away from her, he didn't want her to think that he had thrown his away.

"Of course you wouldn't." She squeezed his hand. "She took advantage of you and your job."

"I felt so betrayed. How could she take away a son from his father? She told me Andrew was better off without me. That I wasn't a good dad. That I'd already been away most of his life. That I had killed people. That I wasn't the kind of man she wanted around her son and that I wouldn't be a good influence on him as he grew older."

Rylla muttered something under her breath that sounded like a bad word. "You didn't believe any of that garbage, did you?"

Nate shrugged. Part of him *had* believed it. A lot of it had been true.

"She was being selfish, Nate. While you were away from your little boy risking your life to protect your country, she was cheating on you. She said those things because she knew they would hurt you and make you doubt yourself so you would give her full custody and she could run away with her new boyfriend. You are still a great dad to Andrew because you've never given up on him, and one day that will mean something to him."

That meant a lot to him. "I shouldn't have said no when you asked me out at Sam and Naomi's wedding. I hate that I hurt you, and I've tried to apologize, I've liked you since we first met six years ago. I know you'd never do what Rachel did, but it's still scary to risk your heart again after it's taken a battering."

"Yeah, it is," Rylla agreed seriously.

"And that's why I keep sending you mixed signals. I might have lost my son but he's still alive, and I know that one day I'll have a relationship with him. But you lost your daughter, and your husband. I hate what Rachel did, and I'll never forgive her for taking Andrew away from me. I don't hate her, she's still the mother of my son, but I would never go back to her, I have no feelings for her anymore. But your husband died. You still love him."

"I do," Rylla acknowledged.

"Sometimes I'm not sure that you could love me and your husband at the same time. I like you, Rylla. I want to date you. But it's scary to think that one day you could wake up and tell me that your heart is always going to belong to Josh. Rachel was never the love of my life, but you could be. And you already found the love of your life. Josh."

"He was," she agreed.

"So do you have room in your life for another great love?"

~

1:59 A.M.

Nate was looking at her with such uncertainty that Rylla couldn't help but reach out and touch him. One of her hands was still encased in one of Nate's, so she lifted her other hand and held it to his cheek. His stubble tickled her palm and she smiled, she knew the answer to Nate's question. There wasn't a molecule of doubt. Although in a way it hurt to let go of her past and the family she would always love, it was also exciting to have hope for a happy future.

She looked him straight in the eye. "There's space for you in my heart and in my life."

Hope lit his deep brown eyes, making them seem like they were glowing. "You're sure?"

"Positive."

His eyes crinkled at the sides as he smiled, and he leaned in and kissed her, softly and sweetly.

"But, Nate, you have to find a way to be okay with the fact that Josh will always be a part of me. I don't want to let him go, he was a good man, and I don't ever want him to be forgotten. He saved my life."

The smile wiped from his face, fear and concern taking its place. "Saved your life metaphorically or literally?"

"Both." Rylla paused and took a steadying breath, she didn't like talking about that time in her life. "You know that my mom tried to poison my dad when I was fifteen."

"Yes."

"Well after that, things got crazy at home. Mila and Elliot were already off at college so it was just me and my dad, and he started to change. A lot. So much that I became afraid that he might end up killing me because he became convinced that I was going to try to kill him just like his wife had. Mila and Elliot didn't believe me when I told them what was going on, they thought I just didn't like Dad's rules like a typical teenager. In the end, I didn't know what else to do so I ran away from home."

"Did your dad ever hurt you?"

"Not really, sometimes he'd get all up in my face and shake me a little, but he never really did anything that hurt me."

Nate's response to that was a guttural growl. "But he scared you enough that you thought living on the streets was the better option."

She nodded. Those weeks on the streets had been the most terrifying of her life. She must have started shivering, although she hadn't noticed because Nate moved to sit beside her then carefully eased her onto his lap. He pulled the sheet free from the mattress and wrapped it and his arms around her.

"What happened while you were on the streets?"

"I saved up as much money as I could, but it didn't last long, and I didn't know what to do. It seemed like I had no good options, I didn't know which way to turn. Nights were the scariest, there was no safe place to sleep, I was just as scared as when I'd gone to sleep in my bed at home. I wondered if I should go back." Everything had been so confusing those few weeks she had spent on the streets.

"What did you do?" Nate asked, his hand stroking up and down her spine, the motion soothing.

"I struggled through each day. I wanted to go to school but I couldn't. If I'd gone back there then my father would get me back. And if he got me back, he would convince everyone that I was crazy like my mom and get me locked up."

"How did you know he wanted you locked up?"

"He told me. All the time. He said it so many times that I actually started to believe it. Maybe he was right. Maybe I really was losing it. My mom was crazy maybe it was genetic, maybe I should have been locked up."

"You weren't crazy," Nate said fiercely.

His protective tone warmed her. "No, I wasn't. But I was a scared sixteen-year-old girl with few options. And I knew the longer I stayed on the streets the fewer options I would have. I wanted an education, I wanted to go to college, I wanted to get a good job. I didn't want to spend the rest of my life on the streets, I knew what would happen to me if I did, but I didn't know how to get my education. I started to wonder whether going home and letting my father kill me was really so bad."

Nate stiffened at her words, and reflexively clutched her tighter. She knew it was hard for him to hear that she had thought death was the best of her options, it was hard for herself to remember those days.

"Were you sure he would kill you if you went back?"

"I was positive. I'd woken up a couple of times to find him in my room holding a knife. I was terrified of him. I knew if I stayed in that house then sooner or later, he would kill me. But I also knew if I stayed on the streets, I would wind up dead sooner or later too."

"How did you survive? How did you meet Josh?"

"I spent most of the day trying to keep out of sight. I didn't know if my dad had reported me missing so I didn't know if anyone was looking for me. Most of the time I hung out at the park. I was so hungry. Starving. I hadn't eaten in days, and I was finally ready to give in. I knew there was only one way I was going to make money. Prostitute myself."

Again, Nate tensed at her words. "Did anyone touch you?" His tone said that if someone did, he would find them and rip them to shreds for laying a finger on her.

"No. I was ready to do it though. I didn't want to, but I didn't see any other way to survive. I was going to do it that night. And then I met him."

"Josh?"

"Yes. He was a youth worker and was out offering kids food, shelter, and help. Lots of kids turned him down, already the life of the streets was who they were, but I jumped at the offer. He took me to a shelter. I had a hot meal and a hot shower and clean clothes. It was heaven. I told Josh everything and he believed me. Mila and Elliot hadn't, so that he did meant everything to me." If Josh hadn't believed her, it would have changed everything. She would have spent however long she lasted on the streets.

"Did you get sent back home?"

"Josh helped me get emancipated. He made sure I had a place to stay at the shelter, it wasn't the best of places, but it was way better than the streets, at least I was safe there. He made sure that I finished high school and applied to college. He was always there for me, he encouraged me, uplifted me, supported me, he was everything to me."

"You were sixteen, how old was Josh?"

"He was twenty-six. I know it's a big age difference, but it wasn't like that. He never took advantage of me. It was never a romantic thing between us at first. I had a crush on him, and he knew it but he never did anything about it. He was just there for me. He didn't touch me until I turned eighteen, then the friendship that had developed between us grew into something more. We got married a little before my nineteenth birthday and then soon after I got pregnant with Elianna." Rylla knew that there were people who thought her and Josh's relationship was inappropriate but she didn't care. They had loved each other and that was all that mattered.

"I'm glad you had him." Nate kissed her forehead, and she felt the truth in his words.

"Josh will always be a part of me but he's not competition to you. I can love him and Elianna, and love you and the family we could have one day." She needed Nate to be one hundred percent in if they were going to start a relationship, she didn't want to fall in love and have her heart broken all over again. He was scared after what had happened with his ex, and she was scared after what had happened with Josh, but if they were going to be happy together, they both had to set aside their fears.

"I want a family with you, Rylla. I know we can be happy together, I can live with part of your heart belonging to Josh, he deserves that and so do you."

She gave a content sigh and snuggled against his strong chest.

Nate shifted uncomfortably beneath her. She could feel him growing hard against her thigh. She had a feeling that this night was going to go further than either of them had anticipated. And she wanted it to.

Deliberately, Nate slid her off his lap. "You should get some rest."

She didn't want rest. Rylla scooted closer, she wanted Nate. She wanted to make love to him. She wanted him inside her. Now.

Entwining her hands around his neck she pulled him closer, whispering her lips across his. She deepened the kiss, he didn't move, didn't respond, then all of a sudden, he groaned into her mouth and was kissing her back just as passionately.

"No." He took hold of her shoulders and pushed her gently away. "We can't."

"Oh, you don't want to?" she asked playfully, reaching between them to run a fingertip along the tent in his sweatpants.

He rolled his eyes and looked down, watching her fingers with a hungry look in his eyes that said he wanted to devour her. "You know I *want* to, but you're hurt, your chest, your neck, we shouldn't."

"I can take painkillers in the morning," she told him. She wanted this, she needed this. She liked Nate, she was already a hairsbreadth away from loving him, why should they wait? After what they had lost they both deserved some happiness.

"Rylla," Nate groaned.

Brushing her lips across his jaw, she whispered in his ear, "Make love to me, Nate."

With another groan, he gave in, laying her down and settling himself on top of her. "You tell me if you're in too much pain," he warned.

"Fine," she agreed, shifting restlessly as her body instinctively tried to get closer to Nate. Right now, she would agree to anything so long as he touched her.

She shuddered out a moan as his lips nibbled at the sensitive spot on her neck behind her ear, and his hand found its way inside her panties.

He groaned as his fingers touched her center. "You're already soaked for me. I don't think I can do this slow, Rylla," he said as one of his fingers slipped inside her making her internal muscles clench in anticipation. "I've wanted this for so long, dreamed about you, I'm not sure I have it in me to take you any other way than hot and fast. This time around anyway."

Hot and heavy was exactly what she wanted. There would be time for slow and sweet later, time to explore each other's bodies, right now she just wanted Nate inside her.

The quicker the better.

"Don't care. I just need you, Nate," she said, lifting her hips when he didn't move the finger inside her, just held it there as though he were savoring the feel of her. "Hurry up."

He smiled and then claimed her lips as another finger slid inside her. He curled his hand around so that his fingers could stroke that hidden spot inside her, and his thumb found her aching little bundle of nerves and teased with expert precision.

Her whole body was trembling, filling with desire, she was so close, already she could see the edges of the tidal wave of pleasure that was coming right for her.

"Stop." She pushed at his shoulders. "I don't want to come until you're inside me."

Nate lifted his head. "Condom?"

"Don't care, we don't need them. I'm on the pill and I'm clean, there's hardly been anyone since Josh and no one in almost two years." She wanted to feel every inch of Nate's rather impressive length without any barriers between them. She hadn't felt this connection with anyone other than her husband and if Nate didn't hurry up and bury himself inside her, she thought she might just burst into flames, that was how hot he made her feel.

"I'm clean too."

"Then what are you waiting for?"

He laughed, and the sound did weird things to her heart, made it swell until it was almost painfully full. It had been so long since someone made her feel this way. Why exactly had she clung to her anger at Nate for so long?

Now it just felt like wasted months that they could have been exploring this thing between them, letting it grow.

Nate shoved his sweatpants down and ripped her panties off her— actually ripped them to pieces—then he entered her in one swift thrust.

Rylla gasped as he filled her, he was so big and it had been so long, for a second it felt like she was being ripped apart, but Nate didn't give her time to dwell. He was moving, thrusting in and out of her hard and fast. His mouth captured hers again, his tongue thrusting in and out in time with his length.

The tidal wave was rushing closer.

Nate reached between them, touched her hard little bud, rolled it between his thumb and forefinger, and then pleasure was crashing over her.

Her toes curled.

Her fingers clawed at Nate's back.

"Nate, Nate, Nate, Nate, Nate," she panted over and over again as pleasure continued to cascade over her in wave after wave until it almost became too much.

She knew he reached his own climax because she felt him coming inside her and for a moment as she hung between earth and heaven, she wished that she wasn't on birth control. Rylla would love nothing more than to be a mother again, to have a partner again.

To have *this* man as her partner.

To have *this* man's baby.

"Thank you," she murmured as tears streamed down her cheeks and she pressed herself against his hard, strong body. Nate had just taken her shriveled up heart and filled it back up.

❧

2:40 P.M.

"How's Rylla?" Heidi asked.

"Battered and bruised but basically all right," Matthew replied. He still couldn't believe his partner had been attacked. When he'd gotten the call his heart had been in his throat. He had jumped straight in his car and driven directly to her house, unable to convince himself she was okay until he'd seen her.

"Nate took her to the hospital today to get her ribs x-rayed and her neck checked. She has a couple of bruised ribs, and one was cracked, but the doctors were happy with the neck wound," Jonathon added.

"She didn't get a look at the man who attacked her?" their boss asked.

"No, it was dark, and she was busy fighting for her life." He had no doubt in his mind that if the killer had gotten her into a car that she'd be dead by now. The Fairytale Killer couldn't take when a woman stood up to him, and he would never be able to control Rylla.

"Why would he go after Rylla?" Heidi asked. "Did he know she'd been working the case?"

"Apparently, he told her that her sister had told him a lot about her," Matthew replied. "We're assuming that Mila tried to convince the killer to let her go by telling him that her sister was a cop and would be looking for her."

"So, he wanted to take her out of the equation so she couldn't arrest him?"

"I don't think so," he answered. "He killed Mila, he wouldn't have done that if he didn't have another target in mind. I think he wants Rylla, I think he envisions her as his next attempt at finding the perfect woman."

"But why Rylla?" Allina asked.

"She doesn't fit his profile," Jonathon said.

"Maybe he's changed his profile," he suggested. "Maybe since what he was originally looking for keeps failing, he decided he should try something else out, and Rylla is definitely very different to the other women he's tried so far."

"If he's changed his mind on what he wants then the decoy profiles we set up are going to be useless," Heidi said.

"They're going to be useless for now anyway, he's going to be fixated on Rylla. If he has decided that she is the woman he's been looking for, then nothing will stop him from getting her. He won't stop until he has her." Which was a truly terrifying possibility.

"He must have been watching her house last night," Jonathon said. "He waited until she was isolated before making a play for her."

Matthew shuddered at the possibility.

"He could still be watching her," Heidi said.

"No, we've been watching her street, he must have decided that since he tried to get her and failed that he'd have to play things differently now. He knows she'll be waiting for him to try again," Allina said.

"Sam has two of his guys keeping an eye on Rylla's house, and said he'll make sure he has two people on her twenty-four seven. And Nate is staying with her. For now, she's safe but this guy is determined, we don't know what he's going to try next. He's never had this happen before. Rylla is different than the others. He hasn't been grooming her online, he knows that she knows who he is and that abducting her isn't going to be easy. We have no idea what he might decide to try, we just know he's going to try something," Jonathon said.

If they could just narrow down who the killer was then they might know what to expect. "Rylla got him last night. She managed to kick him in the face, she must have got him in the nose because there was blood. Kane has her clothes right now. We're just waiting to see if he gets anything he can use to run a DNA test and compare it to the samples we have from Jaden Kite and Hendrick Mint."

"We might have something on Jaden," Allina announced.

"We already know that he owns a limousine company, giving him access to a perfect vehicle to abduct his victims in, but we also found something that might provide him with a way to get the dresses he sent to the women for their dates," Jonathon told them.

Arching a hopeful eyebrow, Matthew asked, "What?"

"Jaden was an only child for the first twelve years of his life," Jonathon explained. "Then his parents broke up, there were lots of accusations thrown around by both parties, an open marriage, threesomes, swingers, affairs. Both his parents wanted custody of him. His dad won and had him for a couple of years, barely let him see his mother, then there were some issues of potential abuse, and the mom was awarded custody. She had remarried and had a daughter with her new husband. Jaden's half-sister was in a bad car accident when she was seventeen. She was left paralyzed from the waist down. Her dream had always been to be a fashion model, but those were shattered by the accident that also left her with bad scarring on her face. So, Jaden bought her a fashion house. He's a silent partner, the business is based in London, where his sister lives with her parents, and is run by her."

"That would certainly give Jaden a way to get the dresses without leaving a paper trail," he said.

"Have we spoken with her yet?" Heidi asked.

"We called her," Allina replied. "But she denies ever having any dresses made for her brother with the exception of Joynelle's wedding dress, and the one she wore for the engagement party."

"Jaden could have gotten to her, told her not to say anything to us," Matthew suggested.

"Yeah, he could have," Allina agreed. "The sister certainly wasn't happy to talk with us and couldn't get us off the phone quick enough."

"Maybe having a sister who could have made the dresses gives us enough for a warrant to get to Jaden's computer." They needed something specific that pointed them to the right suspect. Right now, Matthew just couldn't make up his mind which one of them he thought was their guy.

"I think we need to ..." Heidi broke off as the door was flung open.

"I have bad news," Kane announced as he entered the room.

"Then turn around and walk straight back out," Matthew said, he didn't want to hear any more bad news right now.

"Ha, ha," Kane shot back.

"What is it?" Heidi asked.

"Did you find something?" Jonathon asked.

"Were you able to get enough of his blood on Rylla's clothes?" Allina asked.

"Did you run the DNA tests?" Jonathon asked.

"Did you get a match?" Allina asked.

"Is it Jaden or Hendrick?" Matthew asked. A DNA match would solve so many of their problems.

"If you stopped asking questions, I'd have told you already," Kane snapped as he took a seat at the table.

If Kane was in a bad mood it must be really bad news. And there was only one thing that he could think of that would have Kane in a mood like this. "It's not either of them, is it?"

"I tested Rylla's clothes, most of the blood was hers, but I did manage to find some samples from the man who attacked her," Kane informed them, he always liked to present all of his information without anyone stealing his thunder. "I ran the DNA against the samples we took from Mr. Kite and Mr. Mint when they were booked earlier. Neither of them match. Neither Jaden nor Hendrick are the Fairytale Killer."

"Maybe it wasn't the Fairytale Killer who attacked Rylla after all,"

Heidi suggested, unwilling to accept that their two suspects were now cleared.

"No, he called her princess, he said her sister had told him all about her, and he tried to abduct her the same day he killed and dumped Mila. It was him. And according to Kane's tests the Fairytale Killer isn't either of the men we thought it was," Matthew said.

Which was a completely terrifying prospect. A vicious killer was still free, roaming the streets, they knew there would be more victims, but there was nothing they could do to stop it from happening.

They had no suspects. They were back to square one.

And his partner was firmly in the killer's sights.

～

8:13 P.M.

"Time to ice those ribs again." Nate crouched beside the couch where Rylla was stretched out and pressed the bag of ice against her injured side.

"Thanks." She smiled up at him and winced as she tried to get into a more comfortable position.

"Painkillers." He took her hand and tipped two pills into it, then handed her a glass of water. "Don't argue, you haven't taken anything since breakfast. I've cracked ribs before, it hurts like hell, don't be a martyr, you need to keep your wits about you in case the killer makes another attempt at grabbing you."

He was petrified that might happen. He had no intention of letting that man get anywhere close to her. He wasn't letting Rylla out of his sight any time soon, and Sam had organized for two men to watch Rylla's house constantly. He should feel better knowing she was safe, but he didn't. He kept picturing her hobbling into her kitchen last night, blood all over her.

"Okay, no arguments. For you," she added as she took the glass. He put an arm around her shoulders and lifted them so she could swallow the water.

If it wasn't for the fear that lurked in her gorgeous green eyes, he would have thought she wasn't fazed by everything that had happened. But he knew better. Rylla was an expert at putting on a brave front. To most people she was bubbly and bright and full of energy, but he knew that was an act, and an act that cost her, leaving her mentally and emotionally exhausted by the end of each day. That she fought through everything she had been through with such strength made him admire her so much more.

"I need some ..."

"Chocolate," he finished her sentence, holding out a block of Cadbury's milk chocolate.

"My favorite." She beamed.

"I know."

"So, what's the bad news?" she asked, taking the chocolate and breaking off a row.

That was his perceptive girl, he loved how smart she was, and even hurt and worrying about her safety she kept her cop brain about her. "It's not bad news," he promised, lifting her legs and sitting beside her with her legs resting in his lap.

"But it's not good news either."

He chuckled. "It's not really a matter of being good or bad."

"Well, I can tell from the look on your face that I'm not going to like what you have to say, so just get it over with."

The tense look on her face, and the sudden stiffness in her body, told him exactly what she was thinking. Apparently, since they had spent half the night making love, he now possessed the ability to read her mind. "It's nothing to do with us," he assured her. "We just need to talk about something related to your safety."

She made a face but instantly relaxed. "I don't want a bodyguard."

"Not even if it's me?" He pouted.

Rylla laughed, he loved that sound, when this killer was caught he was going to make it his mission to make her laugh every day. "I prefer to think of you as my boyfriend not my bodyguard."

"I guess I can live with that." He leaned over and gave her a quick kiss.

"Now stop procrastinating and tell me what's going on."

"I was talking with Matthew earlier," he began hesitantly, he knew Rylla was going to resist what he was going to ask her to do.

A small frown creased her forehead. "I don't like you two talking about me behind my back and making decisions for me like I'm some sort of helpless child."

"No one thinks you're a helpless child," he soothed.

"Nor do I like being patronized."

"Sorry. I'm really not trying to patronize you, but you worked this case, you know how dangerous this guy is, I'm terrified that he's going to get his hands on you and turn you into another dead princess." Fear had a physical hold of him, he could feel it like a snake in his belly slithering around inside him.

Rylla's face softened. "I know you're scared, Nate, but he's not going to get me. Sam has people watching the house, and you're here."

She said that with such confidence that his body warmed despite the lurking cold of fear. Rylla believed in him, he didn't want to let her down. He took her hands and held them tightly. "He knows where you live. He was obviously watching the house yesterday because he knew when you went off on your own and followed you."

"If he's watching the house that's great," Rylla said. "That means someone will see him and arrest him."

To him, knowing the Fairytale Killer could still be watching the house wasn't great. It was terrifying. He didn't want this man hunting Rylla, he wanted her far, far away from here. "This killer is determined and organized. Everything he has done so far, he has planned down to the tiniest detail. Now he's fixated on you. He knows where you live, I think it's safe to assume he knows you're a cop since he said that Mila told him all about you." At the mention of her sister her hands trembled in his. "I don't want to see him get you. I think you should go away for a while, until this guy is caught."

"Go away?" She narrowed her eyes suspiciously. "Like to a safehouse?"

"Not a safehouse per se, just a house that's safe, and right now I don't think this house is safe."

"How would he get in here?"

"I don't know, and that's what scares me."

"He'd have to get through two highly trained men with guns outside, then in here he'd have to get through you. I just don't see that happening."

"I love that you have such faith in me, but this guy loves tricks and games, and we still don't know who he is, therefore we don't know how he could get to you. He could be anyone." Matthew had been by earlier to update them on the case, and learning that the two suspects they'd had were now both categorically cleared was not the news he had been hoping for. He had hoped that the blood on Rylla's clothes from her scuffle with the killer would tell them exactly who the killer was.

"If I let him run me out of my own home then he wins," Rylla said.

"If you stay here and let him abduct and kill you then he wins," he contradicted. "Rylla, please, I'm begging you, I couldn't take it if something happened to you. I know you don't want to but I'm asking you to do this for me."

She sighed, and he knew she was going to agree even before she said the words. "Way to play hardball, Nate."

"I'm playing the hardest ball I can because anything less might not keep you alive."

"Just where am I supposed to stay? Your house?"

He would love to take Rylla home with him, but he had a safer place in mind. "Actually, I was thinking of the cabin that Naomi owns. The killer would have no way to know about that place, and if he's still watching your house and tries to follow you then we'd spot him."

"For how long?"

"As long as it takes."

"I don't like this." She pouted making her look seriously adorable.

"I know you don't."

"I don't want to do this, it feels like running away, and if he's intent on getting me he's not going to stop no matter where I am."

"You do what you have to do to keep yourself safe. There is no shame in running away." And he meant either now or when she'd run as a teenager.

"Fine. I'll do it."

Nate felt himself relax as relief flowed through him. "Good."

"When?"

"Tomorrow morning."

"Are you coming with me?"

"Do you really have to ask that?"

She smiled. "No. Thanks for staying with me these last few days."

Five days. They had spent the last five days together. He hadn't left here since Rylla had learned that her sister had been abducted. Already he felt like they were an old married couple, he felt so comfortable with her. "You know there's no place I'd rather be."

"Me too," she said, then yawned. She was tired, between the nightmares and then their lovemaking she hadn't gotten much sleep last night, and she was injured, her body needed rest to heal.

"Bed time," he announced.

"It's not even nine yet," she protested.

"You're tired and you need sleep." Nate lifted her legs and stood, set the bag of ice down on the table, and carefully gathered Rylla into his arms so she didn't have to hobble up the stairs. And because he couldn't get enough of holding her. When this was over, and the killer was caught —or dead—he didn't want to go. He liked seeing her every day, he wanted to go to bed each night with her at his side, and wake up each morning with her in his arms. Was it too soon to move in together? They might have known each other for six years but they had only really been together as a couple a day or two.

"No."

Confused, he looked down at her head resting on his shoulder. "No, what?"

"It's not too soon for us to move in together."

"How did you know that's what I was thinking?"

"Because I was thinking the same thing."

With the woman he knew he already loved in his arms, a shared future they both wanted, and that knowledge that he'd spend the rest of the night holding her, Nate thought that life couldn't get any better than this.

~

10:24 P.M.

. . .

He felt like he was flying.

He had finally found her.

The one.

The one he had been searching for.

He had known it from the moment he grabbed her. When he had touched her, he had felt it, when her blood had dripped down onto his skin it was like nourishment for his soul. They were connected now. Forever.

Rylla Franklin was perfect, she was everything he wanted. When she had completed her training she was going to be amazing. Better than he could have hoped. Better than he could ever have dreamed. He wasn't sure how he had gotten so lucky.

Now he just had to make sure that the police didn't figure out who he was. He couldn't let them stop him. He couldn't let *anything* stop him. He would have Rylla, he would bring her to his special castle and treat her like the princess that she was while he taught her what was expected of her.

Right now, he wasn't quite sure how he was going to get to her. His attempt had failed. He had waited patiently for an opportunity to present itself and been rewarded for that patience when she left her home, alone, to go running. Just as he had assumed, she had been distracted and hadn't noticed him following her in his car. When she had collapsed against the grass, he had gotten himself ready.

He had timed it perfectly. She hadn't heard him come up behind her, she hadn't even known he was there until he had wrapped his arms around her. She had fought him as he had known she would, and she had managed to get away from him three times. Three times but there wouldn't have been a fourth. He'd almost had her, if that man hadn't shown up and given him no choice but to abandon everything, he would have gotten her.

That wouldn't happen again. It had angered him that she'd managed to get a few jabs in, he couldn't deny it. It seemed like training Rylla was going to be an excellent tool to help him learn to get his patience under control. If Rylla had attacked him like that when they weren't out in public, he might have lost it, beaten her in a rage before his mind had cleared enough for him to make logical choices.

That could not happen. He couldn't let himself lose control like that. If he did, he could kill Rylla without even knowing what he was doing. And then what would he do? He would never find someone else like her. He wanted someone with fire inside them. Rylla had a fire burning so brightly inside her he could almost see it from here.

But how was he going to get her?

The cops knew that he was after her because he'd told Rylla who he was. To make things worse Rylla had hurt him. She had kicked him squarely in the nose, possibly breaking it, definitely making it bleed.

That blood had gotten all over Rylla. He had no doubt that she had given her clothes to the crime scene unit, who would have run DNA tests. Those tests would have proved that whatever suspects they had were not the so called Fairytale Killer.

They would be on edge. He was coming after one of their own. They would do whatever it took to keep Rylla safe.

His blood may not point them in his direction, but it would make them more cautious. They would be watching Rylla like a hawk. They already had people watching her house. He'd seen them when he'd driven by earlier.

He couldn't go back there to watch her, he was going to have to come at her another way. He'd have to work out something foolproof. If he made another attempt at getting her and failed again, he would never get another opportunity. They would lock her away someplace he would have no hope of getting to her.

Watching her house and waiting for her to be on her own again was out. Now he was going to have to come up with something more creative. A way to get to her that no one would expect. There had to be something, he just didn't know what it was yet. For now, he would just have to exercise his patience and see what happened next.

Because he knew one thing for sure.

He wouldn't rest until Detective Rylla Franklin was his.

CHAPTER
Ten

August 1st
8:53 A.M.

Rylla paced up and down the small space. She felt claustrophobic.

She had suffered from the phobia most of her adulthood. When she was stressed it made it worse. Right now, she was pretty stressed. She didn't like having to leave her home because some killer had decided to fixate on her. In her mind she kept seeing the bodies of Jeannie Jones, Tillie Schueman, and Georgia Lars. She didn't want to end up like them.

Just like she didn't want to be stuck in this little cabin.

It was too small.

Naomi and Sam had had it built on the property where Naomi used to live. Her house had been burned down—almost taking Naomi and Sam down with it—and although Naomi had moved in with Sam, she liked the quiet and peace of the country and so they'd built the cabin and sometimes came and stayed here.

The Fairytale Killer would have no reason whatsoever to come looking for her at her friend's place. She appreciated Naomi and Sam letting her hide out here, and she should be safe here.

If she didn't lose her mind first.

It felt like the walls were closing in on her. Since no one lived here the place was small, one open plan living, kitchen, dining area, and upstairs there were two bedrooms and a bathroom. That was it. Rylla usually avoided places this small if she could help it. It just wasn't worth the suffocating feeling.

She'd been here before, several times, and she didn't remember it being this small then.

Pacing wasn't helping. Nor was it good for her injured knee, each step sent pain jarring through the joint.

Up and down, up and down. From the front door to the back door and back again. Over and over again. She counted her steps for something to do, hoping the monotonous task would put a stop to the near crushing claustrophobia.

One, two, three, four, five, six, seven, eight, nine ...

"Rylla."

She started as Nate suddenly appeared before her, halting her pacing.

"What's wrong?"

"Nothing." She wasn't going to discuss her phobia with him, it was embarrassing.

"Well, I can't take any more of the pacing so come and sit down." He took her elbow and attempted to maneuver her to the sofa.

She tried to let him. She *really* didn't want to explain her claustrophobia. But as soon as she sat, she felt a rush of cold flush through her body. She shivered. She knew Nate must have felt it too because he was still touching her.

"Rylla, what's going on?"

She couldn't answer even if she had wanted to.

A rush of heat followed the cold, and her entire body broke out into a sweat, drenching her in seconds.

"Are you sick?" He pressed the back of his hand to her forehead. "You are burning up."

She shook her head. She couldn't speak. The walls were closing in on her. There was no air. Little white dots danced about in front of her eyes. She needed to get out of here.

Now.

Staggering to her feet, she shoved off Nate's hands, and hobbled for the door as quickly as her knee allowed.

Outside she bent over, hands on her thighs, dragging in huge, deep mouthfuls of fresh air.

She felt Nate's hand on her back, rubbing circles. His presence helped to calm her, and she appreciated that he didn't ask her any questions and allowed her some time to gather herself. Eventually she felt calm enough to straighten, without a word she turned and wrapped her arms around Nate, leaning into him.

"What's wrong, honey?"

She had to tell him. They were in this together. "Claustrophobia," she mumbled against his chest.

"I knew you suffered from it, I just didn't realize it was so bad. Have you always suffered from it?"

"No. Since the accident."

"Josh and Elianna's accident?"

"Yes."

"What about the accident started it?" His hands were still rubbing circles on her back, and she focused all her energy on that so she didn't fall apart.

"It was raining really badly that day. The roads were slippery. Someone was speeding, they lost control of their car and hit Josh's car. The car flipped, then slammed into a tree. Elianna was killed instantly but Josh wasn't. He was trapped in that car, dying, with our dead daughter, for almost thirty minutes. I can't imagine what that was like. I can't get that picture out of my head. Whenever I'm in a space that feels too small, I think of what it must have been like for him."

"I'm sorry. I'm so sorry you have that image in your head. I wish I could take it away but I can't."

"Just having you here helps," she told him, and felt his lips press to the top of her head.

"I'm always here, Rylla."

"I know."

"Do you think you can manage to go back inside? I don't think he would have followed us here, but we can't be sure, and I'd rather have you inside where he at least can't see you."

Because she wasn't stupid and she had no intention of taking unnecessary risks, she straightened and nodded. "I don't want to but you're right, it's smarter to be indoors right now."

"Together," he reminded her, taking a firm grip of her hand and leading her back inside.

There was no TV, so Nate suggested they play cards, they were just setting up when the door opened, and Sam and Naomi came in.

"What are you doing here?" Rylla asked Naomi. A killer was stalking her, her pregnant friend shouldn't be anywhere near her right now.

"Keeping you company," Naomi replied.

"Really?" She rolled her eyes. "And you're okay with that?" she asked Sam.

Sam just glowered and she suspected that they'd had quite the argument about it.

"I may be pregnant, but I still know how to shoot," Naomi reminded them.

"Is Anton still outside?" Rylla asked.

"Yes," Sam replied.

Although she didn't want Nate to go, she wanted to find out what was going on with the case. "Can you do me a favor?"

"What?" Nate looked suspicious.

"Can you and Sam go and talk to Matthew, see what's going on with the case?"

"I'm not leaving you," Nate said immediately.

"Please, Nate. They just lost both their suspects, you and Sam could help. Anton is here so I'm perfectly safe, and he doesn't even know where I am. Please, Nate," she said again. "I'd feel so much better if you went and helped them. You'll be back here tonight."

"Okay," he reluctantly agreed. "If it will make you feel better."

"It will." She would miss him, but he'd only be gone for a few hours, and she trusted him, he was smart and paid attention to details, he'd be able to help Matthew and the others.

"Stay safe, no risks, promise me." Nate put an arm around her waist and drew her against him.

"I promise." She had no intention of doing anything but stay safe.

Nate kissed her then went to get his keys. Sam followed him to the door.

"I don't get a kiss?" Naomi asked her husband.

"I'm still mad at you."

"How much trouble could I get in sitting here quietly with Rylla with Anton right outside?"

"If you were a regular person, none. Since it's you, I don't even want to think about it," Sam shot back but came and gave Naomi a quick kiss.

"So, I'm not as good company as I'm sure Nate has been but I'm better than nothing." Naomi grinned once the guys were gone.

Rylla couldn't help but smile back. "I guess you're better than nothing."

"So, you and Nate are a couple now?" Naomi asked as she eased her huge self down onto the couch.

"We are." It felt so right to say it out loud, it made it feel much more real like it wasn't just her and Nate holed up in her home playing house.

"I'm so happy, for both of you. You deserve some happiness again, and Nate's great, you two make an amazing couple."

"Yeah, well, you can stop playing matchmaker now," she pretended to grumble.

"True, now I'll get to play wedding planner."

"*You're* going to plan my wedding?" Rylla laughed. "You? I remember when we were planning your wedding, you didn't care about any of those details. Flowers, bridesmaids' dresses, menus, table decorations. Getting you to make decisions was a nightmare."

"None of that stuff was important to me, all I cared about was marrying the man I loved."

Although she still missed Josh every day, the thought of being married again was a good one.

"And maybe one day you and Nate might have children together." Naomi rested a hand on her stomach. "I know you'll always have a special place in your heart for Elianna, but it would be nice to have another baby with Nate."

Rylla's hands moved to her own stomach. "Yeah, it would," she agreed. Her daughter would always be her first born, but it would be amazing to have a child with the new man in her life. Maybe marriage and babies were in her future after all.

~

10:01 A.M.

"We're going to have to start over from scratch, go over everything we know about the Fairytale Killer and make sure our profile still fits. We haven't been able to get a warrant to go through the Happily Ever After Club's list of paying customers because we don't have a name." Heidi Kramer looked frustrated.

Nate didn't know the captain well, but what he did know about her was that she was smart as a whip, efficient, good at her job, and full of energy which she usually released by constantly fiddling with something. Right now, she was vigorously squeezing a sheep shaped stress ball.

While he had agreed to come here because it was what Rylla wanted, and what would make her feel better, it didn't mean he liked being away from her.

And he didn't.

He ached to be back in the cabin with her, where he could keep an eye on her, where he could be there to comfort her, where he could be there to help her deal with her claustrophobia. He trusted Anton to keep any threats away, and he knew Naomi would provide good distractions. He knew she was safe, that was the only reason he had come, but that didn't make being away from her any easier.

"What do we know for sure about this killer?" Heidi asked.

"He met all his victims except for Rylla in the Happily Ever After Club," Jonathon said.

"The name he used for each of them translated to Prince Charming," Allina said.

"But the story he gave each about who he was was different," Matthew added.

"Based on the age of the victims we assume his in his mid to late thirties, but again that's just an assumption," Allina said.

"He somehow found out the dress sizes of each woman because the custom princess dresses he sent them for the dates, and that they were found in, were a perfect fit. Our assumption, especially given that the Drake kids saw someone in their house, is that the killer broke into the homes of his victims at some point," Jonathon said.

"He needed a vehicle that he could transport his victims in, and although we thought limousine because Jaden Kite had access to them, I think it's still a reasonable assumption. It fits with the fairytale theme of the date, and it gives him a safe place to have an unconscious victim stowed away without anyone seeing. And he'd have to knock them out almost immediately because he can't drive and be with them, but he can't bring in someone to drive, so however he sedates them or ties them up he would have to do it as soon as they got to the car," Matthew said.

"Based on the first four victims, he was after someone he believes was cultured and would make a suitable wife. Based on the wounds to the victim's backsides he intends to punish them until they learn his rules. Rylla throws off the profile of what he was looking for," Jonathon said.

"Whatever Mila told him about her was obviously enough to catch his interest," Allina agreed.

Nate didn't want to think about Rylla as this killer's target. If he thought too much about it, he would be back in his car driving out to the cabin, where he would handcuff himself to Rylla and whisk her out of the country until this killer was caught. He had to distance himself a little. Not focus on Rylla as a potential victim. He had to look at this like he would any other case he worked.

So far he'd sat quietly, listening to the cops work, now he asked, "What about Beau Drake?"

"Mila's husband?" Heidi asked.

"Rylla thought he might have been involved in her sister's disappearance."

"Because she didn't want to accept that it was the Fairytale Killer who had kidnapped her sister," Matthew said.

"What if she was right? What if Beau is the killer? What if he was angry that Mila was divorcing him? Rylla said they were going through a bitter custody battle. He wants to find someone who's going to treat him the way he believes he deserves to be treated. He wants to find someone who won't leave him. He wants to find someone more obedient that he can control and dominate," he suggested.

"Then why take Mila?" Jonathon asked.

"Maybe he thought he could kill two birds with the one stone. He starts searching for the woman of his dreams, then he stumbles upon Mila on the website and thinks it would be a good way to get rid of her. He didn't keep her as long as the others, right?"

"Yes, but he didn't keep Georgia Lars long either," Matthew said.

"She made him angry though, didn't she? So, killing Georgia so quickly wasn't planned."

"Maybe killing Mila so quickly wasn't planned either," Allina said. "Maybe he intended to keep her but then she started talking about Rylla and she sounded more appealing.

"Maybe he intended to keep her, maybe he always intended to put her in a position where she couldn't leave him. Maybe he tried with the other women, realized it was actually his wife that he wanted after all, so he took her, thinking if he locked her up he could force her to become what he wanted. Then she starts talking about Rylla and he thinks maybe he married the wrong sister."

"What about the man that the Drake kids saw in their house?" Jonathon asked.

"What if that had nothing to do with this?"

"We believe the killer broke into the victims' houses. We know Mila was on the website, we know the killer was the one who took her, what are the chance that there were two break-ins at her house so close together?" Matthew asked. "If it wasn't the killer then who was it?"

"What if it was a private investigator," Nate proposed. "They were going through a divorce. They were fighting over their kids and property and investments. He would have wanted dirt on Mila, something he could use against her that would give him a leg up in the proceedings."

"Had Beau hired a private investigator?" Heidi asked.

"Yes," Sam answered, speaking for the first time. "This man." He held out a picture of the man Beau Drake had hired to dig up dirt on his soon to be ex-wife.

"Blond hair, brown eyes, could have been the man Emmy and Mac saw," Matthew acknowledged.

"Maybe the killer doesn't break into their homes then," Jonathon suggested. "Hendrick Mint admitted to breaking into Georgia and Whitney's house because he was interested in Whitney."

"At this point I don't think it matters," Allina said. "Do we really think it could be Beau Drake? He wasn't even on our radar."

"Rylla doesn't like him," he said. In his mind that was reason enough to make the man a suspect, he trusted Rylla's judgment on people.

"But she never did anything about it," Matthew pointed out. "If she thought he was abusive or violent toward her sister, or her niece and nephew, then she would have arrested him. But Beau certainly wasn't upset about Mila's disappearance. And he wasn't co-operative about letting us talk to the kids, or about having them help try to identify the man they saw in their house. Which I guess would make sense if it was a private investigator he had hired."

"We know the killer used tranquilizers to knock Jeannie Jones out, and Mila is a doctor, Beau could have gotten access to the drugs through her. And he works in IT, apparently he's very good. I don't think he would have had any trouble making sure he covered his tracks on the website," Sam explained.

"Did you two look into Beau?" Heidi asked.

"Yes." He and Sam had checked the man out on the drive here from the cabin.

"Do we want to know how?" The captain eyed them shrewdly.

"No," Sam said.

"What did you find?"

"There were some charges against him, way back when he was in his teens. For hacking, blackmail, coercion, and sexual assault. Apparently, he would hack into the computer system of his female friends and take control of their computes. He would read their emails, their web browser histories, their online chats, he would activate the cameras on the monitors and use it to watch them in their bedrooms. He then used all of that to blackmail the girls into having sex with him. If they didn't, he would share all their personal information and pictures of them half naked that he'd taken with the cameras of their computers and post them all over school and all over the internet," he told them.

"Nothing between then and now?" Matthew asked.

"No. Non-disclosure agreements were signed between Beau and his family and the families of the three girls he targeted. We assume that the girls' families accepted a substantial amount of money from Beau's family in exchange for not pressing charges, and the whole thing went away. But it shows what kind of person Beau Drake is. He's smart, he's manipulative, and he believes that women are there for the sole purpose of catering to his every whim. That sounds exactly like the Fairytale Killer."

And if they didn't stop him first, then Rylla was going to become his next victim.

~

11:11 A.M.

"You want to go for a walk?" Rylla asked.

Her friend was pacing up and down the cabin and had been for the last hour. Normally Naomi was also a pacer, but right now, at thirty-eight weeks pregnant just waddling around to do the things she had to do was hard enough let alone pacing.

"A walk?" she asked, looking down at her stomach that had just tightened almost painfully. She'd been having Braxton Hicks contractions on and off for the last month. The first time she'd had them Sam had rushed her to the hospital in a panic, terrified their baby was about to come early, now they had both sort of become used to them.

Rylla followed her gaze. "Oh, right."

"I think it's probably safer for you to stay indoors anyway," she reminded her friend.

She really truly understood Rylla's unease, and that constantly being on the move helped to alleviate that tension. She'd been stalked. By a vicious man who wanted to hurt her by hurting other people. She had been confined to her home, with Sam as her bodyguard, and it had almost sent her insane. In the end, she had believed sacrificing herself to the killer to stop another innocent person getting hurt was the preferable option.

But it was so much easier to be practical about things when it wasn't herself that was the target of a killer. When it was her friend playing things safe was of course the sensible thing to do, she didn't want anything to happen to Rylla. She had lost a lot of people in her life that she had loved and cared about, and she didn't want to lose anymore, especially her best friend.

"I guess," Rylla agreed, pausing at a window to stare longingly outside.

Naomi knew that her friend suffered from claustrophobia and that being holed up in the small cabin had to be extremely difficult, so she heaved herself to her feet. "We could go for a short walk, we'll just ask Anton to come with us." She didn't like having to ask people for help, she was much more comfortable being self-sufficient, or taking care of others, but right now, pregnant as she was, she couldn't protect Rylla if the killer managed to track her down.

Rylla's green eyes lit up at the prospect of being out in the fresh air. "You can stay here, we won't be long."

"Oh, no, I'm not being left behind, besides, I'm so bored that anything—" she broke off as another cramp in her stomach gripped her. The Braxton Hicks contractions were getting more frequent, but she couldn't be going into labor yet, she still had another two weeks to go, and she wasn't ready to be a mom yet. She needed those last two weeks to prepare herself.

"Naomi?" Rylla came to her. "What's wrong?"

"Nothing," she assured her friend. "Just let me go to the bathroom and then we can—" again she broke off as she felt a popping sensation in her stomach, and then a trickle of fluid rushed down her leg. Her gaze fell to the floor, as did Rylla's, whose eyes widened.

"Your water just broke. Have you been having contractions?"

"I thought they were just Braxton Hicks, I've been having those for the last month."

"You're going into labor," Rylla said delightedly. "I'll call Sam and have him meet us at the hospital. Anton can drive us."

"No. I'm not in labor," she protested. "These are just Braxton Hicks, and that's probably just pee."

"You're in labor," Rylla insisted.

"No."

"Yes."

"No," she said more insistently.

"Yes."

"No."

"Yes—why am I arguing with you about it? We can go to the hospital and let a doctor decide if you're about to have your baby."

"No, I'm not ready. I'm not ready to have the baby," she said desperately. She was terrified about her abilities to be a good mother.

"It's going to be okay, Naomi." Rylla put an arm around her shoulders. "You are going to be the best mom ever. Seriously. That little baby in there is the luckiest little girl in the entire world to have you as her mommy. I know you're scared. I was scared too. But we're going to get you to the hospital, and we're going to call Sam, and everything is going to be okay."

She nodded, Rylla was right, she could do this. She just needed Sam. She was going to ask Rylla to call now when another contraction came. This one was much stronger than the others, and she cried out, gripping her stomach as the rolling wave of pain buffeted her.

"You all right?"

"Yes," she said, breathing through the pain. She could deal with pain. Pain was fine, it was fear that she was afraid of.

"Okay, let's go, I'll call Sam in the car."

They both looked up as the front door opened, expecting to see Anton. Instead, a tall man with dark hair, and dark eyes stood there.

Naomi knew she'd seen him before but right now she couldn't place him.

"Beau?" Rylla said, confused.

Beau Drake. Rylla's brother-in-law. That's why he looked familiar, she had met Rylla's family before, including Beau.

"Is something wrong with Emmy or Mac?" Rylla asked.

"No," the man said. "They're fine."

"Then why are you here?"

"For you." Beau held up a gun.

Both she and Rylla automatically reached for their weapons, but stopped when Beau cocked his gun.

"I wouldn't do that if I were you. My gun is already out, I'd get off at least one shot before either of you could reach your weapons. And I'm aiming directly at that baby belly."

Naomi put her hands in front of her stomach as if that could save her unborn baby from a bullet. Rylla moved, positioning herself in front of her, so if Beau took the shot, she would take the hit.

"It's you, Beau? You're the Fairytale Killer?" Rylla asked.

"Yes."

"You killed your own children's mother?"

"Don't look so righteously angered," he snapped. "She didn't care about those kids. She was trying to take them away from me. How is that doing what is in their best interest?"

"So, you killed her?"

"It wasn't my original plan. I tried other women first, but I kept failing. I thought if I could get her alone then things could be different between us. But they weren't. And then she kept talking about you, and I thought why not? Maybe you're the better sister after all."

"Turn yourself in, Beau. Don't make this harder for Emmy and Mac," Rylla pleaded.

"Don't bring them into this. This has nothing to do with them."

"Doesn't it? We have a friend outside, he's going to see you here, and he's going to call the cops. Your only choices are turn yourself in or death. Don't make Emmy and Mac lose both their parents."

Beau just chuckled. "Your friend is a little tied up at the moment."

Tied up? Beau had gotten to Anton? That wouldn't have been an easy feat. What had he done to him?

"Let's go." Beau gestured with his free hand at Rylla.

"I'm not going anywhere with you."

"Then your friend dies."

"Leave her alone, she has nothing to do with this," Rylla said.

"I don't want to hurt her, but I will if you don't come with me. You can't cover all of her, Rylla. I can get a shot off, and then another and another, and make sure that she and her baby have a long, slow, painful death."

Rylla was weighing her options, Naomi could feel it. But there was no option. Rylla could not walk away with this man. If she did, she would be signing her own death warrant. Another contraction hit her, and she moaned, momentarily distracting Rylla.

Beau took advantage by firing off a shot that grazed her bicep. "Next shot I aim to hurt her not just graze her."

"Rylla, no," Naomi begged, seeing the look in her friend's eyes. "He'll kill you."

"If I don't go with him then he'll kill *you*, and I can't let that happen."

"No," she protested again, she couldn't live with it if her friend died in her place.

"I love you, Naomi." Rylla gave her cheek a quick kiss then walked slowly toward Beau, her hands held palms up in surrender. "I'll go with you, just don't hurt her."

"I have no intention of hurting her," Beau said as he tossed Rylla a pair of handcuffs. "Cuff your hands behind your back. Properly. If you try and trick me your friend and her baby pay the price."

Rylla caught the cuffs, and with a last hesitation put them on. "You need to call her an ambulance, she's in labor."

"She'll be fine. Someone will find her. You, on the floor by the couch," Beau waved his gun at her.

Naomi wanted to fight, she couldn't just give up and let her best friend walk out the door with a killer, but she didn't know what else to do. She couldn't risk him hurting her baby. She had no choice. As much as she hated it, she walked to where he indicated and struggled down onto the floor. As soon as she was down, the man grabbed her hands, snapping a cuff around her wrist, then around the leg of the couch, and attached the other end to her other wrist.

She was trapped.

Maybe if she hadn't been pregnant and in labor she might have had the strength to lift the couch and get free, but right now she didn't.

She had no choice but to wait here until someone found her.

Catching the look on Rylla's face, Naomi turned big, scared eyes to Beau and begged, "Please, call my husband and tell him to come. You'll still have a head start. I don't want anything to happen to my baby."

With Beau's attention focused on her, Rylla charged, aiming her shoulder at his solar plexus.

At the last moment, Beau turned and fired off a shot.

Rylla dropped instantly.

"No," Naomi screamed. "Rylla."

Leaving her handcuffed to the couch, Beau scooped Rylla's limp form off the floor, and ran out the door.

There was blood. Right where Rylla had fallen. Her friend had been hit.

Another contraction came, gripping her entire body in a tidal wave of pain.

How was she going to do this?

She was all alone, Sam and Nate wouldn't be back for hours, and her baby was coming. There was nothing she could do to stop it. There would be no hospital, no medications, no doctor, nothing. It was just her.

She didn't care about the pain, her only concerns were her baby and her friend.

If anything went wrong, then both she and her daughter could die.

Another contraction hit.

They were coming faster.

She prayed someone found her before her baby arrived.

~

4:42 P.M.

. . .

She woke slowly, and not quite all the way.

She was in a happy place. The sand was soft and warm under her bare toes, waves crashed gently along the shore, people laughed.

Her daddy was there. And her mommy. Her big brother and sister too. They chased each other through the shallows. And jumped over the frizzy white bubbles as each wave crashed then the water was dragged out again.

Then she was swung up onto her father's shoulders and he was walking out into the deeper water with her.

At first she was excited, she loved to be out this deep. But her dad didn't stop. He kept walking. The beach behind her got further and further away.

The water was too deep.

If he let go of her she'd sink underneath the surface.

The waves would get her, tossing her this way and that until she didn't know what was up and what was down.

Still, he kept walking.

Deeper and deeper.

Then he was gone.

She was alone in the water.

It buffeted her about.

Her head went under.

The sound of rushing water filled her ears.

"Rylla."

Someone said her name, but they were so far away. Too far away to help her.

"Rylla."

She was drowning and she couldn't stop it from happening.

"Rylla."

This time the voice snapped her awake.

All the way awake.

Her eyes popped open, and she saw a face hovering above her.

Beau Drake.

Her brother-in-law. She had never liked him, but never in a million years would she have dreamed that he was a serial killer.

"You're awake," he sounded relieved.

"You shot me," she intended it to convey the anger she felt but instead her voice was weak and rough. Her throat ached but it was nothing compared to the pain in her leg. She must have passed out when he'd shot her, then he'd transported her here, wherever here may be.

"I didn't mean to." He pouted like a spoiled child. "You ran at me, startled me. I didn't want to hurt you. I never wanted to hurt anybody."

Part of her thought he really believed that. Beau was so wrapped up in getting what he wanted that he didn't seem to think of anything else.

"I think you're okay," Beau told her. "The bullet went straight through, and your wound seems to have stopped bleeding. I cleaned it and bandaged it, I've got antibiotics and painkillers for you."

He sounded sincere like he really didn't want her to die.

He was crazier than she thought. He really wanted the two of them to be together. But surely he had to know that was never going to happen. Even if he kept her here long enough and managed to brainwash her with a combination of isolation, dependence, and fear of physical harm, that would be all it was. Brainwashing. Survival. There was nothing he could do that would ever make her love him.

"Here, take these." He lifted one of her hands and tipped an assortment of pills into it. He put an arm underneath her shoulders and awkwardly tried to lift her. It was then that she realized one of her hands was cuffed to the bedpost.

"I don't want them." She let the small round pills fall to the mattress. She couldn't know that they were really painkillers and antibiotics, he could be giving her anything.

"I said take them." He switched instantaneously to anger, and for a moment Rylla quivered in fear.

He could kill her before anyone found her or she managed to escape. Anything she said or did could set him off. That was how Georgia had been killed. She had angered him and he had lost control.

Beau grabbed her chin and dug his fingers into the tender flesh of her neck, right above the cut he had given her the other night. Reflexively her mouth popped open, and he shoved the pills inside, then tipped some water in after them. He clamped a hand over her mouth so she couldn't spit the pills out. Her only options were swallow or choke.

She swallowed.

"Good girl." He patted her head as though she were a puppy that had just passed a training exercise.

"How did you find me?"

"Tracking device on your friend's car," he replied smugly.

She should have thought of that. Naomi had met Beau once or twice, he probably thought staking out her house and tagging her car was going to be safer than coming back to her house. "How did you get through Anton?" She knew Anton, he was a big guy, getting through him wouldn't have been easy.

"Told him Emmy and Mac needed you, he didn't bat an eye. He was going to bring me inside, but I took him out."

"Did you kill him?"

"Of course not. I just knocked him out and put him in the trunk of his car. I don't kill people. Only if I have no choice. I couldn't let those women go, they would have reported me. I didn't kill them for fun."

He might not have killed them for fun, but he had still killed them. He would kill her too. She needed to formulate a plan on how she was getting herself out of here. Rylla glanced down her body and saw a crisp white bandage had been wrapped around her left thigh, above the bandage that was still wrapped around her injured knee. The bandage was already stained bright red. Despite what Beau thought the gunshot wound was clearly still oozing blood. How badly was she hurt? Obviously not enough to have bled to death right away, but the injury could still turn out to be life threatening.

Unable to do anything about the wound she turned her attention to the room. It was decked out just like she pictured a fairytale castle would look. The room had been modeled with a medieval theme, and while it was beautiful, and if this was a hotel or a Bed and Breakfast, and she and Nate were spending a romantic evening here it would have been amazing, it was still her prison.

It was a representation of just how far gone Beau really was. He truly believed that he was Prince Charming in search of his perfect princess. When he realized that was never going to be her, he would kill her and move on to the next woman. And then the next, and the next, and the next, until he was stopped.

There were no windows, and only the one exit. The door looked big and strong, but she knew how to pick a lock. All she needed was an opportunity to get away and she would seize it and make it work.

"Did you call an ambulance for Naomi?" Was her friend okay? Had Beau shot her after he had shot her? Even if he hadn't Naomi was in labor, it could be hours before Nate and Sam returned to the cabin. What if there were complications? Both Naomi and her baby could die all alone in that cabin, just like Josh and Elianna had died all alone in the car.

"Your friend will be fine."

"You just left her there? She was in labor."

Her chastising tone obviously upset him because his hand connected with her cheek with such force it sent her head snapping sideways. "You don't speak to me like that," he growled. "If you have something to say you wait for permission to speak, and then when permission is granted you speak to me with the respect I deserve."

She knew she should keep her mouth shut, but she couldn't. "Respect you deserve? You killed four people including the mother of your children. You shot my pregnant friend and left her handcuffed to a couch to give birth alone. You shot and kidnapped me. Why should I respect you? What have you done to earn my respect?"

Rylla had thought that pushing him would result in another hit, but instead his angry face slowly relaxed, and his frown morphed into a smile. He began to stroke her hair. "I was right. You're everything Mila had and more. You're perfect. And one day you're going to realize that I'm everything you've been looking for too."

"That's never going to happen, Beau," she said softly. "You know that. It didn't work with any of the other women."

"You're different than them."

"Maybe, but the result will be the same. I'll never live up to your expectations. I'm never going to love you." Rylla stopped herself before she admitted she was already in love with someone else. Beau didn't know about Nate, there was no reason for him to suspect that the two of them were a couple. But if he knew he could take out his anger on Nate, and she couldn't let that happen. "I'm never going to stop trying to escape, and my friends are never going to stop looking for me. When you finally accept that I'll never be your princess you'll kill me."

Knowing that she would either die in this room or die trying to escape if Nate and the others didn't find her first was heartbreaking. She finally had something to live for. After so many years where she had wished that she had died right along with the rest of her family, she now had hope for a bright and happy future, and that had all been wiped away in a second.

Her eyes grew heavy.

She was sleepy.

There must have been sleeping pills mixed in with the painkillers and antibiotics he'd given her earlier.

She fought against it as her eyes tried to close. If she passed out she would be completely vulnerable, Beau would be free to do with her whatever he pleased.

Rylla was afraid.

She didn't want to die here. She didn't want to break Nate's heart by leaving him just like Rachel had when she'd taken his son from him. She wanted to live.

Hard as she tried, she couldn't fight against it any longer.

Her eyelids fluttered down, then refused to lift up again, and the pills pulled her into the blackness.

~

8:30 P.M.

"I wish we could find something definitive so we can get him off the streets," Nate said as they drove back toward the cabin.

"We'll find something," Sam assured him. He had been in his friend's place before, terrified that the woman he loved was going to be snatched away from him by someone whose intent was to hurt her, and powerless to stop it from happening because they didn't know who it was. Although Beau Drake looked like he could be a viable suspect, right now there was no proof he had done anything to hurt Rylla or anyone else.

"In the morning we'll go and talk with Emmy and Mac, maybe they can give us something," Matthew said. "And maybe Rylla will know something that will help. If Beau is the killer, then we will find evidence, and we will arrest him."

Nate nodded tersely, it was clear he was feeling helpless. He wanted to fix this, but right now they didn't know how to fix it. They would find a way though. They would get the Fairytale Killer off the streets.

All three of them tensed as they turned into the driveway.

There were no lights on in the cabin.

"Did Naomi text you and say they were going somewhere?" Nate asked him.

"No. Did Rylla text you?"

"No. Matthew?"

"I haven't heard from either of them."

"Something is wrong," he said, he could feel it.

"Has anyone heard from Anton?" Nate asked.

"No." And that terrified him. Anton was probably the best body-guard he had working with him. He trusted the man with his wife, and that spoke volumes because there weren't a lot of people he would trust with Naomi's safety. If Anton hadn't contacted them then it was because he couldn't.

Sam pulled the car to a stop, and all three of them drew their weapons as they climbed out. They went to Anton's car first. It was dark, and as they approached, they could see that it was empty.

Anton wouldn't leave Naomi and Rylla alone and unprotected by choice.

He nodded at Nate, and although he could tell his friend wanted nothing more than to go running to the cabin to check on Rylla—a feeling he echoed because his pregnant wife was also in there—he opened the driver's door and popped the trunk.

As soon as they lifted the trunk, they found Anton. He was inside, unmoving, his hands and ankles bound. Sam knew immediately that the man was still alive. Why bother to waste time tying up a dead man?

Still Matthew confirmed it by pressing his fingers to Anton's neck and nodding.

He couldn't wait any longer, he had to check on Naomi. The killer had obviously found Rylla, and just because she was the one he wanted didn't mean he wouldn't kill anyone who got in his way. He had left Anton alive, hopefully that meant Naomi was alive too. Losing his wife and unborn daughter would kill him.

Ignoring Matthew's whispered commands to go slow, both he and Nate took off for the cabin.

The front door was open.

Someone had definitely been in there.

When the light from their flashlights splashed through the open doorway, a voice called out, "Sam?"

"Naomi." Tossing training aside he ran into the cabin, switching the lights on as he went.

The sight that met him was his worst nightmare.

Naomi lay on the floor, cuffed to the couch. There was blood on her arm, and their baby lay between her legs, in a pool of blood.

"Sam," she said again, this time it was more of a sob. "Is she okay? She was crying at first but the last few minutes she's been so quiet."

He didn't remember crossing the room, he was just as Naomi's side, grabbing her tightly, and asking fiercely, "Are you okay?"

She nodded. "The baby?"

Sam turned his attention to his newborn daughter. She was so tiny, and her little eyes were closed. Was she still alive? He reached for her, laying his hand on her chest, and felt it rise and fall, her heart beat beneath his touch. "She's alive."

Naomi sagged in relief.

"Here, we need to wrap her up to keep her warm." Matthew knelt beside him with a stack of towels and blankets, and a bag to wrap the placenta in.

While he carefully wiped the baby down and wrapped her up in the blankets, making sure to keep the placenta and cord wrapped up with her until help arrived, Matthew turned his attention to Naomi, and unlocked the handcuffs that kept her bound to the couch. He held Naomi's wrist and took her pulse, his other hand on her chin, as he peered into her eyes.

"Is she okay?" Sam asked. There was so much blood and mess he was terrified she was hemorrhaging and going to bleed out right in front of him.

"Her pulse is strong, and her eyes are clear. Naomi, I see blood on your arm are you hurt anyplace else?" Matthew asked.

"No. Sam? Are you sure she's okay?"

"She's perfect." He smiled at his wife and placed the baby in her outstretched arms.

Naomi stared at the newborn, transfixed. "She's so beautiful. And so tiny." She traced a fingertip over their daughter's little face, then kissed her.

"Naomi, look at me," Matthew instructed. "This looks like a gunshot. Did he shoot you?"

"Yes," Naomi replied, and Sam vibrated with anger. Who shot a pregnant woman?

"I called an ambulance," Nate suddenly appeared. "I checked everywhere I can't find Rylla. Naomi, where is she? I see blood on the floor."

"He took her." Tears were streaming down Naomi's pale face. "My water broke and we were going to go to the hospital, but then he came. He had a gun, he said if Rylla didn't go with him then he was going to kill me and the baby. Rylla tried to talk him out of it, but then I had another contraction and she got distracted, he took advantage and shot me. I told her not to, but she agreed to go with him. Then he cuffed me and Rylla tried to tackle him, but he shot her. She collapsed, and he just grabbed her and ran. I was so scared, Sam. The baby was coming, and I was worried something would go wrong."

That she had delivered their baby, alone, handcuffed, shot, and after witnessing her best friend's abduction made him love her so much more. She was the most amazing woman. "Shh, it's all right now." His heart was thumping in overdrive, but he exuded as much outward calm as he could manage to help calm his wife. Naomi had started to shake, so he took another blanket and wrapped it around her, then scooped her up and sat with her on the couch, cradling her in his arms.

Matthew gently extracted Naomi's injured arm and grabbed another towel wrapping it around the wound. "Do you know who he is?"

She nodded. "It was Rylla's brother-in-law."

"Beau Drake?" Nate demanded.

"Yes."

"Did he say anything?"

"Just that he wanted Rylla and didn't want to hurt me, but he would if he had to."

"Did he say where he was taking her?"

"No."

"How many times did he shoot her?"

"One."

"Was she still alive?"

"I think so, but I'm not sure."

"Did he—?"

"Nate, stop interrogating her," Sam growled.

"I'm sorry, Nate," Naomi cried. "He got her because of me, because she didn't want him to hurt me."

Nate took a long breath, deliberately calming himself, then he crouched in front of the sofa, resting his hands on Naomi's knees. "It's not your fault, Naomi. I don't mean to be hard on you, I'm just scared. I'm glad you and the baby are okay, and I know Rylla would be too. She couldn't have let him hurt you, you know that."

"What if he kills her?" Naomi's voice was stark. Sam knew his wife, and he knew that if her best friend died to protect her, then Naomi would never forgive herself.

"No," Nate said firmly, holding Naomi's face between his hands. "We will find her. We will. That man will not take her away from us."

Naomi nodded, then sunk against him, still crying quietly. Sam tightened his hold on them. His wife and little girl. His family. He wouldn't be able to relax until he got them to the hospital, and they were checked out, and a doctor told him that they were both okay, but at least he could hold them.

No one messed with his family and got away with it.

He hoped Beau Drake suffered a horrible death for the grief that he'd caused and for laying a finger on his wife.

The baby chose that moment to give a loud cry and begin to squirm. Naomi squeezed the baby tighter, and he squeezed them both tighter.

His girls.

He was so grateful he hadn't lost them.

They were alive.

Alive.
Alive and in his arms.
And he was never letting them go again.

CHAPTER
Eleven

August 2nd
7:07 A.M.

"Thanks for letting us speak with the kids so early," Matthew said as Elliot Franklin opened the door to his house.

Nate still couldn't believe this was happening.

Rylla was gone. She could be dead already.

He didn't want to think like that, but he couldn't stop himself.

He had seen the pictures of the other victims. In his mind he kept conjuring up pictures of what the killer would do to her. How would he kill her? Would it be quick? Would he draw it out and make it as painful as possible? The killer didn't appear to enjoy inflicting pain, but if Rylla made him angry then he would lose control.

They knew she was already hurt.

Naomi had seen her get shot and collapse, and they'd tested the blood on the floor to confirm it was Rylla's.

It was.

At least Beau had spared Naomi and the baby. Though if they

hadn't arrived when they had the baby might not have survived much longer. By the time paramedics arrived the baby's body temperature was low, and overwhelmed, exhausted, and traumatized, Naomi had passed out in Sam's arms. They had both been taken to the hospital, where the baby had been warmed up, and Naomi's wound had been tended to. Now, almost twelve hours later, they were both doing well and resting comfortably, Sam protectively at their side. Nate doubted his friend would be letting his wife or daughter out of his sight any time soon.

He'd thought he had a chance at happiness like that with Rylla. A chance to have a family again, a wife who loved him and would never leave him, who would support his attempts to get his son back, and to give him more children.

But now he might lose all of that.

"Nate." Matthew jabbed him in the side.

He blinked and saw that Rylla's brother, Elliot, was standing holding the door open, waiting for them to enter.

He had to focus.

If they were going to find Rylla then he had to keep it together. If he let his emotions get the best of him, the price to pay could be Rylla's life. And he would not allow that to happen.

"Do you want to go back to the hospital with Sam, Naomi, and the baby? I'll keep you updated," Matthew offered.

"No. I want to be here." He *needed* to be here. He wasn't sitting on the sidelines while the cops worked this case.

Matthew nodded once, and they both followed Elliot inside. Mila's children had been dropped off at their uncle's house two days ago shortly after her body had been found and the family notified. Beau had come by briefly around dinner time before leaving again, and no one had heard from him since.

"Did you think it was odd that you never heard from Beau after he left the kids here? I mean, they'd just been told their mother had been murdered, and he just left them." Nate couldn't imagine hurting the mother of his child. Even after everything Rachel had put him through he would never do anything that would hurt her, hurting her would be hurting Andrew, and he would never hurt his son.

"I tried calling him several times," Elliot replied as he led them into a fancy lounge room full of furniture that looked like it cost more than Nate made in a year. "He wouldn't answer. The kids were upset, they needed their father. Mac slept on the floor at the end of our bed both nights, and Emmy had nightmares, and hasn't been eating."

"Do they know?" Matthew asked.

"About their father and what he did?" Elliot asked, his green eyes blazed just like Rylla's when she was angry. "No, they don't. Are you positive it was him that killed my sister?"

"Yes, I'm sorry. Rylla's friend Naomi was there when she was abducted, she positively identified him," Nate informed him.

"Isn't Naomi pregnant? Did Beau hurt her?"

"Yes she is, and yes he did, he shot her, but thankfully she and the baby are okay and recovering in the hospital," Nate replied.

Elliot shook his head like the whole thing was one big unbelievable mess. Nate knew the feeling. "I still can't imagine why Beau would start killing women."

"Rylla didn't like Beau. What did you think of him?" Matthew asked.

"He wasn't my favorite person, and not who I would have chosen to marry my little sister. I was pleased that Mila was divorcing him and hoping that he didn't wind up with custody of the kids. He's never been particularly interested in them, I'm not even sure why he was fighting for full custody. I guess it was just because he didn't want Mila to have what he thought of as part of his property."

"He wasn't a hands-on dad?" Matthew asked.

"No, quite the opposite. He wasn't even there for the births of either kid. Mila is close with my wife Stacey, and that was who was her birthing partner. After Emmy came along, he and Mila started drifting apart. She wanted to do all the family things that came with having children, but Beau wanted none of it. He wanted to keep living as though he were a single guy."

"How did he treat Mila?" Nate asked.

"He expected her to cater to his every whim. In his mind it was his job to earn a living and bring home the money, it was Mila's job to do everything else. But Mila worked too. She had a full-time job, she did all the cooking and cleaning and laundry, and she did everything for the kids."

"Did Mila love him?" Matthew asked.

"I think she did at first, then she felt like she should stay with him for the kids, but when she finally realized that having their parents stuck in an unhappy marriage wasn't helping them, she filed for divorce."

"Was she afraid of Beau? Did he ever hurt her or the kids?" Matthew asked.

"If he ever laid a hand on those kids she would have walked straight out the door. As far as I know he never hurt her. Physically at least."

"Yet she was after full custody of the children," Nate said.

"When Mila told Beau it was over between them and she was leaving, he lost it. He was so angry, I think that was when she started to become afraid of the kids being alone with him. He just got angrier, threw things, when she tried to call the cops, he took her phone and stomped on it. He started following her around, kept threatening her that she couldn't leave him and get away with it. He would beg her to come back. Saying he wanted to stay married and that it was all Mila's fault that their marriage had problems."

"Why didn't she file for a restraining order?" Nate asked.

"I think she thought it would all just die down. That once Beau got used to the idea, he would accept that she wasn't coming back and move on. Rylla told her that she should do something about it, that she should play it safe, but Mila didn't think it was any big deal. She didn't believe that Beau was a threat to her."

"Rylla was telling the truth," Nate said quietly, squarely meeting Elliot's gaze. "She was terrified that your father was going to hurt her."

"I know." Humiliation flashed through his eyes, and he dropped his gaze to his feet.

"You knew Rylla was in danger, and you didn't do anything to help her?"

"No, back then I didn't believe her, but just before our father passed away a couple of years later, he admitted it. By then Rylla was with Josh, and we didn't approve, and I was too embarrassed about not helping my sixteen-year-old sister and letting her run away from home and live on the streets."

"I get it, I wouldn't have liked my eighteen-year-old sister marrying a twenty-eight-year-old either, but despite what anyone else thinks about it they were in love, they were happy together. I think it's time to let the past stay in the past and move forward. When Rylla lost her husband and daughter she grieved alone, don't make Emmy and Mac grieve alone, give them as much family support as you can. They've lost their mother, and unless Beau gives himself up then they're probably going to lose him too."

"El?" A tall blonde appeared in the doorway. "The kids are ready."

Elliot looked at them and when Matthew nodded, he said, "Bring them in."

"Do you have another photo to show us?" Emmy asked as she entered the room, her brother trailing along behind her.

"Yes, and we have to talk to you about something," Matthew replied.

Both children had red puffy eyes and looked exhausted. Unfortunately, they were about to get news that was even worse than learning their mother had been murdered.

"Is this the man you guys saw in your house?" Matthew held out a photo of the PI that Beau had hired.

"That's him," Emmy said immediately, Mac nodded his agreement.

"Come and sit down," Matthew told the kids, who exchanged glances and then came and perched side by side on the edge of the sofa.

"Do you have more bad news?" Emmy asked. "Did something happen to our dad? We haven't seen him since the day before yesterday."

"We need to ask you some questions about your dad," Matthew began.

Emmy bounded to her feet, apparently understanding where the conversation was headed. "My dad didn't kill my mom," Emmy screamed at them, bolting for the door.

Elliot stopped her. "I'm sorry, honey, but Aunt Rylla's friend Naomi identified him as the killer."

"Naomi?" Emmy echoed like if Naomi said it then it must be true as opposed to the rest of them who were probably lying to her.

"Yes, she was there when your dad took Aunt Rylla," Elliot told her.

Emmy's eyes grew wide. "Dad took Aunt Rylla?"

"Took her where?" Mac asked.

"Why would he do that? Why would he hurt Mom? I don't understand." Emmy's eyes were darting from person to person seeking something that told her it was all a big mistake.

"We don't really know why," Matthew said. "But we need to stop him, and we need to find your aunt before he hurts her."

"Do you think he'll kill her?" Emmy whispered.

"Yes," Nate answered honestly when everyone else hesitated. "You guys stayed with your dad the night your mom had her date, right?"

"We did, but dad went out for a while. He asked a neighbor to come and stay with us for a bit," Emmy answered.

Interesting, they hadn't known that. There had been no need for Matthew and the others to look into Beau's whereabouts at the time his almost ex-wife was abducted because he hadn't been a suspect.

"And you stayed with your dad while your mom was missing?" Matthew asked.

Emmy nodded, she was trying to be strong, she was trying to be grown up, but she was looking very young and vulnerable right now.

"Do you remember your dad going someplace while you were staying with him?" Nate asked. They already knew that Beau Drake was the Fairytale Killer, that wasn't in question, all they needed to know was where he was keeping his victims. He was terrified that Rylla didn't have long left. Even if Beau didn't kill her right away, they didn't know how serious the gunshot wound had been, she could have already bled out.

"Dad didn't go anywhere," Emmy said.

"Nowhere?" Matthew repeated.

The girl shrugged. "Well work I guess while we were at school, but otherwise he was home with us."

They all looked to Mac for confirmation, and the little boy gave a scared nod, clearly not understanding the implications of that.

"So, he was home with you the whole time," Nate checked again.

"Uh huh. Why is that important?" Emmy looked confused.

Because it meant that Beau was keeping his victims somewhere on his property. That he had kept his children's mother prisoner in his home at the same time his children were there. That Rylla was most likely there right now.

~

7:38 A.M.

It was time to make her move.

Rylla had been spending most of the time pretending to be passed out. Beau kept giving her pills, but she was just pretending to swallow them while hiding them in her mouth between her teeth and her cheeks and spitting them out as soon as he left the room.

He seemed to truly want to make her better and was genuinely contrite for shooting her in the first place. He was all over the map.

Right now, though, she didn't have time to figure out why he was doing what he was doing, her focus was getting out of here.

The downside to refusing to take the pills was that her leg was burning hot and raging with pain. She hadn't taken any painkillers or antibiotics since that first lot he'd given her. She was sure the wound was infected, and it hurt so badly that it was hard to concentrate.

But she had to concentrate.

She had to get out of here.

She wanted to go home to Nate. She wanted to know that Naomi and the baby had survived. She wanted her life.

So, she had to fight.

Earlier while she had been alone, she had managed to work free the handcuff key that she had scooped up back at the cabin. When she'd attempted to knock him over and he'd shot her she had collapsed. By some fluke she had landed right on top of one of the handcuff keys, she had scooped it up and tucked it away into the sleeve of her shirt.

Again, luck had been on her side. When Beau had picked her up the pain in her leg had made her black out, but while she was unconscious and Beau had transported her here and tended to her he hadn't found the key.

Ignoring the pain that still gripped her leg, she tried to wiggle herself up so she could reach the cuff on her left wrist.

With one twist of the key she was free.

While she wanted to go running straight for the door, she needed to take a moment to steady her swimming head.

Walking wasn't going to be easy, she wasn't even one hundred percent sure her leg could bear weight, but it wasn't like she had a choice. If she didn't get out of here, then Beau was going to kill her. She didn't know when, it could be hours, it could be days, it could even be weeks, but she knew it was inevitable.

After just a few precious moments of rest, Rylla shuffled to the edge of the bed and slowly stood.

Immediately her bad leg buckled, and she fell back against the mattress.

She didn't have time for this.

Gritting her teeth she climbed back to her feet, and by sheer force of will she remained standing. Hobbling—something she was getting used to doing since Beau injured her knee the other night—as quickly as she could to the door, she reached into her hair and began to pull it loose from the ties and pins she'd used to secure it in a messy bun. Thankfully it was summer, and her thick mass of red curls were too hot to leave hanging down her back so she always kept them pinned up and off her neck.

Using bobby pins she had the lock to the door picked in minutes.

Sagging in relief against the door, she had done it, she was free.

Again, she didn't have time to rest for too long, she had to keep moving.

Pushing the door open she was met with a set of stairs leading down. Clutching the railing she managed to stagger down the steps and found herself in a garage. It was messy and full of tools and boxes and other odds and ends. Ignoring all of it she went for the door. As soon as she opened it, she gasped.

She immediately recognized where she was.

This was Beau's house.

She had been here before when Mila had asked her to pick up the kids for her so she didn't have to see her almost ex at a court ordered custody exchange.

Rylla's heart soared with hope. She was in the middle of a busy family neighborhood, there should be someone around to help her.

She was about to start for the nearest house when an arm wrapped around her and yanked her back.

"You got out." Beau's voice in her ear was more resigned than surprised.

"I won't ever stop trying, Beau. I'll never love you. You're sick. You need help. Think of Emmy and Mac, let's go straight to the police station, you can turn yourself in and we can get you the help that you need."

"I don't need help. What I need is a woman who knows how to be the perfect wife," Beau said as he yanked her arms behind her back and handcuffed her.

"No one like that exists," she insisted. "You're looking for something that you can never find. No woman is going to measure up to the standards that you've set."

"Maybe you're right," he said slowly, dragging her backward and closing the door. "Maybe I can't find what I want. Maybe there's no such woman."

Although it sounded like he was agreeing with her she had the feeling in fact he wasn't. "Let's get you help, Beau," she pleaded.

"I think I know what I was doing wrong," he said as he turned her around and hefted her over his shoulder walking with her through the garage and into a small room at the side. "You, and Mila, and all those other women were too old. You're past the point of being able to learn. Maybe I need someone younger."

Fear gripped her, was he going to go after his daughter next? Right now, she wouldn't put anything past him. He was so consumed with getting what he wanted that he was completely disregarding the thoughts and feelings of anyone else. "Don't hurt Emmy, Beau."

"I'd never hurt my kid." He sounded offended and dropped her into a large hole in the floor. The ground back here was dirt, and beside the shallow grave was a pile of dirt. He was going to bury her alive. For a claustrophobic like herself that was about the most horrifying way imaginable to die.

"Don't do this, Beau," she begged. Between her hands cuffed behind her back, her cracked ribs, and her injured leg, she was struggling to get up but couldn't.

"I'm sorry, Rylla. I thought you could be the one. I was so sure of it. When I first grabbed you on the street the other night, I felt it in my bones. But I was wrong. You can't give me what I want." He picked up a shovel and tossed the first load of dirt on top of her.

"Think of your kids, you already took their mother from them, don't make them lose you too. Please, Beau. When my partner eventually finds you, please turn yourself in, don't make him kill you."

Beau had ceased listening to her, she could tell. He was focused on his task, tipping shovelful after shovelful of dirt onto her. With each one the feeling of claustrophobia grew until she too was consumed.

Rylla wanted to beg him to stop but she knew that nothing would convince him to let her live, he'd already dug this hole, he had intended to kill her even before he saw that she had escaped.

The dirt was soon crushing her.

The pressure on her injured lungs was agony.

She couldn't move.

The dirt was inching closer and closer to her face.

Beneath it her skin crawled with terror like a million spiders were scuttling all over her.

She wanted out of here right now.

She'd thought she could save herself. And she almost had. She'd gotten out of that room, she'd gotten to the door, she'd been so close.

But close wasn't good enough.

Now she was going to die alone just like Josh had.

She was never going to get to tell Nate she loved him.

Dirt rained down on her face and she frantically shook her head backward and forward, trying to dislodge it.

But it was coming too quickly.

Raining down upon her.

Faster and faster.

There was no escaping it.

Rylla turned her head as far to the side as she could and tucked her mouth as closely as she could to her shoulder, hoping to carve out at least a tiny pocket of air.

Why?

She wasn't sure.

She knew she was going to die in this hole, there really didn't seem much point in dragging it out, in trying to scrounge just a few measly extra seconds.

And yet she couldn't not fight.

The dirt was all over her head now. In her ears, covering her eyes and plunging her into darkness, edging closer to her mouth and nose.

Rylla was about to surrender to the fear and let death carry her away to join Josh and Elianna when she heard a voice.

~

8:12 A.M.

"That's Rylla." Nate intended to go running straight for her, but he was grabbed from behind and physically prevented from making a mad dash to the garage where Rylla was standing at an open door.

"Stop," Matthew hissed in his ear. "You can't just go running blindly in there."

"*Rylla* is in there."

"Exactly. We have to play this smart. He could be in there too."

"Then why would he be letting her stand at an open door where she could get to help?" he demanded.

"I don't know, but we have to go in carefully, otherwise he could kill her."

He was going to risk it when Rylla was suddenly yanked from view. A moment later the door was slammed closed.

The arms around him tightened and he struggled against them. He had to get to her, he had to save her, he couldn't lose her. He couldn't be this close to her and just stand here and do nothing to help her.

"Stop," Matthew growled. "If you go running in there like this you're going to get her killed. Is that what you want?"

Nate stilled. Not because he wanted to. Not because the fear swirling inside him like a blizzard had stilled. But because he knew that the longer he fought, the longer it was going to take to get to her.

"You are not a cop," Matthew reminded him. "You don't have to be here. I can have you removed in a moment. You're here *only* because I know you love her, and because you're trained, you know what you're doing, and you've done hostage recovery before. But if you can't keep your emotions in check and hold it together for Rylla's sake, then I *will* cuff you and stick you in the back of the car. Understand?"

If agreeing was going to get them into that garage quicker then he would agree to anything. "Yes."

"All right." Matthew loosened his grip, and when he didn't make a move to dart toward the garage, Matthew released him altogether. "We go in slowly, and carefully."

Guns drawn, they made their way down the drive toward the huge double-story garage at the back of the property. There was definitely enough space in there to hold someone captive. And if he had gone to the trouble of soundproofing then no matter how much the women screamed for help no one would ever hear them, even here in the suburbs.

At the garage door, Nate waited for a signal from Matthew then eased it open and stepped inside. The space was messy, and he could hear someone mumbling to themselves somewhere inside. He couldn't hear Rylla. Were they too late? Had Beau already killed her?

Fighting to keep it together, they made their way toward the voice.

In a smaller room off the large one they found them.

Beau had a shovel in his hand and was throwing dirt into a hole at his feet.

Rylla was nowhere to be seen.

Just because he couldn't see her didn't mean he didn't know where she was.

She was in the hole.

Being buried alive.

That was horrific enough, but for Rylla, a claustrophobic, it would be even more terrifying.

He prayed with every fiber of his being that she was still alive. That he hadn't lost her by mere seconds. If Rylla died because Matthew wouldn't let him come running straight back here, he would never forgive him. Or himself.

Beau obviously hadn't heard them and was still muttering to

himself, something about how he needed to go younger, that a younger woman was the answer, while he continued to shovel dirt onto Rylla.

"Beau, it's the police, put the shovel down," Matthew announced their presence.

He turned, surprised and confused, then angry. "Go away."

"We're not going anywhere, Beau," Matthew said. "Put the shovel down and put your hands behind your back."

"She's already dead," Beau sneered. "The hole is all filled in."

Nate was close enough to see that the hole was indeed mostly filled. If Rylla wasn't dead already they had minutes at the most to get her out of there before she suffocated.

"It's over, Beau." Matthew somehow managed to maintain an outward calm that was currently eluding him. "We know what you've done. You're going to prison. Don't make this any harder on your children than it already is."

"What I've done?" Beau echoed. "All I've done is try to find the same happily ever after as everyone else. I didn't do anything wrong."

"You killed four women," Matthew reminded him.

"You have no proof," he growled.

They were wasting time. Beau Drake clearly believed that abducting, holding captive, and then killing four women was perfectly reasonable because he wanted to find a wife that behaved in the way he thought she should. He was never going to see things any differently. Rylla's time was quickly running out. They had to make a move.

"You drugged a man and left him inside the trunk of a car. He identified you. You shot and handcuffed a woman in labor. She identified you too. You shot your sister-in-law and brought her here. We saw her. She's in there. Don't let her die too."

Beau paused, seeming to weigh up his options. Apparently, deciding he wasn't walking out of here unless it was in handcuffs, he gripped the shovel and stood over the hole, the edge of the shovel positioned where Nate assumed Rylla's head was.

Beau lifted the shovel high then began to swing it down.

Nate fired.

Beau dropped.

The shovel clattered down beside him.

He ran to the hole, shoving aside Beau's dead body, and began to dig.

He started where Beau had been aiming the shovel, clawing at the dirt, moving it as quickly as he could.

Matthew bent and slapped handcuffs on Beau even though they both knew he was already dead, then came and helped him dig.

The grave was shallow, and it didn't take them long to uncover Rylla's face. As soon as he could reach it, Nate dug his fingers into her mouth and scooped out the dirt that was there. Then he put his fingers to her neck.

"Is she alive?"

"I've got a pulse but it's weak," he replied.

"Ambulance is already on the way," Matthew replied, moving down the hole to dig out the rest of Rylla's body so they could get her out of the hole.

Nate cradled her head in his hands. She was still, her eyes closed, dirt streaked her face and rested on her long eyelashes. He checked her head and neck but couldn't see any injuries.

"Rylla? Can you hear me?" he asked.

She didn't respond.

Beneath the dirt her skin was hot to the touch, chances were wherever Beau had shot her the wound had become infected.

"Rylla, come on, honey. Answer me," he begged.

"She's free," Matthew announced, scooping enough of the dirt off her that they could get her out of the hole.

Nate gathered her limp body into his arms and picked her up, carrying her out of the garage and laying her down on the grass outside. Now that she was free, he could see a blood-soaked bandage wrapped around her left thigh. Matthew knelt beside them and unwound the tattered material to reveal the gunshot wound, the edges of which were red, and ragged, and enflamed.

"She's going to need to go straight on antibiotics." Matthew stood. "I'm going to grab water from the car and clean out what dirt I can."

Rylla was so still. And she looked so frail and vulnerable lying on the grass in her dirt-stained shirt and shorts. Nate had to put his hand on her chest so he could feel her heart beating and her chest rising and falling with each breath, to try to convince himself that she was in fact alive.

"Wake up, Rylla," he begged again. "Come on, honey, you're scaring me. Wake up. Please, honey, wake up now. I love you, Rylla, you have to wake up now."

Matthew returned with a bottle of water and fresh clean bandages, and began to pour water on the angry looking wound, cleaning it as best he could, then winding a long compression bandage around it.

Then finally, beneath his touch, she began to stir.

"Rylla, it's Nate. I'm right here, baby." He wanted his voice to be the first thing she heard so that she would know she was safe. "You had me so scared." His voice was stark, the fear hadn't left him yet, as the adrenalin drained out of his system, realization of just how close he had come to losing her began to really sink in.

She began to cough and gag on the dirt that was still in her mouth and throat, her dirt laden eyelashes began to flicker.

"Don't open your eyes yet," he cautioned, holding out his hand to Matthew for some of the water. Matthew handed over a bottle and a square bandage, and Nate tipped some over the material, soaking it, then using it to clean away the dirt from her face so that it didn't get into her eyes.

"You love me?" were the first words she spoke. Her voice was rough from the dirt she had inhaled, but it was the most beautiful sound he had ever heard.

"For years now," he told her, pulling her into his arms.

"I love you too," she said, and snuggled further into his hold.

He'd been wrong, her voice wasn't the most beautiful sound he had ever heard, the woman he loved telling him she loved him too was. And then the second most beautiful sound filled the air. Sirens. Help was here. Rylla was alive and was going to be okay, and she was his, all his.

~

4:53 P.M.

. . .

Rylla's first concern when she woke was that it had all been a dream and she was going to find herself back in Beau's creepy castle.

But then she felt Nate's presence.

It hadn't been a dream.

She was alive.

He had saved her.

Her eyes felt heavy, but she opened them anyway. She didn't want to sleep anymore, she'd been asleep ever since she had been bundled into the ambulance. Now she wanted to be awake, she wanted to revel in the amazing feeling of being alive.

Nate was in a chair beside her bed, his hand loosely held hers, and although his head was tipped back to rest on the back of the chair, as soon as her eyes opened, he straightened and turned in her direction. When he saw she was awake he beamed at her.

"Hey, how are you feeling?" He leaned his elbows on the edge of the bed and reached over to kiss the tip of her nose.

"Better."

"Really?" He raised a doubtful brow.

"Really," she assured him. Whatever was dripping into the back of her hand from the IV was doing its job.

"I never want to live through something like that again." Nate's brown eyes were still filled with fear. "Don't you ever scare me like that again."

Rylla patted his hand. "I'm sorry, Nate. But you know I didn't have a choice. There was no way I could let him hurt Naomi and the baby. You're sure they're all right?" Checking that her friend had survived had been one of the first things she'd asked about after Nate and Matthew had dug her out of what would have been her grave.

"Positive," said a voice from the door.

She turned to see Naomi sitting in a wheelchair, a small bundle wrapped up in blankets sitting in her lap.

"Is that her?" Rylla struggled into a sitting position, her entire body felt weak and empty.

"Yep." Naomi couldn't take her eyes off her baby girl as Sam pushed her over to the bed.

"What's her name?"

"Daveli Rylla Zeeke," Naomi replied.

That name was perfect. "After David and Eli."

"And you, you saved our lives." Naomi's brown eyes grew teary. "How can I ever thank you for that?"

"You don't need to thank me." Rylla looked from the baby to the look of wonder on Naomi's face. She remembered when she had looked at Elianna that way, almost unable to believe that something so perfect, something so small and precious, was all hers to love and take care of. For a long time, she had thought she would never again hold a child that was all hers in her arms. It had been too painful to even consider. But now she couldn't wait until the day that she gave birth to a baby that was half her and half Nate.

"Well I am, all three of us are," Naomi indicated the baby and Sam, who stood protectively at her side. "Want to hold her?"

"Of course." Nate elevated the bed further and Sam picked up Daveli and passed her over.

Rylla smiled down at the little girl, her tiny round nose, her soft dark hair, and her pink cheeks. She was beautiful, and she was so touched that Naomi and Sam had named their daughter after her.

"Knock, knock."

She looked back to the door to see the last person she expected standing there.

"Elliot." She and her big brother hadn't been close since he left for college. As kids she had adored him, looked up to him, followed him around everywhere he went until he'd get so sick of her. But then he and Mila hadn't believed her when she'd told them about their father, then they had been angry that she wanted to become an emancipated minor, and they hadn't been supportive of her relationship with Josh. It had been like three strikes and they were out. Although she spent time with her nieces and nephews, her relationships with her siblings had remained strained.

That had never really bothered her. She'd still been hurt by Mila and Elliot's betrayals and hadn't been in any hurry to forgive them. But now things were different. Now she wanted to grab hold of her family and keep them close.

"We'll give you two some time," Nate said, lifting Daveli from her arms and leaning over to kiss her lightly on the lips. He looked so good with a baby in his arms.

When Nate, Sam, and Naomi had gone Elliot tentatively came over to the bed. "You're all right?" he asked.

"Yes," she replied, suddenly nervous around the brother she had known all her life. She wanted to fix things between them, but she didn't know how to make the first move.

"You and this Nate guy, you're a couple?"

"Yes."

Elliot nodded, looking as awkward as she felt.

This was ridiculous. They were brother and sister. It shouldn't be this hard for them to have a simple conversation.

"Elliot, I—" she started.

"Rylla, I—" Elliot said at the same time.

They looked at each other and laughed. The tension broken.

"I'm sorry, Rylla. I should have believed you. You were a good kid. I should have known that if things at home were bad enough to make you run away then you were telling the truth."

With that apology the last of the hurt and betrayal melted away. "It's okay. Emmy and Mac, do they know?"

"Yeah, they were the ones that helped Nate and your partner find you. When Matthew called to tell us they'd found you and were bringing you here, we sat them down and told them their dad was dead."

"Those poor kids." She couldn't imagine what Emmy and Mac were feeling right now. It was one thing to lose both your parents, but another for your dad to kill your mom and three other people.

"I think they should stay with you," Elliot announced.

"With me?" Rylla was shocked. "I thought you would want them to stay with you."

"We have four kids, I would love to have them stay with us, but I think they'll be better off with you."

"Really?" The thought of becoming a parent again was both terrifying and exhilarating.

"You'll be a great mom to them, Rylla. Just like you were a great mom to your daughter."

Her brother's faith in her meant a lot. Emmy was only a little older than Elianna would have been

"I'm here, Rylla. Any time you need me. Any help you need with the kids all you need to do is ask. I already told them that once you're better, and you go home, that they'll be moving in with you. They're happy about that. They're in shock and they're going to need time and love and help and support, but they're strong kids, they'll find a way to survive just like you did. I should go, you look like you need to rest."

Elliot kissed her forehead then left. Alone, she let her eyes fall closed. She was so tired. Tired but happy. Although a little nervous. She and Nate had only just started dating. How was he going to feel about becoming a parent to her niece and nephew? Especially given that his own son had been cruelly ripped away from him.

She heard the door to her room open and knew it was Nate.

He must have thought she was asleep because she heard him sit down in the chair beside her bed. When he took her hand, she opened her eyes.

"I thought you were asleep." He reached out and tucked a stray lock of hair behind her ear. His fingers lingered on her cheek, and she leaned into them.

What if he walked away when he found out about the kids? She couldn't blame him if he did. Dating was one thing, loving her was another, agreeing to become an overnight father was on a whole different level.

"What's wrong, honey?" he asked, sensing her tension.

She may as well get it over and done with and just say it. If he walked away so be it. "Emmy and Mac are going to come and live with me."

"Okay." He nodded calmly.

"Okay? You're fine with helping me raise two traumatized kids? Emmy is going to be a teenager in a couple of months, and Mac is almost the same age as your son."

"Rylla." He took her hands in his. "I can't wait to marry you and have children with you. So, we're having the kids a little earlier than I thought, and in an unconventional way, but Emmy and Mac are great kids, and you are the perfect person to help them through this difficult time. I want to be there for you and for them. We're in this together. I love you, and if raising your niece and nephew is what you want to do then it's what I want to do."

How had she gotten so lucky to fall in love twice in one lifetime with the two most amazing men on the planet?

"I love you." She ran her fingers through Nate's hair and drew his face down to hers so she could kiss him.

"I love you too," he whispered across her lips. "And I can't wait to get you home so I can show you just how much."

Rylla laughed. "We're going to have two kids living in the house," she reminded him.

"You're right, we definitely need a lock on our bedroom door."

She laughed again, then yawned, it was getting harder and harder to keep her eyes open.

Nate climbed onto the hospital bed and stretched out beside her, draping her arm across his chest. "Sleep now, Rylla."

She snuggled into him and finally let her eyes fall closed. As she drifted off to sleep, she felt a contentment she hadn't felt in years. Falling asleep in the arms of the man she loved, she could definitely get used to that.

Ready for more serial killers?!
In the third book in the Storybook Murders trilogy while investigating an unrelated case Detective Matthew Greer stumbles upon Grace Bennett who has been missing for five and a half years!

Fable Killer (Storybook Murders #3)

Also by Jane Blythe

Detective Parker Bell Series

A SECRET TO THE GRAVE

WINTER WONDERLAND

DEAD OR ALIVE

LITTLE GIRL LOST

FORGOTTEN

Count to Ten Series

ONE

TWO

THREE

FOUR

FIVE

SIX

BURNING SECRETS

SEVEN

EIGHT

NINE

TEN

Broken Gems Series

CRACKED SAPPHIRE

CRUSHED RUBY

FRACTURED DIAMOND

SHATTERED AMETHYST

SPLINTERED EMERALD

SALVAGING MARIGOLD

River's End Rescues Series

COCKY SAVIOR

SOME REGRETS ARE FOREVER

SOME FEARS CAN CONTROL YOU

SOME LIES WILL HAUNT YOU

SOME QUESTIONS HAVE NO ANSWERS

SOME TRUTH CAN BE DISTORTED

SOME TRUST CAN BE REBUILT

SOME MISTAKES ARE UNFORGIVABLE

Candella Sisters' Heroes Series

LITTLE DOLLS

LITTLE HEARTS

LITTLE BALLERINA

Storybook Murders Series

NURSERY RHYME KILLER

FAIRYTALE KILLER

FABLE KILLER

Saving SEALs Series

Prey Security Series

Prey Security: Alpha Team Series

Prey Security: Artemis Team Series

IVORY'S FIGHT

PEARL'S FIGHT

LACEY'S FIGHT

OPAL'S FIGHT

Prey Security: Bravo Team Series

VICIOUS SCARS

RUTHLESS SCARS

Christmas Romantic Suspense Series

CHRISTMAS HOSTAGE

CHRISTMAS CAPTIVE

CHRISTMAS VICTIM

YULETIDE PROTECTOR

YULETIDE GUARD

YULETIDE HERO

HOLIDAY GRIEF

Conquering Fear Series (Co-written with Amanda Siegrist)

DROWNING IN YOU

OUT OF THE DARKNESS

CLOSING IN

About the Author

USA Today bestselling author Jane Blythe writes action-packed romantic suspense and military romance featuring protective heroes and heroines who are survivors. One of Jane's most popular series includes Prey Security, part of Susan Stoker's OPERATION ALPHA world! Writing in that world alongside authors such as Janie Crouch and Riley Edwards has been a blast, and she looks forward to bringing more books to this genre, both within and outside of Stoker's world. When Jane isn't binge-reading she's counting down to Christmas and adding to her 200+ teddy bear collection!

To connect and keep up to date please visit any of the following